Quick & Dirty

Whitley Cox

Whitley Cox

Ebook ISBN: 978-1989081037

Cover Design: EmCat Designs

Editing: SkyDiary Productions

For Alicia!
You, lady are true friend.
xoxo

Contents

PROLOGUE   VI

1. Chapter 1   1

2. Chapter 2   12

3. Chapter 3   21

4. Chapter 4   31

5. Chapter 5   40

6. Chapter 6   53

7. Chapter 7   62

8. Chapter 8   70

9. Chapter 9   82

10. Chapter 10   89

11. Chapter 11   98

12. Chapter 12   106

13. Chapter 13   116

Epilogue   128

PROLOGUE

Tate

My eyes darted around the lobby of the hotel. Something was off. Something didn't look right, but what? I needed everything to be perfect, beyond perfect. I needed everything to be immaculate—spectacular. Despite the fact that my hotel only brought in the elite of the elite, I wanted the reviews to be glowing, and Parker Ryan, acclaimed travel journalist and hotel reviewer, must not be disappointed.

Everything and anything he wanted, he was going to get.

And if I happened to make a friend along the way, all the better.

My therapist said I'm lonely and I need to make friends.

I wasn't sure I agreed, but whatever.

I was too busy to be lonely. My days were full. It was my responsibility to make sure that my guests were happy and my staff was taken care of.

It's impossible to make friends or be *lonely* when you're the Big Kahuna and work eighty hours a week.

I had no time for either.

I'd arranged for Mr. Ryan to stay in the most luxurious villa, the presidential villa. He'd get daily massages, deep-sea sport fishing with our best guide, a sunrise hike up to the Belvedere Lookout, tableside dinners by the executive chef and, if he was up for it, spear-fishing, parasailing and skydiving with yours truly.

Yes, everything must be perfect.

I needed to impress Parker Ryan, and I needed to impress him big time.

It didn't matter that my resort was one of the most sought-after holiday spots in the entire world and that only the elite one percent of the population could afford to come here, to the tropical island haven of Moorea; I had other properties, and they needed the exposure, too.

So if Parker Ryan wanted to come here to Moorea and interview me, he was going to get star treatment all the way.

He just couldn't take my picture.

I continued to stare at the framed painting of a tropical sunset hanging above some wicker chairs. Something was off; there was imperfection afoot.

Ah ha!

It was crooked.

I hustled over and fixed it, then I noticed some dust on the top of the frame. Using the handkerchief from my breast pocket, I began to dust.

Muttering to myself, I took to dusting the entire sitting area.

"This is not my

fucking job. Where is housekeeping?" Probably off doing their job; they'd get to this room later. I immediately chastised myself for my thought.

My staff was actually fantastic, and I had nothing to complain about.

I was letting the nerves get to me. I'd just never agreed to an interview before, and it was stressing me out. I prided myself on my ability to remain under the radar and out of the public eye. I maintained an anonymity most people with my level of wealth found difficult to keep going.

I could walk into a bar anywhere in the world right now and no one would know who I was, no one would know that I'm Tate McAllister—a billionaire and hotel magnate. And I intended to keep it that way.

I glanced at my watch as I continued to dust, desperately trying to rub out a smudge on the glass top of the side table. No smudges. There would be no smudges in my hotel's review, none.

Shit, it was closing in on go-time. Mr. Ryan was going to be here soon. Damn it!

I lifted my head up from the glass and was dumbstruck.

A vision.

She was Illuminated like a redheaded angel with the afternoon sun glowing around her in an ethereal halo as she sashayed her way in through the open doors.

The warm breeze snagged the hem of her skirt and flipped it into a jet stream of ivory behind her, while dark crimson tendrils got swept up on another sudden gust and danced around her head like an arc of fire.

She made a half-hearted attempt to tame her wild mane, but then, when her efforts proved futile, she gave up.

When she stepped farther into the lobby and out of the sun's radiance, I was suddenly sent into a fit of panic.

Her face was nearly as red as her hair, and her eyes were filled with what could only be described as white-hot seething rage.

Without a second thought, I raced up to her. "Hello, and welcome to The Windward Hibiscus Hotel. Is there anything I can help you with?"

Blue eyes the same color as the crystal-clear ocean outside flashed up at me, full of flames . . . and something else.

"Yes!" she said with a huff, her perfect little freckle-covered nose lifting into the air just a touch. "You can take me into the nearest broom closet and fuck me senseless."

Chapter One

Parker

"Hey, it's me again. Look, I know you're pissed, but it's really for the best. You weren't making me happy. I need a woman who has more spark. More fire. More passion. You're like a dead fish, really. I think you might have some daddy issues there, *darling*. Not enough hugs growing up or something." His syrupy-sweet voice made me wish there was an app where you could reach inside your phone and throat-punch the caller on the other end. How I wanted to just watch him choke and gasp for air, his smarmy eyes bugging out as his hands found their way to his neck and he looked at me in panic.

Motherfucker!

Daddy issues?

Fuck him. He knows nothing about me. NOTHING!

But like the mouse that keeps going back to the same freaking trap, I put my ear back to the receiver.

"I need someone who is going to be there for me when I need her, you know? Besides, were you even happy? Half the time I can't even tell. Happy, mad, sad. For a woman who doesn't get Botox anymore, you sure have a face like one. Anyway, I just wanted to let you know I've put all your things in a box and had my chauffeur drop it off at your apartment."

Swallowing the taste of bile that had suddenly formed a thick film on my tongue, I deleted the message on my phone before his voice could continue.

Fuck him!

Fuck Xavier Rollins and his millions.

Fuck Xavier Rollins and his beautiful downtown penthouse apartment.

Fuck Xavier Rollins and his nice cars, his family's private jet, his enormous yacht.

Fuck him and fuck everything else.

Fuck everyone else.

Fuck everyone he knew, he worked with, fuck them all.

I was done.

I'd wasted three years of my life with that asshole.

Three fucking years. And apparently during the last year (but who really knew? It could have been the whole damn time) he'd been screwing everything with two X chromosomes that batted heavily mascaraed eyelashes at him. His assistant, his secretary, his kid's nanny, his ex-wife apparently from time to time.

You name the bitch, and chances are Xavier had slipped his pasty-ass body between her thighs.

And yet the bastard had the audacity, the *audacity* to dump *me*.

"I'm not sure it's working anymore," he'd said on New Year's Eve as we ate dinner in one of Xavier's New York restaurants. The entire place had been closed down for a private party hosted by Xavier himself. The room was packed with New York's most elite socialites and celebrities, all "friends" of the eccentric millionaire and giddy as can be to be part of such a lavish event.

"You're never around. You're always off working. And you're, well . . . " He actually had the decency to grimace slightly. "You're not exactly warm or *adventurous* in bed, darling. I need a woman who's willing to, you know . . . "

I shook my head and blinked at him a few times before deciding to open my mouth. "No, I don't *know*. What is it you would like me to do?"

I scanned the nearby tables, hoping nobody was eavesdropping on us, but it was a party, it was New York, it was Xavier Rollins.

People were listening.

They always were.

Bringing my voice down a little lower and leaning closer to him, I swallowed before speaking. "Can we not discuss this here, please, Xavier?"

He took a sip of his rye and tonic while simultaneously giving a half-wave and a smile to Gigi Hammond across the room. She winked at him and bit her lip the way a woman does when she wants you to bite her "other" lips.

"No, we'll discuss it right here. I want a woman who is adventurous."

"I'm a travel journalist. I go on adventures for work. You're not making any sense."

He coughed slightly while his eyes took on an almost bored, glazed-over look. "Yes . . . but not in bed."

Suddenly my cheeks felt as if they'd gone up in flames. "Please," I said with a hiss, "let's not talk about this here."

He flicked his wrist again as if I were not more than a pesky fly buzzing around his head, a mild irritation he could just bat away. "I'm sorry, darling, but you're boring. You're boring me. I want a woman who is around more. You're like a dead fish. Cold, boring, lifeless. We're through."

I shook my head, still not entirely able to process what was happening but nonetheless feeling the harsh sting of his words.

Cold.

Boring.

Lifeless.

A dead fish.

A distant ringing sound began going off in my ears, and my chest hurt.

Was I having a heart attack?

A stroke?

I shook my head and shrugged. "What kinds of things in bed are you wanting? You've never said anything. You want me to quit my job and just follow you around like some *groupie*?"

"Not a *groupie*." He got a wistful look in his eye. Xavier had always wished he could be a rock star. Live the life of a rock star. And despite the fact that he had millions of dollars and hobnobbed with the richest of the rich, partied with rock stars and movie stars, models and politicians, he *wasn't* a rock star. He was heir to The Handy Dandy Soap Company, a big household cleaning supply company that his grandfather had founded decades ago. Sure, over the years Xavier had bought up restaurants and a couple of nightclubs, made a bit of a name for himself, but no matter how much he tried to run, he couldn't escape The Handy Dandy Soap Company or his nickname, "Bubbles."

"Not a *groupie*," he said again. "Just a doting girlfriend."

"I am. When I'm home."

"Which is not enough and why this won't work any longer," he said blandly. "You're not what *I* need. You're not *who* I want." He raised a hand and signaled the waiter for another drink. "You. Me. We're through, darling. I've moved on and so should you."

My bottom lip dropped and nearly hit the table. "You're dumping me? Here? In front of everyone?" I asked. "All because I'm not adventurous enough for you, which by the way is the first I'm hearing of your discontent with our sex life."

He looked about ready to get up and leave.

Bored out of his tree and wanting to find a more lively conversation companion. "That and the fact that you work too damn much."

"But you suggested I take this job. It was your idea. I like what I do." Only when I said the words out loud, they tasted foul on my tongue, because the truth was, I didn't really like my job anymore.

I was tired of it.

Tired of the travel, tired of never being home more than a few days a month, tired of living out of a suitcase, tired of eating at restaurants.

I wanted to cook my own meals, sleep in my own bed more than two nights in a row, and have a closet full of clothes I could stare at while complaining I had nothing to wear.

But I also wanted to do something worthwhile.

I'd never understand these millionaires' and billionaires' wives who did nothing all day long, simply because they didn't have to. Even if Xavier and I got married one day, I would still want to work in some way. Devote my life to charity work or fulfill my lifelong dream of writing a book.

I couldn't simply spend the rest of my days playing tennis, getting my nails done and making wait-staff feel like garbage at the country club bistro.

No, I needed more.

He lifted one shoulder cavalierly. "It was either now or tomorrow morning. But I would rather take Felicity home with me tonight. So now it is." And as if on cue, his little assistant, *Felicity* with her size zero waist, Double-D chest and mile-long legs, sauntered up in a barely-there black leather miniskirt and matching crop top. Jesus Christ, how old was this chick? Xavier was forty-seven; was he old enough to be her father? I wouldn't doubt it.

Felicity perched on his knee and wrapped one svelte arm around his back, her coal-black eyes fixing me with a lethal stare.

What the fuck?

We used to be friends . . . sort of. She and I had grabbed lunch in the past. I babysat her cat, and it'd barfed all over my Aubusson rug. And now, all of a sudden, she's his new fuck buddy and I'm chopped liver?

"So . . . what? You want me to stay the rest of the night at the party, or should I just go?"

I didn't know what to do.

People would be wondering why I'd left.

It'd be all over social media by morning, if not sooner.

The breakup, the speculation as to why.

Rumors, some true and some not, flying out from every moron with opposable thumbs and a cellphone, trying to somehow cash in and weigh in on a very public breakup.

And then the memes would start.

I'm sure people were snapping pictures of us at this very moment.

My mouth hanging open like a codfish, Xavier sitting there all smug with his hand up Felicity's skirt, her siren-red lips nibbling on his ear as if it were some piece of decadent chocolate and not old-man ear with hair sticking out of it.

Well, now I wanted to barf as well as scream and throw things.

Fucking Xavier Rollins.

Fucking *Bubbles!*

"Oh, no. Of course not. That would be incredibly awkward for me . . . and for you. You can go."

I gawked at him.

He was dismissing me?

Three years I'd wasted with this asshole.

Three goddamned years, and I meant that little to him that he was breaking up with me in a room full of people with his mistress perched on his lap like a puppet in a crop top. I continued to just stare at him, stare at what I was *losing*.

And then it hit me.

How had I not noticed any of this sooner? The greasy, poufy hair, the semi-squinty brown eyes, the nervous twitch in his left eye — I'd been blind to it all.

Blinded by love.

Because even though I'm not sure I'd ever said it to him, I did love Xavier.

At least I thought I did.

"Did you hear him, Parker?" Felicity asked with an almost giggle, well, more like a cackle. "He said you can *go.*"

And you can go straight to hell, you traitorous little bitch!

But I didn't say anything. Over the years I'd learned that it wasn't always important to have the last word. Sometimes the best thing to do was gather up what remained of your dignity and leave with your head held high.

I reached for my purse and my coat, then, with nearly a hundred pairs of eyes on me, I walked out of the "XR" restaurant, hailed a cab and didn't look back.

And now, two weeks later, I was on the tropical island of Moorea and about to interview a billionaire.

"Stupid fucking Xavier . . . " I muttered after I thanked the man from the shuttle for retrieving my suitcase from the back of the van. I clicked the handle up and headed to the lobby to check in. "Stupid fucking Xavier. I can be warm. I can be adventurous!"

I rolled my suitcase down the slate path toward the big open doors, the rhythmic *clickity-clack* sound of the wheels on the exposed rock drowning out the din of hotel lobby noise while the strident cry of a random tropical bird punctured the air like a car backfiring in a quiet street.

I scanned the entrance into the hotel, not quite sure what exactly I was looking for but knowing I'd know when I saw it.

"Stupid fucking Xavier," I said again.

Maybe I'd just sleep with the first man who said "Hello" to me.

How was that for adventurous?

Rock his world, give him all the warmth and attention Xavier said I never gave him.

I'd give it to a complete stranger.

Yeah, I'd have sex with a complete stranger.

Quick and dirty sex to get over my breakup.

An innocuous tropical fling.

Nobody knew me here.

Yes, I was here for work, but no one besides me and the owner of the hotel knew that. And as long as he didn't find out what I was up to, I could have a different man in my bed every night if I wanted. I was here for ten days; that's ten different men.

This place could be my rebound playground.

The further I got into the lobby, the more I liked my idea.

I was going to fuck away my worries.

Fuck away my problems.

Use someone else to exorcise the plague that was Xavier Rollins from my mind, my body and my soul.

Now I just had to find the right guy . . .

"Hello, and welcome to The Windward Hibiscus Hotel. Is there anything I can help you with?"

Eyes as green as the surrounding mountains flared with curiosity and perhaps a dollop of fear. But I hardly took notice of his eyes and their long camel lashes, because the rest of him was just that handsome . . . no, handsome wasn't the right word . . . yummy? Delicious? Sex on a stick? No, he wasn't a stick. Too much muscle to be a *stick*. A sex god? Yeah . . . this guy was a walking, talking, sex god. He just had to be. Tall and dreamy with just a hint of danger.

Muscles, toned and hard, threatened to rip right out of his crisp white dress shirt, while stubble, thick and impeccably groomed, covered his jaw, cheeks and upper lip.

Oh mama! You, you are exactly *what I'm looking for.*

Without even thinking, I gave him my best assertive stare. "Yes!" I said with a huff, lifting my head just a tad to look him in the eye. He was a good six inches or so taller than me. "You can take me into the nearest broom closet and fuck me senseless."

"Uh . . . " he replied, his dark brown eyebrows nearly shooting clear off his head.

I shook my head and shrugged. "Or I can go find someone else. A pool boy or landscaper." If I were to guess by the nice designer shoes, expensive shirt and the way he greeted me, he was probably high up on the management chain. But that was okay, I could slum it just this once.

Hotel managers had needs, too.

And if anything, I'd bet he'd be even more discreet than a guest, not wanting it to get back to his boss, Mr. McAllister.

I watched as his eyes slowly, appreciatively raked my body from head to toe, a big smile spreading across his mouth as his gaze landed on my breasts.

I made a noise in my throat, and his head snapped back up.

"So? Broom closet?"

Hunger glittered in his eyes while challenge curved his lips. "Well, if you're a guest, we can just check into your room."

I shook my head. "I am a guest. But no, no names for now. Broom closet, or I'll find someone else."

His chest shook with laughter as he grabbed my hand without hesitation. His other hand reached for my suitcase, and soon he was pulling both me and it down a wide and airy corridor, past a few restaurants, what looked to be a spa, a couple of banquet rooms and a library before he stopped in front of a big wooden door. Reaching into his pocket, he fished out a key ring and, after a few seconds of fumbling, slid the key into the knob. It clicked, and he pushed the door open.

"I think a lady deserves more than a broom closet, don't you think?" We were in a small but very nice room with a baby grand piano, a loveseat and two chairs. "This room is soundproof. It's where musicians who come here to play practice and warm up."

The room was windowless, but the walls were a soft gray, and three of the four held big, beautiful paintings of the islands and ocean. So, even though there was no view of the outside, the room wasn't suffocating or stuffy.

I spun around to face him, swallowing hard at just how gorgeous he was.

And the look he was giving me—pure lust.

He left my suitcase near the door and took a couple of steps toward me. "You can back out, you know. I won't judge you." Another few steps. The gap between us closed quickly. I licked my lips. "Unless sex with a random stranger was on your list of things to do while you're on the island."

My eyes went wide as they roamed his rock-hard body, finally landing on the front of his pants. I could see the telltale bulge, and I licked my lips again. He crept forward until we were less than a step away from each other, his body radiating heat and pheromones in such volume I was starting to feel a little woozy.

"Do I get to know your name first?" he asked.

I shook my head. "I'm a guest. You work here. I'm sure you'll find out eventually. But for now, no names. Just . . . this." I grabbed him by the collar of his shirt and pulled him forward, rising up on my tippy-toes to get at his mouth.

His lips crashed down onto mine as his hands made their way around my body, skimming my waist and hips, cupping my butt, bringing my pelvis closer to his.

A growl rolled up from the depths of his chest and into my mouth, electrifying my body.

He rocked against me, and I felt his hardness between us.

Sparks shot through me, zinging out and landing between my legs.

I couldn't stop the moan that flowed from the back of my throat, and I grinded my body into his, loving the rush of adrenaline and the rush of need that coursed through me, awakening every cell and nerve ending.

I hadn't felt this alive in years, maybe ever.

Xavier certainly never made me feel this way.

Compared to this man, kissing Xavier had been like kissing a wrinkled mole rat.

I let my hands travel up and around to his hair. It was lush and soft, with just a slight wave. I pulled ever so slightly, and he groaned against my lips, his mouth opening wider to let his velvety tongue sweep in and explore the recesses of my mouth.

This was good, so good, but I wanted more.

I'd asked him to fuck me senseless in a broom closet, and although we were several steps up from a broom closet, the rest of the request needed to be fulfilled.

Letting my hands drift back down, I snaked them between us and went to work on his belt, needing to free him, to see him, to feel him.

Was he big?

Was he circumcised?

Did it matter?

Picking up on my vibe, he cupped my butt even more firmly and hoisted me up onto his hips, driving the two of us forward until my back and head abruptly hit the wall with a dull *thud*. He hiked my skirt up with one hand while I continued to work his belt and zipper.

Finally, he was free.

I couldn't help but take a peek, and holy fuck, he was big.

Like huge!

My eyes flicked back up to his, and he grinned wide and cocky at me before finally shrugging.

But then responsibility kicked in. That bitch.

"Uh . . . condom?" I asked.

Sex hadn't been on the agenda for this trip, so I wasn't packing.

"Just a sec," he murmured, pressing a knee between us and against the wall while shoving a hand into his pocket, his other one still firmly holding onto my butt cheek, long, nimble fingers digging into my plump flesh.

Seconds later he came up victorious, a little black foil packet held between his finger and thumb.

My feet hit the floor as he put me down. "Start without me. I'll be with you in two shakes." He ripped the pack open and quickly sheathed himself.

Start without him?

His gaze wandered back up to me and my chest heaved from the heat of his stare. "I said start without me. Touch yourself. I want to see you touch yourself."

Well, this was not going at all how I had thought.

His hand came forward, and those strong fingers wrapped around mine. Then he ruffled up my skirt and guided my hand beneath the front of my panties.

"Are you wet?"

I swallowed.

Holy fuck, this was so hot.

And holy fuck, was I ever wet.

I nodded. "Yeah."

"How wet?"

My lips parted slightly, and my eyes threatened to roll into the back of my head when he pushed my fingers a little deeper and I brushed my clit.

"Really wet," I said, surprised at how out of breath I was.

"Hmmm..." he hummed. "Let me see." He pushed my fingers out of the way and began to explore on his own. My breath caught, and I moaned when he started rubbing delectable little circles around my clit, only to push farther down toward my core, dipping inside for just a moment before pulling back out.

Playing with me, toying with me, gliding around with incredible ease.

Exploring my pussy as if he owned it, as if he were mine and I was his and we hadn't just met five minutes ago.

"Now, how do you taste?" He pulled his digits free, but not before delivering one final pinch to my clit.

I jerked, and my legs nearly flew out from under me.

His chuckle was diabolical and deep, smooth like warm honey.

I watched as his pupils took over his irises, black invading green the moment he slid those two wet fingers into his mouth and sucked off my arousal.

I don't think I've ever been more turned on in all my life; the way he looked at me, in his eyes, in his mind I was completely naked, on my knees with his cock in my mouth.

The thought ran rampant through my brain, but I quickly pushed it away.

No. Not this time.

Maybe if he could keep a secret from his boss, we could do this again and I'd do that, but right now it was about fucking. Hard and fast, quick and dirty.

"Mmmm . . . so sweet," he hummed, his tongue darting out to run along the seam of his sensuous lips, lapping up the last drops of me.

My heart felt like it was seconds away from beating clean out of my chest, while my lungs burned and my mouth was desert-dry. I let my eyes drift back down his body, landing on the thick, pulsing rod between us, encased in latex and poised to fuck. And again, my brain taking a backseat to my libido, I leaped up on to his hips and captured his lips with mine.

He growled against my mouth as his hands made their way to my butt again.

He tilted his hips and rocked against me while I used one free hand to move my thong to the side.

Then, with a grunt and an inhale from the both of us, he was inside me.

"Oh God!" I cried, my body taking over and starting to move as I rode his length up and down while his arms bunched and flexed under the strain of having to hold me up.

"Fuck!" He snarled, his lips traveling along my cheek and neck before finding rest in that sweet spot where the neck meets the shoulder.

He nipped at my skin, alternating between gentle kisses and savage bites.

All the while, his hips continued to hammer into me, his pelvis shoving me hard against the wall in unrelenting thrusts. I took each and every one, my body relishing the brutality of the way he took control, took possession.

I bowed my back and pressed into him, my nipples hard, achy peaks against the fabric of my bikini top.

He lifted his head from my neck and began to drop kisses along my collarbone, reaching inside my halter top and bikini top with one hand to draw out a diamond-hard bud, latching on and tugging with his teeth. I gasped from the delicious bite of pain.

Yes, more!

My body was a maelstrom.

Everything felt incredible, from the way he kneaded my backside to the way his cock stroked inside me, coaxing out the orgasm with hard, measured thrusts.

His mouth was hot and wet on my skin as he continued to suckle and lash at my nipples, alternating between harsh bites and soft licks, until I was gasping for air and practically begging him to stop, but also to never stop.

I was close.

So damn close.

My clit throbbed, and the orgasm that brewed like a hot tropical storm in my belly was getting ready to unleash itself, preparing to devastate everything in its path and leave me as no more than a shell of a woman in its wake.

"Come for me, baby," he whispered, his breath warm against my skin as his lips traveled back up to my neck. "You're close. I can feel it. Let go."

He wedged a free hand between us, found my clit, pinched, and that was it.

That Was It

My body short circuited.

I shut my eyes and threw my head back against the wall as the sensations swamped me.

Pleasure upon pleasure upon pleasure rippled in never-ending and growing waves throughout my entire body.

I cried out.

But the words came out as no more than a choked and garbled sob as I said "yes" and "more" over and over again, until I wasn't sure I knew any other words in the English language.

I wasn't even sure I knew my own name or where I was or why I was here.

My only answer would have been "to fuck this man," whoever he was.

I was just starting to come down from my cloud when the realization hit me.

He hadn't gotten off.

"Um . . . do you still need to get off?"

His laugh wrapped around me like a warm blanket, and my body went lax against him. "I got off, baby. Yours was just a hell of a lot better than mine, and you didn't even notice."

My cheeks were on fire. "Oh . . . I'm sorry."

He continued to laugh and I found myself laughing right along with him. "Don't be. That was some of the hottest sex I've ever had. And the way you come . . . the way you taste . . . holy fuck, woman."

Now I was certain my cheeks were aflame.

I resisted the urge to touch them and make sure no embers flickered across my freckles.

Swallowing, I motioned for him to let me down. "Well . . . uh, thank you."

He pulled the condom off, tied it and then shoved it into his pants pocket.

"Thank you, Miss . . . "

I shook my head. "No names, please."

Jesus Christ, what had I done?

Now that the endorphins were starting to wear off, things were not looking nearly as fun or hot.

I'd just had sex, albeit world-rocking, coma-inducing sex, but it'd been with a complete stranger.

And I needed to keep it that way.

I was coming off a breakup; I had no room for relationships or romance in my life.

This was a one-time thing.

I wasn't going to spend the next ten days screwing random guys.

No, I had a job to do.

What on earth had I been thinking?

"I'm going to find out your name eventually, you know."

I shrugged and smoothed down my skirt. "I know. But can you just *pretend* you don't know it? Can we just behave, for the next ten days, as if this never happened? Ships passing in the night. That kind of thing." Regret settled like a lead balloon in my stomach, and I watched as his face, for just a fraction of a second, fell in disappointment.

"We can *pretend* or do whatever you like. You are the guest, and we aim to please and see to your every whim." He plastered on a giant panty-dropping grin and finished doing up his belt. "Now, I'll let you go first, then I'll wait a minute and leave after you when the coast is clear. I highly doubt you will ever see me again anyway. I'm incredibly busy over the next several days seeing to a VIP guest."

I gave him a small smile, followed by a nod. "All right, then, well . . . uh . . . thanks again." I grabbed my suitcase handle and opened the door, poking my head out and scanning the hallway to make sure no one was around. Once I'd determined the coast was clear, I glanced back over my shoulder at him one last time.

He winked.

Who the hell winks these days?

Nobody winks anymore.

But he winked, then followed it up with another big, sexy smile.

I couldn't stop myself and smiled back. Then, with a pit the size of a grapefruit in my stomach, I pushed the door open and headed up to reception.

"Parker Ryan," I said, trying to feign nonchalance as best I could, as though not ten minutes ago I hadn't been forced up against a wall and impaled by a sexy demigod in expensive shoes and a tight shirt.

The front desk woman's eyes went wide. "Oh . . . *Miss?* Miss Ryan. We've been expecting you. Yes, of course, welcome to The Windward Hibiscus Hotel. We're so happy you've decided to come and spend your time at our resort. If there is anything, *anything* at all that you need, please do not hesitate to call and let us know. We have a twenty-four-hour concierge service, and even though we're on an island, there's not much we can't accommodate."

I glanced at her name tag it said "Janessa." Smiling, and hoping my cheeks were not as red as they felt and I didn't have the words "I JUST HAD SEX

WITH A STAFF MEMBER" stamped on my forehead, I said, "Thank you." A man dressed in the customary beige pants and navy polo shirt with the hotel logo and name emblazoned in the top right corner, came over and offered me a complimentary smoothie in a glass. I thanked him and sipped it greedily. Sex with a stranger was parching. Mmm coconut and something I couldn't quite put my finger on.

"It's guava, Miss," Janessa said, taking in my creased brow as I continued to sip through my straw.

"Is that what it is?" I hummed. "It's delicious." I finished off the delightful glass of liquid heaven and set the empty vessel down on the front desk. "Now I know I'm supposed to go and meet with Mr. McAllister, but I was hoping to freshen up first. If I could be shown to my room, I'd really appreciate it."

Her French-tipped nails *tippy-tapped* on the keyboard, and her round face with rosy cheeks stretched into a big smile. "We actually have you in our presidential villa for the duration of your stay. Mr. McAllister wants you to spend your time here in the lap of luxury. You have an unencumbered view of the ocean as well as fresh fruit trees right outside your door next to your own private veranda. The veranda has full privacy as well, if you're one of those who chooses to tan topless."

I smiled ruefully. "I'm not, but good to know. Thank you."

She nodded as she reached for a key card from a big stack, swiping it through a reader to load it with my room number. "All right then, Miss Ryan, if you'll just follow me, I will take you to your villa so you can freshen up." She sashayed out from behind the desk and went to reach for my bag. I let her, and then the two of us took off back down the same hallway I'd just come down. Past the same door I'd just ducked out of, the door to the room where not fifteen minutes ago I'd had the most intense, incredible and unforgettable sex of my life, all with a man whose name I refused to learn.

Chapter Two

Not that I dress to impress, because in my line of work, people are trying to impress me, but for some reason I wasn't happy with my current outfit and desperately wanted to change.

When I'd selected my clothes before my flight, the white, flowy skirt and wide-strapped blue halter top seemed acceptable. With four-inch cork wedge sandals and some chunky jewelry, I was beachy casual but also professional.

I was in French Polynesia, on the island of Moorea in Tahiti, the definition of tropical; a pantsuit or pencil skirt and nylons were out of the question, especially in this heat.

But this was also the nicest hotel I'd ever stayed in, and I've stayed in some real posh places.

Everything was top of the line, spotless and impressive.

I didn't need to count the threads to know that the sheets were going to feel like silk against my skin, or to read the price of the booze in the minibar to know that there wasn't going to be a thing in there under fifty dollars, or more likely a hundred.

This place was paradise for plutocrats, and for the next week and a half, I got to live like a magnate as well.

I jumped into the lavish stone and smoked-glass shower and washed off the smell of airplane from my skin, subsequently, and to my dismay, also washing off the smell of my tryst. I closed my eyes under the pulsing water, my hair neatly tucked up under a plastic shower cap so that I didn't have to waste time drying it. I'm pretty sure I was already going to be late for my meet-and-greet with Mr. McAllister.

Washing my body, I let my soapy hand wend its way down my torso, dipping two fingers between my legs.

He'd made me touch myself.

No man had ever *ordered* me to do that before.

No man had ever *watched* me do that before.

Sure, from time to time when the need hit me, I'd take care of myself in the middle of the night.

I had packed my battery-operated boyfriend on this trip, and he sat dutifully in my suitcase waiting to be called upon when needed.

But I'd never touched myself in front of a man, never had him guide me, order me, and then blatantly taste me, reveling in my flavor as he licked himself clean of my wetness.

Who was that man in the "broom closet"?

Would I see him again?

Did I want to?

I rubbed decadent little circles around my clit at the memory of his touch, of his lips, his hands, his . . . before I knew it, I was a panting and wanton mess, biting my lip as my second orgasm for the day overhauled my body and made me cry out while the warm water pelted my skin into supple butter.

Within fifteen minutes I was dressed, with freshly applied makeup and a new outfit.

This time it was a sexy but professional short-sleeved wrap dress, with a black, white and turquoise floral print.

My mother said it aged me when I'd worn it to our family reunion this past summer.

She'd said it made me look close to forty-five and not the youthful thirty-two I actually was.

But then this was coming from the woman who at forty-nine (yes, you got that right, my mother was only two years older than my ex-boyfriend) still walked out of the house wearing denim miniskirts and spaghetti-strap tank tops that showed off her bra strap and sometimes even the lace on the cups.

I took one final glance at myself in the big floor-to-ceiling mirror, pinched my cheeks, slathered on some peachy lip balm and was out the door

The well-groomed grounds toward the main hotel area were pristine

Freshly cut grass, ponds and streams, although manmade, looked as though they'd been put there by Mother Nature. Palm trees and vegetation galore quilted the property, while the chirp and warble of tropical birds filled the balmy afternoon air.

Besides the main hotel, which looked fairly standard, all the outbuildings were stylized in the traditional French Polynesian fashion, with domed roofs and evenly spaced posts supporting the beams. I would have to ask Mr. McAllister if the rooftops were thatched with the traditional sugarcane leaves, or if they'd decided to go with something a little more modern.

I had no idea what to expect with Mr. McAllister.

I'd tried researching him online before I came but couldn't really find much, and no picture.

He was a billionaire, I knew that, but as far as how he'd made his fortune and what other things or properties he owned, I didn't know. I'd mentioned him to Xavier when I'd been initially booked to go and review the hotel, and he hadn't even heard of Tate McAllister, let alone The Windward Hibiscus Hotel. But when we'd Googled the place, both of our eyes had nearly popped out of their sockets.

If I were to guess, I would say he was an older gentleman, possibly a recluse, having made his money through various lucrative real estate investments over the years. Only to buy this hotel late in life and choose to run it while spending the rest of his days living the dream in the heart of paradise.

White hair, tanned skin, possibly a little looser around his neck, maybe some wrinkles and spots on his hands from spending too much time in the sun.

Undoubtedly, he was probably smart as a whip, maybe a bit old school.

But was he kind?

Generous?

Now that he'd made his billions, did he just sit on them on an island paradise and bark orders at his staff, or was he a philanthropic man giving back to society?

I had no idea if there was a Mrs. McAllister, or children; Wikipedia had given me zilch. So, even though everyone was going to be bending over backwards to try to impress me, I still wanted to make a good impression. Especially if I was being granted the opportunity to meet with the owner himself, something not even Xavier Rollins or Wikipedia had managed to do.

I was wearing the same cork wedges as before and tread carefully up the path toward the main hotel again. Janessa at the front desk had given me instructions to get to Mr. McAllister's office. I took the elevator up to the top floor then made my way to the solid teak door with the bronze engraving that said "MCALLISTER" in a no-nonsense bold font.

There was no receptionist or secretary out front, so all I could do was knock, hoping that I wasn't disturbing him from a nap or taking his pills. I teetered back and forth on my heels, my stomach doing a series of somersaults as I heard the tread of heavy footsteps on the other side of the door. The knob jiggled, the door opened, and I looked up.

The afternoon sun was glaring in from behind him, casting his body into a shadowy glow, but I couldn't mistake that smell, tropical but manly with just a hint of minty freshness, that warrior frame, that orbital pull as if he were the moon and I the tides. It was him.

"Uh . . . " we both said.

I blinked a couple of times. I hadn't realized how dark the hallway was until the light from outside stabbed me in the retinas. "I'm, uh . . . I'm here to see Mr. McAllister. Is . . . is that your boss? Your father?"

Oh, shit, had I just slept with the owner's son?

His lip twitched for a second. "No. Not my *boss* or my *father.*"

"Well, is he here? I have an appointment. I'm . . . " I swallowed. Damn it, I was going to have to tell him my name.

He fucking works here, you nit, of course he can find out your name. You're staying in the presidential villa, the whole entire hotel staff knows who you are.

"I'm . . . I'm Parker Ryan from *The Decadent Traveler Magazine.*"

Now it was his turn to appear flustered.

No, I'm going to say he was beyond flustered.

The man was downright stupefied.

"You're a woman?" he managed to finally say.

"What gave it away?" I snorted. "Does Mr. McAllister prefer to do interviews with men?"

Shaking his head, he opened the door wide and invited me inside with a sweep of his arm. His office was a continuation of the opulence outside, not a stapler or picture frame out of place: white leather couches, chrome desk, all set to the backdrop of wall-to-wall floor-to-ceiling windows, nothing but the blue Pacific sparkling like millions of diamonds for as far as the eye could see. He wandered over to the big glass and chrome desk, hesitated for just a moment, hovering his butt over the leather desk chair before letting out a big exhale and finally taking a seat.

He gestured for me to take a seat on the opposite side of the desk.

I did so, crossing my legs and watching as his eyes followed, lingering on my exposed calf and, when the fabric parted at the slit, the bottom of my thigh.

"So, is Mr. McAllister busy? Did he send you to answer my questions and show me around instead?"

He pursed those sexy lips of his in thought for a second before he gave almost an indiscernible nod and pushed himself back up to standing, and extended a big hand across the desk at me. I stared at his fingers; those fingers had been inside me. He'd licked those fingers clean of me.

A need for more of those fingers hit me in the gut (and lower) like a roundhouse kick.

Slowly, I leaned up and took his hand. A sudden jolt of electricity ran from his hand to mine, and I fought the urge to pull away from the shock. He must have felt it, too, because his green eyes lit up and amusement tilted his lips.

"Hi, Miss Ryan. *I'm* Tate McAllister . . . *owner* of The Windward Hibiscus Hotel, and it's a *pleasure* to make your acquaintence."

My mouth dropped open like a guppy's. Holy crap. I'd just slept with the *owner!*

"*You're* Tate McAllister?" I squeaked. "But you're . . . you're . . . "

"Young? Attractive? The man you assumed was a concierge and ordered to fuck you in a broom closet less than an hour ago?"

My tongue was sandpaper.

His lips turned up into another wickedly sexy grin. "I am the owner, yes. But I will admit that you're not the only one who is surprised here. I had assumed by your name that you were a man, and I have planned a series of activities for you during your stay that I am now re-thinking."

My feminist back instantly went ramrod-straight. What kind of *activities* had he planned for a man that as a *woman* I would be unfit to do? Bikini contest judge? Jock-strap tester? Mustache trimming competition?

I gave him my best steely stare. "And what *activities* had you planned for *Mr.* Parker Ryan?"

He managed a sheepish smile and looked down at his lap for a moment. "Well, deep sea fishing, a sunrise hike to the top of the mountain, spear fishing, scuba diving, skydiving, parasailing . . . "

My eyes narrowed in on him. "Insert feminist rant here," I said snidely. "I can do every one of those things."

He struggled to hide another smile. "I'm sure you can. Have you ever been scuba diving before? Fishing?"

"Well, no, but . . . " Shit, he had me there. "I-it can't be *that* difficult."

"It's not. I'll teach you."

I shifted in my seat and felt my thighs glide across each other.

So that's where all the moisture in my mouth had gone.

Damn it.

Suddenly images of Tate and I out on a boat, him shirtless and standing behind me, helping me reel in a big . . . crap, what fish were out here? Salmon? Bass? Marlin? Helping me reel in a big *marlin*, his arms around mine as we grunted and groaned with the strain of hauling our catch on board. I licked my lips and re-crossed my legs, hoping to God that my pebbled nipples weren't visible through my dress, because they sure as hell ached.

"Okay."

"However, I would also like to schedule you for some more pampering things as well, now that I know you're a woman, a hard-*working* woman, no less. I'll book you in for a few massages, scrubs, facials, manicure and pedicure. Do you do yoga? Pilates? Meditate? We have it all. Private or group classes. Whatever your heart desires, we have it."

Whatever my heart desires?

What did my *heart* desire?

I knew what my *body* desired.

What my body craved, and that was more of Tate McAllister.

Hard, sex god, Tate McAllister.

I just continued to nod like a bobble-head on the dash of a car. His one dimple winked at me again as he smiled and chatted, and his eyes gleamed with all kinds of mischief and promise.

The not-so-distant memory of the way his hands, his lips, his tongue, his teeth, his . . . felt on my skin, inside me, had my eyes glazing over and my pulse picking up speed.

"You okay?" he asked. "Miss Ryan?"

I shook my head and blinked. "Oh, uh, yeah, sorry. Jet lag."

He nodded once. "Would you like to postpone things until tomorrow? You're welcome to return to your villa and sleep."

"No, no. I'm fine, thank you. If you don't mind, I'd like to start off by interviewing you first. And then we can do a tour and discuss the next week or so."

"You'd like to *start* off with interviewing me? How about discussing what just happened downstairs, now that we're no longer just John and Jane Doe. We're going to be spending an awful lot of time together over the next ten days. Best to clear the air, don't you think?"

I let out a big exhale, avoiding his penetrating stare and instead choosing to look behind him out into the endless ocean. The sky was a brilliant blue, while the sea was more of a deep and alluring cobalt, swirling like a marble with hints of turquoise and green and darker patches where there was reef and shallows. He was living in paradise, living the dream.

Finally, I let my eyes drift back to his.

He was waiting for me.

Patiently waiting for me to collect my thoughts, my nerves and whatever else was plaguing me.

Was he always this patient?

"I'm coming off a harsh breakup. My ex left a message on my phone, and I listened to it in the shuttle. I was in a terrible mood when I walked into the hotel and wanted to make it better. I can't be the first person to use someone else, use sex as a way to lift spirits or make themselves feel better. You could have said *no.*" I shot him my best challenging glare, but he met it with another amused and confident smirk, his eyes continuing to twinkle.

"But I didn't."

"No, you didn't."

Silence.

Awkward, awkward silence.

Well, awkward for me.

He seemed to be thoroughly enjoying himself.

Jesus, you could cut the sexual tension in the room with a knife.

The A/C was humming in the corner, but I was still rather warm, my face was surely flushed, and I'm pretty sure my chest and neck were rosy, too. Nearly as red as the beautiful single hibiscus he had in a short glass vase in the corner of his desk.

I swallowed again. "Look, it was a one-time thing, okay? Quick and dirty sex with a stranger was all. Just because we're no longer *strangers* doesn't mean it has to get weird. You helped me out of a funk, and from what I can remember, you seemed to enjoy yourself as well."

"I did," he said smugly. "More than I've enjoyed myself in a very long time."

Crap.

"Yes, well, be that as it may, it can't happen again. I'm here for work. You're the owner. It was a one-time thing."

"One-time thing, eh?"

Eh? Was he Canadian? I'd have to ask him. Wikipedia had been useless.

I nodded. "Yes."

"Quick and dirty sex with a stranger?"

Why was he repeating everything I'd just said?

"Yes." I nodded again. "Quick and dirty. But it's not happening again. Now, if you don't mind, I'd like to start the interview, get down to business."

He cocked his head ever so slightly. "Get down to business . . . "

Okay, now he was just starting to piss me off, repeating me like a flippin' mynah bird or some petulant toddler.

I let out an exasperated sigh. This man was incorrigible. "Let's begin then, shall we?" I asked, opening my shoulder bag and whipping out my digital recorder and notebook.

Tate smiled wide and leaned back in his chair, an ankle rested on his knee, and he tucked his hands behind his head. "Ask away, lady."

"Okay." I swallowed. "So, how did you come to own The Windward Hibiscus?"

"I bought it a few years back. It was a rundown three-star hotel that I bought for a steal, and I've spent the last six years turning it into one of the most elite and coveted resorts in the Pacific. *The billionaires' haven,* as it's been nicknamed."

I nodded. "And how have you come to have such wealth? How were you able to come up with the capital to pay for the place?" I watched as his eyebrow twitched half an inch on his forehead, and I found myself suddenly backpedaling. "I—I'm sorry if this question seems a tad intrusive. It's just that nobody knows who you are. Nobody knows anything about you, how you've come to own one of the most exclusive resorts in the world. I mean, you don't even have a picture or biography on Wikipedia. And this *is* my job. It's why you brought me here. To interview you and review the resort." Crap, I just had this feeling he was going to be one of those "off the record" bozos.

This time, his grin stretched nearly clear across his face. It reached his eyes, and the corners crinkled, making him not only handsome as hell, but also adorable. "And I'd like to keep it that way, if I may?"

I looked down into my lap. Normally, I was much more confident than this. He was flustering me. I was so off my game.

"Off the record?" he asked taking pity on me.

Fuck!

My head snapped up. That amused smirk was still on his face. He was enjoying this little dance far too much. I nodded. Even if the world didn't get to know, *I* wanted to know.

"Fine. Off the record."

My answer seemed to suffice so with a curt nod he started. "I *inherited* my starter money. My father left us when I was small, and my uncle, my mother's brother, stepped in and was the male father-figure in my life. He never married, never had any children. If I were to guess now, I'd say he was gay, just based on a few puzzle pieces I've put together over the years, but he never came out to anyone. He was successful in real estate, and when he died, he left everything to me. After taxes, my inheritance was just shy of five million dollars. I paid off my mother's house and bills, set her up comfortably, then invested the rest. A few years later, I found out that my father had died. Apparently, as shitty as he was a father, he was just that shrewd of a businessman . . . "

His lips twisted wryly as if weighing the next thing he was going to say. "And a philanderer. I have three half-siblings spread across the world. He left his fortune, which was rather substantial, to the four of us. He never raised any of us as far as I know. Knocked our mothers up and left a few years later, so I guess it was his way of 'making amends.' I received around ten million from his estate. And I've only met one sibling so far, but he received the same amount. I'm assuming the other two inherited something as well. I'm still trying to find them."

Wow. I simply nodded, my mouth agape but encouraging him to continue.

He did. "Combined with my investments, some shares I'd purchased and lucrative business decisions, I was able to buy The Hibiscus, with a small loan from the bank as well, of course."

She finally found her voice again and decided to ask one her burning questions. "And why did you decide to turn it into an elite resort?"

"Because I like my privacy, and I respect when others do as well. Our security rivals the Pentagon. Everyone, if they wish, can check in under an alias. Every *legal* whim, fancy and proclivity is seen to. Men can bring their mistresses here and never worry about being found out. Women can bring their boy-toys and leave the fear of being discovered at the airport. We are discreet, private and full-service."

"But all of that comes for a price," I said, perhaps a bit too rashly. That comment about *mistresses* had ruffled my feathers something fierce, and I was suddenly looking at Tate McAllister with less *fucky* eyes and more *screw-you* eyes. I bet he had mistresses up the wazoo.

"Of course." He shrugged. "Luxury, privacy, *discretion*, nothing worth having is *free* in this day and age."

"So, what about your personal life? *Wife? Ex-wife? Girlfriends? Children?*"

Based on what had transpired in the soundproof room not an hour ago, I sincerely hoped that my first and third questions were going to be a hard "NO." I couldn't imagine being "the other woman."

He shook his head. "No. There's been no time." There was a sadness to his smile, but he quickly quelled it and flashed me another super sexy one with straight white teeth. That expression seemed to live on him. "That's not to say I don't enjoy the *companionship* of women. I just don't have anyone *special* in my life. No wife. No ex-wife. No *girlfriend*. No children." His head tilted to the side, and he suddenly reminded me of a curious puppy. "What about you?"

I shook my head. "What about me?"

"Husband? Ex-husband? Boyfriend? Children?"

What the hell?

We weren't here to interview me.

This was not a back-and-forth thing.

I was the one asking the questions, not him.

But somehow, I knew by the way he was looking at me, by the curve of his mouth, that he wasn't going to take a head shake or "No" for an answer. That if I wanted more answers, I'd have to give him something.

I shook my head again. "No. I've never been married. No *boyfriend.*" That one still hurt. "I told you I'm coming off a bad breakup. And no children." That one was like a punch to the gut.

He barely nodded as he stood up from behind the desk and sauntered his big gladiator frame around to the front, perching on the corner just a foot or so away from me. I had to look up to see his face and nearly swallowed my tongue when I did.

The man was smoldering, green eyes with flecks of gold twinkling, full of mischief and dirty secrets.

Oh, Mr. McAllister, I'm sure you have *loads* of dirty little secrets.

That's when I noticed a couple of blond hairs on the shoulder of his white dress shirt. I hadn't noticed them before, but from where he was sitting now, the sun hit him just right and illuminated them like strands of gold.

A taste of panic rifled through my body. I wasn't blonde, he wasn't blond, and they were much too long to be his anyway. Maybe four or five inches long. A woman's?

"Hmmm," he finally said. His sounds of amusement affected me far more than he could ever realize. I loved the little rumbling noise he made at the back of this throat. It was primitive and wild. "So, anything else you'd like to ask me, on or *off* the record, Miss Ryan?"

I ran my tongue between the seam of my lips again before putting my pen between my teeth and lightly biting down in thought. "I don't think so, at least not for now. Perhaps a quick tour?"

Tate extended his hand, and at first, I wasn't sure why. Did he expect us to hold hands and wander around the resort?

Another handshake?

But he was offering to help me to my feet.

I'm such an idiot.

I extended my hand, and that surge of electricity from earlier rushed through my body, making me practically convulse on the spot.

Did he feel it, too?

He had to.

It was a shock, an actual shock.

Like when you rub your socked feet along a carpet, touch something metal and then shuffle over and touch someone else.

He helped me to my feet, and I quickly pulled my hand back, even though my body was screaming at me not to. But my brain overthrew the battle, and I released his hand only to find it at the small of my back, ushering me out the door not a second later.

"Just this way, Miss Ryan. I'll show you the pools, the grounds, the restaurants. And if we have time ... the grotto. And then we have 'reservations' "—he chuckled as if having reservations at his own restaurant was funny—"at the Tiki Lounge this evening."

"*We* do?" I asked, following him to the bronze-doored elevator.

"Well, yes. It's not very often I invite a journalist here to experience the lap of luxury and document their stay, let alone interview me. So, I figured the least I could do was give you what you're after, an all-access pass ... to *me.*"

The elevator doors parted, and he motioned for me to join him inside.

I stepped forward like a robot. The words *all-access, to me, quick and dirty* rolled around in my head until they no longer even sounded like words.

They were more of a chant, a mantra, an ... *order.*

Chapter Three

I WATCHED THE ELEVATOR doors glide shut, then all I felt was hot.

Hot and bothered as this menacingly attractive man, who smelled so damn good I could hardly stand it, looked down at me with those searing eyes of his.

I swallowed hard and refused to glance up at him.

This was not going to happen.

This could not happen.

It shouldn't have happened in the first place, but it had, and now I had to live with it.

But I was going to make damn sure it didn't happen again.

As if they were a piece by Monet I studied my feet as the elevator descended.

But I could sense him watching me.

He leaned back ever so slightly to glance behind.

The pig.

Was he really so obviously checking out my ass?

Jesus.

Yeah, it was so not happening again with us.

No way.

No how.

Suddenly he dropped to a crouch.

"What the heck are you doing?" I asked, taking a half step to the side.

"Just a second." His voice smooth while amusement and triumph glittered in his eyes. Before I could blink, protest or step away, his hand wrapped around my ankle, and he lifted up my foot. I stumbled on my one leg and, without thinking twice, reached out and put my hand on his broad, warm shoulder.

Strong, hard . . . oh, God, so *hard*, muscles flexed, able and true beneath my fingertips.

"What are you doing?"

He reached for something with his free hand, the one that wasn't currently caressing my leg, and lifted something off the bottom of my shoe. He held it up a second later. "You had toilet paper stuck to the bottom of your heel."

"Oh . . . " Instant mortification flooded me. I'd been wandering around the resort with bathroom tissue on my shoe like some twenty-something drunk chick at a bar.

He set my foot back down on the floor then slowly, ever so slowly, way *too* slowly, let his fingers trail up my calf to the back of my knee and bottom of my thigh, beneath the hem of my dress before he finally let go, standing up to his full height.

I tried not to shiver.

My nipples were already so hard they could cut glass, and I was sure he noticed.

The fabric of this dress was *quite* thin.

I hadn't realized it, but I'd closed my eyes from his touch, the heat of his fingers, the softness of his palm as it grazed my searing skin.

Tingles of need and longing zinged through me in every direction like poorly organized fireworks.

If I wasn't careful, I was going to set the entire hotel on fire.

My lips parted just barely, while my chest rose and fell in quick and erratic succession.

My breathing shallowed, and I fought the urge to squeeze my legs together and not let the low groan that was building at the back of my throat break free. I licked my lips and swallowed hard, waiting, hoping, envisioning him running that hand up even further and then plastering me against the wall of the elevator and taking me just like he had downstairs an hour ago.

I wasn't sure how long I had my eyes closed, but when I finally opened them, Tate was standing beside me again, grass-green eyes ignited with lust, pupils dilated and nostrils flaring. The man was in full-on rut, and if I didn't get out of the elevator soon, I was going to let him have me any way he wanted to.

Swallowing again, I let my gaze flick down to the tissue in his hand before drifting back up to his face. "Uh, thanks."

He shook his head slightly, but his expression, his thoughts were completely tangible. "No problem at all, *Miss Ryan.*"

"Parker," I said softly. "Please call me Parker."

Another barely discernible head movement; this time, I was pretty sure it was a nod. *"Parker."*

The elevator dinged and the doors parted.

A wave of cool air from the lobby whooshed forward, sending a rush of goosebumps chasing across my skin.

His hand fell to the small of my back again, and he escorted me out and to the front doors.

The palms ahead of us swayed gently in the tropical breeze, inviting us out into the glorious Tahitian sunshine.

"We'll start off with the recreation center, then the spas, the restaurants, the beach and finally the pool and grotto. Does that sound okay to you?"

I was waiting for him to remove his hand from my back, but he didn't.

Instead, he shifted his placement and let his fingers graze the top of my hip as he careened us around a corner and off in the direction of a big outbuilding. I could feel the heat from his palm through the dress, and his fingers bunched just a touch, trying to hold on. I was hyperaware of his touch; it was consuming my every thought.

It conveyed possession and control effortlessly, and it was making me incredibly hot.

"Sounds good to me," I said with a swallow, unsure how to pull away and not entirely sure I wanted to.

****

As promised, we finished the impressive tour next to the biggest, most beautiful VIP pool, where loungers and cabanas were set up. Staff scurried around and saw to every imaginable whim of the demanding guests while soft music played over an expertly hidden sound system. A few people were still milling around, some in the water, others on the deck. Off in the shade of a big white cabana, a couple of gentlemen were getting massaged by two tiny Thai women.

The men on the tables were rather large and *quite* hairy, and for some reason, as hard as I tried, I just couldn't look away.

I gawked as the little women poked and prodded them with their knees and elbows, getting in between the rolls and making the grown men whimper and wince in pain.

Tate caught me watching and chuckled. "They may be small, but they're mighty. Have you ever had a Thai massage?"

I nodded. "Yeah, they're intense."

He laughed again. "That's one way to describe them." His hand fell back to my hip, and he turned me toward what looked to be a mound of round rocks purposely designed into a big hill and then covered with foliage and flowers. But when we wandered around it a little more, I saw that there was an opening and the pool continued on into the mound, making it more of a tunnel.

"And that's the grotto," he said finally, pointing inside. I couldn't really see much as it was rather dark, but it appeared as though you waded through the small channel and then it widened and opened up inside. There may have also been some built-in underwater seating, but the shadows and lack of lighting inside made it difficult to determine. I'm sure in the coming days I'd make my way in there and find out for myself.

"And what's so *special* about the grotto?" I asked, allowing him to lead me away and back in the direction of the main hotel building.

He lifted one shoulder. "What happens in the grotto stays in the grotto."

"Who the heck are you, Hugh Hefner?"

He laughed. "No. I don't need a little blue pill."

My face was an inferno.

No, he certainly didn't, that I could attest to.

I'd gotten so used to his hand at my back or on my hip that when he moved it to open the door for me, a sudden emptiness flooded me and I longed for him to put it back.

His warmth, his touch, they had become comforting, and even though I'd just met the man, I felt safe standing next to him as he chatted animatedly about his eco-resort for the immensely wealthy.

I wasn't quite sure what was happening or *going* to happen between Tate McAllister and I, but one thing I did know was that the man could kiss, the man could fuck, and even though he'd simply been showing me around the resort, I'd had a wonderful afternoon with him.

I followed him inside, but we didn't stop.

Instead, we continued on through the lobby and to the left, through another series of doors, and then into what could only be described as Oceanian opulence to the Nth degree. The restaurant was breathtaking, all open concept beneath the French Polynesian-style domed thatch roof, so the evening breeze and lullaby of birds could cool off and entertain all the guests. Through the restaurant we walked, past tables of content diners with big fruity tropical drinks of deliciousness in front of them while the flame from a big grill in the center of the space flew up at random intervals, threatening to singe the rafters.

I let out the breath I'd been holding as Tate pulled a chair out for me on the patio. It would appear we had the best seat in the house. A perfect view of the sunset. "Wow, I can see why you live here. This is extraordinary."

His eyes danced emerald fire as he smiled at me and took his own seat. "It is, isn't it?"

I hadn't even been given a chance to order a drink, or even my meal, but somehow within seconds of sitting down, a delicious and funky-looking cocktail was placed in front of me, complete with a little umbrella and a wedge of pineapple. Moments later, the most decadent-looking meal was rolled over, only to be finished tableside by the executive chef himself.

In no time at all, I was dabbing at the corner of my mouth with my cloth napkin. I sat back, staring at the empty plate in front of me. "Well, that was incredible. I can't remember the last time I had anything that tasted so good."

Tate's ghost of a smile made my heart rate skyrocket. "I hope you don't mind that I ordered for us. I just, well," he lifted one shoulder, "wanted to impress you."

I grinned back and brought my fancy shmancy drink to my mouth, letting the straw rest between my lips as I looked at him over the rim. "Well, I'm impressed. That was delicious. I've never had barracuda before. And that certainly won't be the last time I try it, either."

His sexy flash of a smile made me instinctively squeeze my thighs together and hope to God he didn't notice my nipples pearl beneath my dress.

He lifted his beer bottle in the air, expecting me to join him in a toast.

I clinked the bottle with my cup.

"What are we toasting?" I giggled.

"I'm not sure yet," he said. "But I'm sure by the end of your stay here, we'll have a lot to celebrate." He winked again, tipped his beer back and finished it off.

****

Still not used to the time change, and an early riser by nature, I found myself wide awake and staring at the ceiling by five in the morning.

Not one to waste time or energy, I tossed on a bathing suit, wrapped a robe around my body, then headed off to the lap pool located just off the main lobby.

I flashed my key card in front of the panel, and the light blinked green while the door clicked open.

Pentagon security indeed.

I was half-expecting a retinal scan or, at the very least, a fingerprint.

It was quiet as I slowly padded my way inside. My flip-flops made a godawful racket as I wandered across the tile.

I relished the idea of having the space to myself.

Even though swimming laps was probably one of the most antisocial forms of exercising, I wasn't interested in making small talk or having to dodge another guest.

But when I rounded the corner to the pool, my heart sank. I wasn't alone.

Someone else was using the pool.

I stood at the edge for a moment and watched as the lithe body in a black Speedo, black swim cap and blue goggles did the front crawl like an Olympian.

He glided through the water, muscles flexing and contracting with each rise of his powerful arms while the water shimmered on his back and arms under the dim pot lighting overhead.

Then I noticed the tattoo.

Black and tribal and taking up nearly the entire top half of his back, it was beautiful and oh so sexy.

My breath caught before I could stop it; whoever he was, he was magnificent.

"Good morning."

I shook my head and looked down. He was directly below me, hanging on the edge of the pool, removing the goggles and flashing me that same wickedly dirty grin as yesterday.

"Oh . . . ah, morning," I said.

"This pool is closed until six," he said smoothly, water dripping down his face and neck in provocative rivulets.

My mouth dropped open. "Oh. Okay. I-I can go. My key card worked. I didn't see a sign on the door, but I can go."

His wet lips curled into a wry smirk as he blinked a few droplets off his lashes. "Your key card worked because you are in the *presidential* villa, and whoever is in the presidential villa gets to do whatever they want. Time doesn't apply to you. You can use whatever you want, whenever you want. And besides," he turned to face the pool for a quick second, "there is more than enough pool to go around. I can share. It's kind of nice to work out in peace, don't you think?"

I nodded. "Yes. Peace."

He didn't wait for me to answer or decide. He just pulled his goggles back over his eyes then pushed off the wall, streamlining nearly three quarters of the pool before he needed to start moving his arms.

I chose to stay.

There were four lanes set up for laps. Plenty of room for the two of us to swim next to each other. I stripped off my robe and grabbed a towel from the rack before I set up camp on a bench. All the while my eyes never left Tate or that tattoo. I pulled my swim cap and goggles out of my bag, tucked my hair up, had one brief thought of running my tongue over that gorgeous ink and then dove in.

It was wonderful to be in the water again.

Xavier and I had been broken up for almost two weeks, and I sorely missed the pool in his condo building.

I had a membership at the YMCA and would go back to the pool there once I returned home, but there was something so nice about a private pool.

Nobody stared at you or clogged or dawdled in your lane. Come to think of it, I was probably going to miss Xavier's pool more than I was going to miss Xavier.

I did my fifty laps and stopped at the end. Tate had kept to himself and swum two lanes over. I hadn't heard a peep from him, but every so often I'd catch a glimpse of him out of the corner of my eye when I came up for air—the man was a machine. Hauling my dripping butt out of the water and up the ladder, I pulled off my cap and goggles and then headed off to the sauna, desperately trying to avoid watching Tate's firm ass twist and flex as he continued swimming. How many laps was he going to do?

I wasn't in the sauna five minutes when the door opened.

"Nothing like a nice bake after a refreshing swim, eh? Limber up the muscles for the day to come?" He sauntered in with the practiced swagger of a playboy, his towel slung over his shoulders and faint goggle lines rimming bright eyes. But I barely took notice of any of that. It was the tight black Speedo that left absolutely nothing to the imagination that had me practically swallowing my tongue and suffering from quick-onset dry mouth.

I nodded only to hastily look away. "Uh . . . yeah. H-how many laps do you do?"

"A hundred."

"Every day?"

"Yes." He took a seat one bench below me and a tad over. He brought his water bottle up and took a healthy swig.

My eyes fell back to the tattoo.

It looked like a series of black swirls and etchings and patterned lines.

I'd never seen anything like it before, and I couldn't draw my eyes away.

His skin practically glowed from the water and his muscles flexed and bunched as he continued to chug. I swallowed and licked my lips. I wanted to trace that entire tattoo with my finger.

No, wait, with my tongue!

Yeah, my tongue.

I wanted to lick every square inch of that gorgeous ink.

I watched as his throat jogged with his swallow.

Damn, even that was sexy, and of course, I'd forgotten to pack a water bottle.

"You want some?" he offered, lifting the bottle to me.

I took it from him. "Thanks."

Why did I get a sudden rush knowing that my lips were going to be touching where his lips had just touched? We'd already kissed. Hell, we'd done *more* than just kiss. But the idea of drinking from Tate's water bottle was turning me on. Not to mention that Speedo of his, and that sexy as hell tattoo, and his abs, and his pecs, and his biceps and legs . . .

"So, you swim a hundred laps, every day?" I asked again, feeling the need to make chit-chat, otherwise I was just going to continue staring at his body, let my fantasies run wild, inevitably start to drool and possibly have a spontaneous orgasm.

Yeah, chit-chat, harmless, boring, sexual-tension-free chit-chat was a must.

Reluctantly, I handed him back the bottle and then, damn it, my eyes fell back down to his crotch.

Get it together, woman!

"Yep. It's a great way to start the day. Though, sometimes I take Sundays off."

I shook my head. "Were you a swimmer. Like in college?"

He nodded. "Yeah, I was on the swim team in university. Qualified for the Olympics even, but that was right around the time my uncle got really sick, so I bowed out and went to take care of him."

"Oh. Wow. That's very noble of you."

Lifting one shoulder casually, he made an indifferent face, as if the past was the past and he didn't want to talk about it, or didn't want to draw attention to his compassion; either way, I was drawn to his modesty. To his quiet power and the immense force it wielded.

The man was a magnate, a billionaire, and yet he still seemed to be so humble and down-to-earth.

The Richie Riches I hung out with in Xavier's circle never would have given up an Olympic dream or even a business opportunity to go and take care of a sick relative; they'd have just hired out the job.

But not Tate.

Tate was different.

"In the end it was for the best," he said with a sigh. "I prefer to swim to keep fit, and that's it. The training regime was insane."

Now I didn't know what to say. No matter how hard I tried to look elsewhere, my eyes just kept drifting from his back to the front of his bathing suit and the bulge that sat there tempting me. I knew what was hidden inside, a serpent . . . and like Eve and that damn apple, one taste was *not* going to be enough.

"Wh-what is your tattoo?" I asked, desperate to take the thoughts that were currently cannoning off one another in my head out of the gutter. Fat chance of that. I'd jumped headfirst into the gutter the moment I asked this hunk of a man to take me to heaven and back in a broom closet.

"Hmm? Oh, it's Samoan. It symbolizes the ocean and waves. These here," he ran his long, capable fingers over a well-defined shoulder blade, "these are meant to be sharks' teeth. Which is fitting, considering that early on in my diving career, I was attacked by a tiger shark." He spun around to show me his full, perfect body and then pointed to a series of scars on his left hip. "See, teeth marks."

My eyes went wide. "Oh my God. You were okay, though?"

He nodded. "Oh yeah, it wasn't a very big tiger shark, just an aggressive one."

I licked my lips again, the urge to trace my fingers over every line of the stunning ink work making my hand twitch. I lifted my thigh and tucked my fingers beneath my leg to stop myself from reaching out. "Well, it's beautiful."

A dangerously sexy smile spread across his face. "Thanks. A buddy of mine, he's Samoan, and when I went to visit his family with him a few years ago, he took me to his uncles's tattoo shop and I had it done. I wasn't sure about getting something so cultural on my body, especially since I'm not Samoan, but Malakai was insistent. He says I'm family, and even though I'm as white as they come, he knows how deeply embedded French Polynesia is in my heart." His Adam's apple bobbed heavy in his throat at the mention of family. "It was an honor."

I looked down at my thighs.

The silence between us was deafening, as was the pounding of my pulse inside my ears.

Not to mention the voices in my head that were screaming at me to touch him, hell, they were telling me to do more than just *touch* him.

"You know," he started, making my head snap up from where I'd been staring to blatantly at his crotch, "I don't see why we can't make the most of your time here. Make one another feel good for the next ten days. You said you're coming off a rough breakup, and I'm unattached. Isn't it pretty much *necessary* to have an endless stream of mind-blowing, meaningless sex after you break up with someone?"

An endless stream of mind-blowing, meaningless sex?

No matter how hot the sauna was, my cheeks were hotter.

He moved over on the bench and pushed himself up, his forearms flexing with the weight of having to hold up his body. A second later, he was next to me on the bench.

"I mean, if you say *no*, I'll obviously respect your decision and back off." His lips twisted, and he reached out and fingered a strand of my damp hair. "But something tells me you're not totally sure if you *want* to say *no*. Am I right?" His voice was dark and low, almost gravelly. It kissed across my skin, licking and biting, tasting and teasing and I wasn't even touching him.

I swallowed and squeezed my thighs together, biting back a whimper from the ache I felt deep in my belly and my swollen clit.

"Quick and dirty, wasn't that what you said?" His voice now tortured me. Every word, every syllable sent shards of need directly to my erogenous zones and made them spark alive.

All I could do was nod as I watched a sinfully delicious bead of sweat emerge on his sculpted upper lip.

I wanted to lick it off; I wanted to lick every damn inch of the man.

"Well, ten days is quick, and what I'd like to do to you is all kinds of *dirty*, so . . . " His eyes flicked up to mine while his hand landed on my bare thigh and squeezed. I inhaled abruptly from the heat of his touch. I couldn't stop it, I couldn't control it, they had a bloody life of their own; my eyes drifted down once again to his crotch. I rolled my bottom lip between my teeth and watched as the bulge in his Speedo started to grow, lying thick and eager against his pelvic bone, desperate to break free of its Lycra prison.

Oh my freaking God.

"Tate . . . " I breathed, unable to form a complete sentence, let alone a complete thought.

"You can say *no,* Parker."

He stood up on the bench below and positioned himself in front of me, spreading my legs and moving into the V. His fingers made their way up my thighs and waist, finally resting on my shoulders, hooking beneath the straps of my swimsuit.

"Say *no*, Parker, and I'll stop right now."

Slowly, excruciatingly so, he drew the damp straps of my suit over my arms, exposing my breasts, then my stomach. His eyes drifted up to mine for a second before he bent his head low and latched on to a nipple, drawing the tender bud between his teeth and tugging. I arched my back to give him better access, my eyes fluttering shut like a vintage doll's as a moan built in the back of my throat. Dear God, the man's mouth was diabolical. Hot and wet and so freaking wonderful. His tongue flicked over the achy bud, and I choked on a sob.

"Tell me *no,* he said again, moving over to the other nipple and delivering the same erotic torment. "Tell me *no.*"

I buried my hands in his hair and pulled his head up. His gaze snagged mine.

"No," I breathed, tugging on his scalp just hard enough to make his eyes go wide in surprise. "No. Don't stop." I smashed my lips against his and wedged his mouth open so I could ram my tongue inside, taking what he was offering and then some. Our tongues plunged and swirled in a hypnotic dance all their own, exploring the deep recesses of each other's mouths while teeth gently nipped and hands roamed and deftly removed clothing (not that he had much). Once we were naked, he backed away, and I mewled in discontent before I could stop myself.

"I don't have a condom," he said matter-of-factly.

My face fell.

Then what the hell were we starting?

"But that doesn't mean I can't make you scream." Then, without any further ado, he knelt down on the wooden bench, spread me wide and dove in, ears deep.

I nearly came on the spot.

Xavier had never been an overly generous lover, not that he didn't go down on me, but when he did, it wasn't for long.

He'd claimed I wasn't adventurous in bed, but when it came to sex, the man liked three positions: missionary, spoon, and me on my knees.

So to have a man like Tate, a man I hardly knew, eat me out with such fervor and fascination was enough of a high to send me to the moon and back multiple times over.

His energy was endless, and the claim he had over me, his possession of my body, was overwhelming.

I wanted this man more than I'd ever wanted anything in my life.

I wanted his hands all over my body, his mouth on my breasts.

I wanted everything and all at once; I wanted it all.

Within minutes, I found myself gyrating against his face, loving the way his beard scratched my throbbing lips and inner thighs as he lapped at my core, drinking down my juices and groaning as I poured my arousal into his mouth.

Using two well-placed fingers, he stroked my inner walls while his tongue ran circles around my swollen and needy clit.

I began to lose focus on the rhythm, and my hips jerked randomly, weak from having to keep my thighs spread and on his shoulders. I tried to delay my destination just a little longer, enjoy the journey and the wicked pleasure this talented man was giving me, but it all just felt too good, too damn good.

Another finger probed my core, and then he did something no one had ever done before; he drew his chin up between my lips and rubbed his beard against my clit.

The pain, the new sensation, the pleasure, oh God, the pleasure, so much pleasure, it was all too much—I detonated.

My hands found their way back into his hair, and I pulled on the ends, shoving his face deeper into my pussy, wanting more of the delicious torture, wanting him to get his fill, to get my fill.

I heard him growl between my legs, and an arm came up and hooked around my waist, the fingers making their way to the top of my mound.

He spread my lips wide and rubbed his chin up and down again, making filthy little circles around my clit until the nub was swollen and hard and I came again.

I shook like I was having a seizure.

Every nerve ending and synapse fired at the same time as the rapture roared through me in growing waves.

From the tips of my toes to the top of my head and back again, I was lost to the moment, to the endless parade of exquisite sensations eclipsing me.

I was lost in Tate.

Finally, after what felt like hours, if not days, he popped his head up, a Cheshire cat-like grin on his face, his lips and the whiskers on his chin glistening with my release.

I reached for him and pulled him down to me, swiveling around so I was laying down on the bench and he was on top of me. His cock was notched at my core, while his arm muscles bunched and bulged with the weight of his big frame.

Tate shook his head. "I don't have a condom, Parker."

I nodded and swallowed. "I know . . . I just . . . "

A smirk caught on the corner of his kissable mouth. "Just the tip?"

My nod was frantic; I thought my neck might snap. "Y-yeah . . . j-just the tip . . . please. I *am* clean and on the pill . . . "

His pupils dilated until there was nothing but black in his eyes. "I'm clean, too," he said, lifting his hips up with a grunt. Then before I could blink, he slammed into me.

Chapter Four

WHEN I GOT BACK to my villa, there was already breakfast waiting for me. A plate of fresh tropical fruit, toast, poached eggs and fresh coffee.

I didn't even remember ordering room service, but then perhaps it just came with the villa, much like my all-access pass to the grounds.

Or maybe Tate had ordered for me?

But either way I dove right in, as I was famished from swimming . . . and other rigorous activities.

I was still getting over the jet lag and time difference, so at Tate's suggestion I was going to spend the morning at the spa, getting pampered and massaged into butter, then wander around the grounds during the afternoon interviewing staff and checking things out.

Followed, of course, by the remainder of the day spent lounging by the pool or on the beach working on my tan.

Just because I was technically working didn't mean I couldn't indulge in the hot sun and the flattering bikinis I'd packed.

I was just coming out of the spa, feeling like a new me, with pink paint on my toes, a fresh face and limber limbs when I was snatched by the wrist and hauled across the hallway, a hand firmly held in front of my mouth. I wanted to scream but couldn't.

I tried to catch a glimpse of my captor, but he had me in such a tight grip I was locked solid staring straight ahead.

A door was opened, and I was ushered into complete darkness.

Holy crap, I was being kidnapped!

I kicked and punched at my assailant but kept getting air and no contact.

Oh my God, I was going to die.

I could see the headline now: *Xavier Rollins' Ex Found Dead on Tropical Beach.*

No name.

No details.

Because in the end, I didn't matter.

I was just Xavier's ex.

That was all.

Would anyone even miss me?

But then the panic inside my veins ramped up.

I was at a resort for the elite; no way in hell would Tate let my murder or death get out. I'd be tossed out into the middle of the ocean to cover up the scandal.

Fish food.

Shark bait.

Would anyone come looking for me?

Would my mother start to wonder and ask questions?

I didn't call her that often; it might be months before she started to worry.

My heart was threatening to beat out of my chest, and I thought I might pass out from how heavy I was breathing.

This was it.

I was going to die.

At least if they did find my body, they'd find it with perfectly pedicured toes and freshly exfoliated skin . . . that is, if the fish didn't eat my flesh first.

A very inappropriate giggle bubbled in my chest.

Jeez, Parker. This is NOT the time to laugh.

Suddenly the hand on my mouth left only to be immediately replaced by lips.

Sensuous lips, sexy lips, lips I was coming to know *very* well.

My body began to relax as curious hands roamed across my freshly scrubbed skin.

They pushed the slit of my robe wider, and fingers delved into my core.

Among other things, like a pedicure, body scrub and facial, I'd also allowed the esthetician at the spa to give me a waxing.

It'd been a while, and things were getting a tad "overgrown." I heard him inhale when he found me hairless, followed by a growl of approval.

It was wild.

Our bodies raged at each other in the darkness, hands and mouths exploring and caressing while his beard chafed my cheeks and his teeth nipped at my lips until I was sure they were bruised.

"You're insatiable," I whispered as he slid two fingers inside me. "Twice in the sauna . . . and now."

"I'm under your spell, Miss Ryan." He hauled me away from the wall a few steps, turned me around and pushed my head down until I was bent in a ninety-degree angle, my hands braced on something hard like a bench or wooden chest. I heard the quick zip of his zipper and the swish of pants dropping to the ground followed by the tear of a condom wrapper. We hadn't used one in the sauna, but I could understand his need to not want to make a mess in here... wherever we were.

Two fingers trailed through my slit, drawing my wetness up and around my lips.

He plunged those fingers inside me, scissoring back and forth while continuing to pump.

I squeezed my muscles around him and rode his hand, loving the way he felt, but wanting more.

He read me like a book, and soon the fingers from his other hand were alternating between rough circles and dirty pinches on my swelling clit.

I moaned from how good it felt, how good being with Tate felt.

The excitement of him whisking me off to have sex, pretending to kidnap me only to then worship my body a few seconds later, making it hum and cry out for more—it was intoxicating.

No man had ever treated me like this.

No man had ever desired me this way.

Made me feel craved and needed.

He was a master at seduction, and for the next ten days I was going to let him seduce the bejesus out of me.

"Fuck me," I panted, my breasts jiggling beneath me as I swayed in his hands, lightheaded from how incredible it all was. My orgasm right around the corner. "Now!"

Slowly he withdrew his fingers, and although I knew what was coming next, I couldn't stop the whimper that passed my lips when I was suddenly devoid of his touch. Firm and nimble fingers gripped my hips, kneading and massaging. I pressed into his hands, breathless and desperate for him to take me.

"PLEASE!"

He grabbed his cock, angled it at my cleft and then sheathed himself to the hilt in one solid thrust. "Oh fuuuuck," he sighed.

"Yes!"

"Parker . . ."

"Harder."

He picked up speed and hammered into me, hard measured thrusts, stroking across my entrance and deep into my channel, hitting the right spot inside me, the spot that very few men can reach or even find.

The spot that made me feel like I needed to pee and that my eyes were going to roll into the back of my head and never come back.

I bowed my back and pushed my ass further up, welcoming him, taking all of him. One of his hands snuck around in front of me, and he wedged his way inside my robe; fingers found a nipple, and he started to pluck and tweak, pulling until they were both hard and aching, my breasts heavy in his palm.

Lifting one hand from where I was braced, I moved it down my body and delivered delightful little smacks to my clit.

"Are you smacking your clit?" he asked, his voice hoarse and strained.

I could tell he was close.

His cadence was starting to wane.

"Yes," I breathed.

"Fuck, that's hot."

"Harder!"

He did as he was told, and within a matter of seconds, we were both coming, panting and snarling as our releases took hold.

He angled himself over my body and his teeth grazed my shoulder, tender bites that hurt just enough to let me know how good he felt, how unhinged he'd become. How wild I made him.

I loved it.

I wanted every bite, every bruise, every chafe.

He pulled out and moved away.

A moment later, the light flicked on.

I shut my eyes from the harsh glare.

We were back in the same room as before, the soundproof room where he'd taken me yesterday.

My hands had been planted on the bench for the baby grand piano; I could still see sweaty prints on the shiny black varnish.

Tying off the condom, he shoved it into his pocket and then did up his pants while I went to work adjusting my robe, tucking my breasts back inside.

"Hello." I grinned.

"Hi."

"Kidnapper routine, huh?"

He nodded, his smile making me weak in the knees. "Yeah. Do you have Stockholm Syndrome yet? Do you sympathize with your captor? Do you want to stay?"

I laughed out loud. "If by 'sympathize' and 'stay' you mean want my 'captor' to take me like that every day, then, yes."

His eyes glowed salaciously as he prowled forward. "That can be arranged, you know."

My arms drifted up to rest on his shoulder. We were nose to nose. "I'm sure it can. Seeing as you're the big boss man and I'm in the presidential suite and have an *all-access pass.*"

His nose rubbed against mine as he pushed my back against the wall again, his knee urging me to spread my legs so he could settle between them. "You have *all access*, baby. Whatever you want, whenever you want it."

"Hmmm," I hummed. "I like the sound of that. A girl could get used to such treatment."

Something, a shadow perhaps?

Sadness?

I couldn't quite put my finger on the emotion that passed across his face, removing that sinister twinkle from his eyes, but it was only for a second.

He quickly tossed on another grin and gave me one of those winks he was becoming famous for.

The man was a master at many things, I was learning, and one of those was hiding his true feelings. Happy on the outside, and something else on the inside.

Who was Tate McAllister?

Would I get to know the real him?

His hand roamed down between us, and he flicked my clit. My whole body jerked in his arms, and he laughed.

"Enjoy it, baby. I am here to *serve.*" Then he drove his tongue into my mouth, and the whole erotic dance started all over again.

****

About an hour or so later, after my wobbly legs took me back to myroom and I picked out a suitable outfit for the day—a Granny Smith apple-green halter top and a white jersey knit skirt that came just below my knees—I knocked on the door of the big glass greenhouse.

It was tough to tell if anyone was inside.

All I could see were green plants aplenty and a few bags of fertilizer stacked up against the wall.

"Hello?" I called out, wondering if it would be okay for me to walk inside or if I should wait to be invited.

I knew I had *all access*, but I wasn't comfortable just sauntering into a space where staff might not be aware a guest, let alone a VIP guest, could be lurking.

All access or not, I wasn't about to intrude or catch someone unaware.

I turned the knob and was nearly knocked flat on my butt by the gust of warm air from inside.

It was hot outside, but it was sweltering inside.

I took a step over the threshold, instantly worried that my green halter top was the wrong choice for the afternoon.

I was sure I'd have sweat stains by the time I left.

There was a big wooden table to my left, stacked four feet high with empty terracotta pots of various sizes, while a scattering of gardening tools—pruning shears, hand spades, a hoe—took up the remainder of the table.

I bunched my knuckles and knocked three times on the worn wood.

"Hello?" I called out again. "Anyone here?"

"Come on in!" hollered a voice from inside the dense jungle. "Be with you in a moment."

"I can come back later if you're busy," I said, not sure who I was talking to or where they were.

The entire space looked like a ripe patch of the Amazon. Big leafy plants and trees grew up the rafters, while rows and rows of tables to the left held seedlings in small pots.

"Hello!" A round and rosy brown face with big straight white teeth popped out from behind a frond. The man's fingers were caked in dirt, while another smudge ran just above his eyebrow. "Hi, I'm Alejandro." He went to shake my hand but, when he saw how dirty his hands were, made a regretful face and then tried to wipe them on his pants. "Sorry, I was busy transplanting."

I shook my head with a smile. "Don't worry about it. I'm Parker Ryan. I'm with *The Decadent Traveler Magazine*. I'm here doing a feature piece on Mr. McAllister and The Windward Hibiscus. Mr. McAllister said I could interview some of the staff, and I was hoping I could ask you a few questions?"

His smile was wide and genuine as he nodded. "Sure, but, uh . . ." His eyes fell on his water bottle on the edge of the table. "Not here. Let's go outside. It's hot in here."

I chuckled a grateful thanks as I followed him back out into the fresh air, where the breeze welcomed us with open arms. We found a picnic table under a palm tree and sat down.

"So, how long have you worked here?" I asked, clicking my digital recorder on.

"Since it opened," he answered before tipping back his water bottle and taking a healthy swig. "Six years."

"And do you enjoy working here?"

"Lady," Alejandro started. I leaned forward, thinking he was going to give me something super juicy. "This is the best *fucking* place to work in the world."

Well, that wasn't at all the answer I had been anticipating.

I lifted an eyebrow. "And what makes you say that?"

"I came from nothing. Most of my family is still back in The Philippines, just barely scraping by. Mr. McAllister hired me, then brought my wife, my brother, his wife and all of our children, all four of them over. We have jobs, and the kids go to school in town. We have a place to live. You see those suites up there, all the ones that *don't* face the ocean?" I nodded. "That's staff. A lot of us live here."

"Do you ever get home to see the rest of your family?"

He nodded. "We get six weeks of paid holiday a year."

"Wow."

"And benefits, and a pension. And our kids are guaranteed jobs in the hotel when they turn fourteen."

I shook my head. "But what if your children don't want to end up in the hotel industry?"

His grin was so genuine, so excited that I felt myself sharing in his joy and smiled just as wide. "That's the thing. Mr. McAllister has set up a scholarship fund for all his staff's children. They can work here if they want to when they finish school, but if not, he's offering to help with their college as well."

I'm not sure why, but I found myself looking for questions to ask that would paint Tate in a less saintly hue. The man just sounded too perfect.

"Do you find working in the service industry rewarding?"

His back went poker straight, and he fixed me with an almost steely glare.

Oh, fuck, I'd hit a nerve.

Foot firmly embedded in mouth.

"Miss Ryan, I am not at all *ashamed* of what I do. It is an honest job, and I make an honest living and provide for my family. Mr. McAllister is the best boss I could have ever asked for. He takes care of his staff. Hell, I'd clean toilets, wipe the ass of a pompous billionaire if it meant I could work here."

My eyes fell to my lap. "I—I'm sorry. I didn't mean it like that. I apologize."

"Did you know that we get roughly fifty applications a week to work here? And if more people knew about the resort, we'd probably get more. Did you know that Mr. McAllister makes a point of hiring refugees and people fleeing from their country for safety? He sponsors visas, brings over entire families, gives them jobs, trains them and sets them up with a new life?"

I shook my head.

"There is no shame in working in the service industry. We all need jobs. Just because you don't fold someone else's laundry or scrub toilets for a living doesn't mean you're better than me or my wife."

I shook my head again. "I—I never said that. I know I'm not." This interview had taken a disastrous turn south. "I apologize if that's how my question came across. That wasn't at all what I meant."

It wasn't, was it?

Had being with Xavier, the king of the snobs, turned me into a snob?

Was I the duchess of snobs? A baroness of snobs?

I'd tried so hard to distance myself from the life I'd grown up in back in Mississippi, where no one ever got out and made a better life for themselves.

No one except me.

I even hired a speech coach to try to lose my drawl.

I'd been that determined to rid myself of my past.

But in doing so, had I become a snob?

Did I look down on those in the service industry?

My mind zoomed back to the moment I'd met Tate.

I'd thought he was a manager.

I'd considered it *slumming* when I slept with him.

Oh my God, I *was* a snob.

I was no better than Xavier and his minions.

A giant pit of regret and shame started to build in my stomach, while my throat closed up and heat wormed its way up my face.

Xavier had turned me into a monster.

I'd turned me into a monster.

The scowl on Alejandro's face softened. "I'm going to tell you something." His eyes flashed to my digital recorder poised in my hand. "Off the record."

Nodding, I flipped the "off" switch. "Of course. Off the record."

"Good," he said, taking a sip from his water. "Why do you think Mr. McAllister caters to the richest of clients?"

I lifted a shoulder. "Because he understands their desire for privacy and discretion and that people are willing to pay whatever is asked for their secrets to be kept secret?"

He shook his head. "He caters to those people because they're willing to pay what he charges, and he has to charge what he does to bring in enough money to do what he really wants to do, and that's help people. He's sponsored so many families and their visas. He's paid for surgeries, flights home. He's kept families together that under any other circumstance would have been torn apart. He is a good man. Did you know that aside from being a hotel for the elite, it's also an eco-resort?"

I nodded. Tate had said that they had solar panels on the roofs, collected rainwater during the rainy season and recycled more than any other resort in Tahiti. He also said that when he bought the property, he'd signed on with a contractor who primarily did restoration using repurposed or eco-friendly materials. No endangered rainforests had been pillaged to build his plutocratic paradise.

Alejandro nodded. "I'm not sure what you're looking for, lady, but there isn't a thing wrong with Mr. McAllister or this place. Everyone who works here is happy, and everyone who comes here is happy."

His face faltered for half a second, but the journalist in me caught it.

I had to tread lightly here if I wanted to explore that drop of the mask any further. "I'd like to apologize again, Alejandro, if anything I've said has offended you. That was never my intention. I don't judge those who work in the service industry. What you and your wife do here is invaluable and noble. And I'm so happy you and your family are healthy and thriving and enjoying life. And also that you're able to be together. I'm very sorry if my words were construed any other way. It's just, well, no one in the world knows anything *about* Mr. McAllister. And very few are privy to having stayed and experienced the beauty that is The Windward Hibiscus, so I'm just trying to ask the right questions and learn as much as I can. Paint an overall picture of the resort."

"Not everyone here is happy, you know?" he finally said after having pursed his lips in thought for a moment.

"What do you mean?"

"I mean, I don't think Mr. McAllister is very happy."

"What makes you say that?"

His slightly chapped lips twisted in thought for a second. "I think he's lonely."

He had more than three hundred guests here at any time and close to four hundred staff. How on *earth* was the man lonely?

"Why do you think he's lonely?"

"When he smiles, it doesn't reach his eyes. At least that's what my wife says. She says when you're genuinely happy, you don't smile with your mouth, you smile with your eyes. And he doesn't have anyone. No friends, no family. His friend Malakai, he used to run the surf shop, he moved back to Samoa last year when his mother died. So now Mr. McAllister has nobody. He's too busy taking care of everyone else here, making sure we're all happy, our families are happy, that *his* happiness suffers."

In my head I was snorting and thinking of a thousand cynical things to say. But instead I kept my face neutral and remained as professional as I could. "I'm sure he's had girlfriends over the years."

"Maybe." He shrugged. "He keeps to himself a lot, though. As friendly as he is, I would never sit and have a beer with the guy. He's the boss. The big boss."

I couldn't stop myself; I had to ask. "And is that a line that *he's* drawn?"

Alejandro's eyes turned fierce again. They were such a deep, dark brown I had a hard time deciphering pupil from iris. "Stop looking for things that aren't there, lady. The line is there because *we* put it there. The staff. We don't want to ever make him feel like he can't reprimand us or take the actions he needs to take. If things got too friendly, it would blur the line between employer and staff, and the last thing we want to do is take advantage of him. If an employee turns out to be shit, half the time Mr. McAllister doesn't even find out about it. We get rid of the dud ourselves, or management does."

Get rid of as in *kill?* Oh shit, now my mind was going all over the damn place. First the "kidnapping" and now this. I really shouldn't have watched that mafia movie on the plane.

"We've all been given a chance here at a better life, and like hell are we going to screw it up." He checked his watch. "I should probably get back to work, though." He stood up with a light groan. His knees made a soft popping sound and he gave his neck a quick side-to-side tilt to work out the kinks. All the while his eyes remained fixed on me. They weren't threatening, but they certainly held a warning. "Mr. McAllister doesn't want the world to know what he's doing because the world doesn't need to know. He's not after the success for the fame. But he also doesn't want to be taken advantage of, and the world is full of scammers."

I stood up as well and followed him back toward the door to the greenhouse. The world is definitely full of scammers . . . and slimeballs and assholes.

I'd been in love with an asshole.

"I won't print any of this, I promise. And I plan to give Mr. McAllister my write-up before I submit it to my editor so he can take out what he doesn't want printed."

That explanation seemed to suffice, and he gave me a curt but friendly nod. "All right, then."

I offered him my hand. He shook his head, as his hands were still dirty, but I reached for his palm anyway. "It's just a little dirt." I smiled. "Thank you, Alejandro. I really appreciate you taking the time to speak with me."

He glanced down at his mud-caked shoes before lifting his head and focusing back on my eyes. "You're welcome, Miss Ryan." Then, with another solitary head bob and a small smile that didn't quite reach *his* eyes, he ducked back into the greenhouse.

Chapter Five

I SPENT THE REST of the day in quiet contemplation while basking in the hot sun on the beach.

I had a lot of thinking to do.

A lot.

It seemed that every time I turned around, a new side of Tate McAllister was being revealed, and every side was more and more appealing.

But then I also had a dilemma on my hands.

What on earth was I going to write?

If I didn't include some of the truth, it would come across as a linear, run-of-the-mill travel piece, and that was not what I was known for.

I was known for getting into the nitty gritty, going into the history of the places I stayed, the people, the guests, finding out what made them all tick as they created the utopia that changed every time a new plane landed and new guests arrived.

By the time dinner rolled around, I was exhausted and sporting some pretty stellar tan lines.

After he'd kidnapped me and had his way with me in the soundproof room, I hadn't seen hide nor hair of my bodacious billionaire.

I was just towel-drying my hair from the shower when there was a knock at my door.

Tossing on a robe, I went to answer it.

"Dinner time!" he sung, wheeling in a big cart with a bottle of champagne chilling on ice and two covered dishes.

My eyes went wide. "Y-you brought me dinner?"

He continued on through the living space and out onto the private veranda. I followed him.

"Correction. I brought *us* dinner." He leaned over and gave me a quick peck on the lips, as if he did it every day, the doting husband home from a hard day at the office.

Only instead of coming home to a warm meal prepared by yours truly, he brought home the bacon *and* fried it up in the pan.

Or his kitchen staff had.

I really didn't care either way.

"Oh."

"Go get your pajamas on or whatever. It's not going to get cold with the covers."

I did as I was told, then joined him a few moments later.

"I hope you don't mind that I ordered for you again," he said, removing the warming covers. "If you don't like it, I can have something else here in a flash."

I took a seat and smiled, thanking him when he placed the linen napkin on my lap. The cool evening breeze off the water was soothing against my damp skin, a balm after the baking I'd done earlier in the day.

"I'm sure it's going to be delicious. There's not much I don't like. And dinner last night was incredible."

He took his seat across from me and poured us each a flute of bubbly, raising his glass in a toast, just like the night before. "Now we have something to toast and celebrate."

"We do?" I asked, lifting an eyebrow.

His grin was filthy, and I had to stop myself from tossing him down on the table, ripping open his dress shirt and riding him like a pony.

"Absolutely! To quick and dirty."

I rolled my eyes.

"Ten days of nothing but hot sex between two strangers."

Shaking my head, I clinked my glass with his and took a sip, eyeing him over the rim. His eyes held a promise that made my entire body ignite and caused a pleasant warmth to bloom between my legs. They were eyes that said, "I'm going to fuck you six ways from Sunday, and then twice on Sunday!"

Suddenly, as if hit by a falling coconut, I got a wonderful little thought.

He'd made such a big deal about the grotto yesterday, perhaps we could explore the cave of debauchery this evening. Heat filled my cheeks as I looked down at my delicious dinner; I was no longer hungry for food.

"What naughty little thought just popped into that head of yours, Miss Ryan?"

I ran my tongue between the seam of my lips before answering him.

His nostrils flared as he watched me squirm in my seat.

The man was just as turned on as I was.

"I, uh . . . I was wondering about that grotto you spoke so passionately about yesterday. Perhaps if it's free tonight, we might, I dunno . . . check it out?"

Not even a second passed before he snatched his phone from his pocket and was texting someone. Three seconds later, he stowed his phone again and dazzled me with a smile that made my whole body tingle.

"Done! Oh, Miss Ryan, I knew there was something *special* about you. And it wasn't just your direct and blunt need to be taken hard and fast in a broom closet."

I looked back down at my plate and pushed the piece of perfectly cooked fish around in the sauce. I was sure if I looked in a mirror right now, my face would be as scarlet as the letter "A."

"Bashful now, are we?" He chuckled.

"No. I just . . . I dunno, now I'm all self-conscious."

"About what?"

Sighing, I put my fork down and finally lifted my head to look him in the eye. "This is NOT me. I am not direct, *especially* when it comes to sex. I don't ask for sex. Ever. I never initiated it in my past relationships. No man ever asked me what I wanted, what my fantasies were. I was never made to feel as though I *could* initiate."

"What are your fantasies?" he asked without hesitation, those bright, soulful green orbs of his piercing my soul and shredding any self-doubt inside me. I felt as though with Tate I could be real. I'd just met the man, and already he made me feel more alive, more interested in changing and growing as a person than any other man.

"I—I don't even know. I've never really thought about it before."

"Of course you have. Don't lie to me Parker, not ever. I'll never judge you, never think you're weird or perverted. Just tell me. What is your *ultimate* fantasy?"

I stared at my champagne as if it were a glorious thundering waterfall in the middle of the desert and I was a lone and weary traveler who'd been wandering aimlessly for days without a drop to drink.

"Drink your champagne," he ordered.

I snatched up the flute and chugged it, watching him over the rim of my glass. He just sat there with the faintest hint of a smile on his face while his eyes danced hot and wicked back at me.

I put the empty flute back down on the table and let out a content *"ah."*

"Fantasy, Parker."

Dear Lord, the command in his voice sent a new rush of need zipping through my body. My toes curled and I squeezed my thighs together. This man was going to be the end of me . . . or the new beginning.

"I, uh . . . I've always wanted to have sex outside."

"You've never had sex outside before?" he asked, unable to hide the surprise in his voice. "Ever?"

I shook my head. "No. I've always had it inside, in a bed. I think I've only ever had sex *not* in a bed once, maybe twice. And that was on a couch. I've been with some pretty even keel guys."

"So that's why you want to go to the grotto?"

I nodded. "A tame start, but yeah."

He shook his head. "And that's your *ultimate* fantasy?" There was skepticism in his tone, and frankly in my heart as well. Was that my *ultimate* fantasy? To be honest, I'd never really given it too much thought.

My sex life had so far not really offered me much in the way of creative thinking.

I didn't watch porn, didn't read smutty books.

I wasn't sure what else there was.

I nibbled on the inside of my bottom lip for a moment in thought. "I want to explore and be adventurous inside *and* outside of the bedroom. To be honest, my sex life has been rather mundane. Whether it was because of me or the men I was with, I don't know. If I were to guess, I'd say it was probably me. The word 'boring' has been tossed around a few times. But I'm not entirely sure what kind of things I'd be into because I don't know what there is."

Eyes searing hot and so full of passion blazed back at me.

He didn't say anything for a moment, and I began to squirm under his gaze as my mind raced in a billion different directions with what he could possibly be thinking.

I swallowed hard and licked my lips, waiting for him to say something.

To say anything. Good or bad, I just wanted the man to speak.

But he was silent and just continued to stare at me.

"Eat your food, Parker," he finally said, the same alpha dominance back in his tone. "Because tonight, baby, you're going to need your strength." Then he put his head down and dove into his fish, leaving me sitting there staring at the top of his head with a gaping mouth and a puddle in my panties.

****

"So what, you just text someone and they shut down this whole section of the resort?" I asked as Tate led me down the slate path from the copse of villas to the common area of the resort. Solar-powered lanterns on four-foot metal poles hung every few feet and guided our way while the delightful squawk and titter of nocturnal birds added a subtle soundtrack to our short journey.

"Yep. I'm the boss. I can shut down the entire resort if I want to. But I don't, because that's not how you make money. But I can certainly say that this section is off-limits for the rest of the night." A cocky smirk jiggled at the side of his mouth. "Besides, this section of the resort usually closes at sundown anyway, unless there is a private party or a guest requests VIP access. We can't have people just wandering into the grotto at all hours. There aren't any cameras in there, unlike the rest of the resort, so if something happened, we'd be liable. We always need to know when it's in use."

I nodded. Made sense.

The lights beneath the water of the pool that connected to the grotto shone bright blue and drew my eyes, while my senses filled with the decadent scents of the evening.

A hint of fire.

Fresh fruit.

Sweet and smokey.

A grill master was probably tending fresh pieces of pineapple and mango over glowing embers.

Add in the heady aroma of salt and warm sand whooshing up from the sea; flowers aplenty, fragrant and sweet and wonderful. My senses were in heaven.

And of course, the best smell so far—Tate. I'm not sure what cologne or soap or aftershave the man wore, but it was driving me absolutely bonkers, fresh and manly with just a hint of citrus and splash of mint from his mouthwash or toothpaste.

The way it wrapped around me as we held hands and made our way around the pool deck toward the grotto, I had to stop myself from swooning and collapsing into his arms like a fair maiden.

This man would make me lose my head if I wasn't careful. But then, maybe I wanted to lose my head.

"Is there a way inside besides through the water?" I asked. We had stopped on the pool ledge, and the mouth to the grotto lay before us. A tunnel into the depths of the unknown, into the darkness, into the . . . forbidden.

My core clenched at the sudden deluge of thoughts that took hold of me.

Tate was going to fuck me outside, in the grotto, in the pool.

His hand squeezed mine before he released it. "Nope. Let's get wet."

He started to unbutton his shirt.

I just stared.

He snorted though his nose when he caught me watching him. "Yes, I know

I'm handsome, but take your clothes off, Parker. You can ogle me once we're both down to our bathing suits."

My face quickly caught fire, but I did as I was told.

Tate just laughed.

Once we were both undressed, me down to my lilac bikini and Tate to his blue board shorts, he slipped into the water and held his arms out for me.

I let him take me, his hands landing on my hips as he swung me around and then down into the pool.

It was only about waist-deep, and the temperature was absolutely perfect.

Our hands linked together again beneath the water, and he tugged me forward and into the grotto.

We continued to wade further inward for a moment or two, lights built into the rock wall guiding us forward into the cavern, deeper into the cave of sin.

A slight bend, and the entrance was no longer visible.

I looked ahead, and another bend masked the exit as well.

When we continued around the corner, the hollow opened up, creating a room of sorts.

A small ledge with a swirling basin to the right, rimmed with pot lights overhead, drew my attention.

There was a natural-looking hot tub next to the basin and a large flat bit of slate rock to step out on to. A small waterfall rushed down the wall, landing in the swirling basin, making the water beneath it froth and bubble.

It didn't thunder loud and proud like a real waterfall, but it made enough of a constant rushing sound that the pulse thudding inside my ears was not nearly as loud, but that didn't mean the voices in my head weren't screaming at the top of their lungs.

You go, girl! Get yours! Take the plunge. Adventures! Quick and dirty! Tear off his shorts!

But then the self-conscious voices were there, too. And just as loud, if not louder than the cheering squad. *Dead fish! Dead fish! What if you bore him? You're bad in bed. You're not adventurous. This isn't you.*

Tate squeezed my hand as we made our way over to the swirling part of the pool. "You okay?" The spray from the waterfall landed on his skin and beaded on the fine blond hairs of his arms, making him look as though he were covered in diamonds.

I threw on my biggest smile and blinked back the water from my eyes. I nodded. "Absolutely. Just telling some voices in my head to shut up."

He released my hand and placed both of his hands on my hips. From there he lifted me up and placed me on the ledge. Shouldering my knees apart, he wedged his way between my legs.

"I can feel your heat," he said roughly. His hand came up, and he cupped me, his thumb rubbing back and forth across my clit atop the fabric of my bikini bottoms.

My lips parted, but nothing came out.

"Is this *really* your only fantasy, Parker? Sex outside?" His thumb continued to rub, and I let my eyes close.

My head fell back for a second, and I just allowed the sensation to wash over me.

Pleasure.
Sex outside.
Yes!
"Parker?"

My head snapped back up. "Yes?"

"Is this really your only fantasy?" He dipped his head and started twirling his tongue around the top of my thigh. Wet and scorching hot, it sent a frenzy of need racing across my skin.

"No," I whispered.

"I didn't think so," he hummed. "Tell me what else you dream about, Parker. Tell me your dirtiest, darkest, most depraved fantasies. Let me see if I can make them a reality."

He nipped my inner thigh with his teeth, and I inhaled quickly from the snap of pain.

Yes, so much more of that.

More teeth.

Teeth everywhere.

"I . . . oh God, yes . . . " He'd moved his mouth over to my core and had sucked my clit into his mouth. The fabric still between us somehow made it all the more erotic.

"Tell me, Parker."

"I . . . I want to sit on your face. I want to deprive you of your orgasm for so long your balls turn blue, and then I want to fuck you with my tits and have you come all over my face," I finally blurted out, the pleasure he was giving me causing my filter to dissolve and nothing but horny frankness to burst free.

His head popped up. "Seriously?"

I sobered for a second.

Was that *too* filthy for even him?

Had I scared him off?

He said I could tell him anything.

He said he wanted to make my fantasies a reality.

The truth was, even though I'd never really watched porn or read any dirty books, I still had an imagination, and on those long, lonely nights when I was alone in my hotel room for work, my imagination got a little smutty.

My high school boyfriend had asked me if he could come on my face back when we were sixteen.

We hadn't even had sex yet; it'd been strictly hand stuff, and we were branching into oral.

But he liked to watch porn, and apparently "all the actresses did it and enjoyed it," so in his infantile mind, he figured "all women must do it and enjoy it." I'd said *no* because I was sixteen and grossed out by the thought.

Inevitably, a month or so later we broke up.

Such is high school.

But all these years, the thought had rattled around in my mind.

Yet, I'd never met a man whom I could look at and say, "Yes, the thought of you coming on my face appeals to me," until Tate.

And wasn't that what these ten days were all about?

Unleashing my darkest fantasies and my deepest desires?

I'd never see him again.

He kept himself out of the limelight and off the radar, and I certainly didn't want the world knowing my depraved business.

It was the perfect setup.

A week and a half of rediscovery, orgasms and companionship, and then I could return to New York and sort my life out from there.

"Yes," I said quietly, tossing my shoulders back.

I was looking toward the ceiling at first, but then my eyes slowly shifted lower, the erection in his shorts drawing my gaze like a magnet.

"Holy fuck," he said. "That's hot." His grin grew wide and dirty. "You *are* a wild and nasty little thing, aren't you? A closet pervert."

I shook my head and laughed. "Uh, no. Couldn't be further from either of those things, actually."

His smiled turned more was impish than dirty and stirred something so primal, so savage inside me I had to resist the sudden urge to grab his ears and ram his face back between my legs.

"Oh, I think you're far dirtier than you let on. We just have to peel back the stiff layers of prude to get at your sweet, soft, corrupt little core." He hummed thoughtfully. "Well, best start fulfilling those fantasies, hmm?" His fingers found the strings of my bikini bottoms, and in seconds I was laid bare and open for him, my pussy lips swollen and glistening with my arousal from his earlier attention.

I reached behind me and untied my top, tossing it next to the other scrap of material.

My breasts tumbled out, and my nipples hardened to stiff peaks, red and desperate for his touch, for his teeth, for his tongue.

Quickly, Tate removed his shorts, and a second later, his erection was bobbing hard and happy in the water in front of me, the thick head a dark plum and so full of blood.

It was demanding I take him in my mouth, demanding I taste him. Lick that delicious salty drop of pre-cum off and let it slide down my throat.

"I thought I was supposed to deprive myself?" he said gruffly, his eyes following mine. With a knowing and sultry grin, he took himself in his palm and started to stroke his cock from root to tip. Back and forth his hand ran the length of him, the veins pulsing, his crown growing an even darker purple.

Mesmerized, I continued to watch him.

"You like this?" he asked, his voice thick with longing.

"Yes."

"You want to suck my cock, baby?"

"Yes."

"Hmm, I want that too. Here," he helped me down off the ledge and into the water.

I hadn't noticed before, but in the basin where we were standing, there was a series of circular steps beneath the water, running down deep into the pool like a funnel. Tate was standing on the uppermost step and guided me down two steps so that I was face-to-face with his length.

"Suck it, Parker. Just for a bit. I won't come, I promise. But I want to feel your lips around my cock. It's all I've been able to think about since you walked into my hotel with a scowl on that beautiful face of yours. I wanted to make you fall to your knees, ram myself to the back of your throat and make you smile as you heard me moan your name."

Holy mother of God, the man knew how to talk dirty.

I was surprised steam didn't start to rise around me in the water.

My skin, my entire body was on absolute fire.

I inched closer to him and flicked my tongue out against the tip.

His breath caught, and I smiled.

Opening my eyes, I looked up at him, our gazes locked as I spread my lips and took him deep inside my mouth to the back of my throat.

Humming softly, I wrapped my lips around his shaft and sucked.

Back and forth, I savored the taste of him.

The saltiness, the sweetness.

He was perfect. His scent enveloped me, and I moaned again from how good it felt to take Tate in my mouth, how much I was enjoying bringing him this kind of pleasure.

He fisted a clump of my hair and began to work my head, setting a quick and hard pace that worked for him.

My lashes fluttered shut, and I let him take the reins.

I brought one hand up and ran it further down his cock, past the point I wasn't able to take in my mouth, while my other hand came up and gently tugged on his balls.

They were so soft, hairless, and as I brought him out to my lips and sucked fervently on the tip of him, they tightened in my palm.

While still stroking him with my hand, I shook my hair free of his grasp and dipped my head lower, bringing one ball into my mouth and swirling my tongue around it before sucking gently.

I moved on to the other one a few seconds later and hummed again.

"You're incredible," he grunted above me.

His hands came up and under my arms, and he pulled me from my spot in the water and plunked me back up on the ledge. Then, with the grace of a pole vaulter, he placed one hand on the ledge and swung his big, sexy frame up and out of the pool until he was standing next to me.

I blinked up at him, the water from the falls still spraying around us and catching periodically on my lashes.

He slid onto his butt, then lay down, his head resting on his bunched up shorts. "Come on over here, gorgeous, and bring that sweet pink pussy of yours. Sit on my face."

I blushed at his filthy candor but did as he said.

Shuffling over the few feet to where his head was, I lowered myself down over his face.

My knees brushed his ears.

His breath was warm on my center, and when his tongue darted out, a shiver soared through my body.

Yes. All of this. I want all of this.

"Lower," he said as his hands came around my hips and his fingers dug into my ass, urging me to sink deeper over his mouth. He kneaded my cheeks and rocked me forward. Lips—decadent, sensual, plump and talented—sucked on my clit and pulled.

His tongue started to lash back and forth across my tender bud.

He feasted on my sensitive core until I was gasping and forced to hinge forward over his head and plant my hands on the cool slate rock.

I bucked and thrust against him, loving that delightful brush of his beard on my labia as they glided across his lips. He made his tongue go rigid, and with the swiftness and speed of a jackhammer, he started to jut it in and out of me, fucking me hard and fast, until I was a quivering mess and but a breath, but a blink, but a thought away from an orgasm.

I pressed my forehead against the rock, spreading my legs wider so his tongue could fuck me deeper. He brought his hand up from where he'd been gripping my ass and started to flick my slick and engorged clit, twiddling it against the back of his finger quickly. Then just when he knew I needed that extra push over the edge, Tate brought my nub between his thumb and forefinger, pinched, pulled, flicked again, and I detonated.

No.

Detonated is the wrong word.

I fucking exploded.

I went off like a missile shot directly into a warehouse full of fireworks located in a city doused with lighter fluid.

Pleasure, ecstasy, rapture.

You name it, I had it.

God?

Yeah, I think I met him.

Angels with harps?

Heard them loud and clear; those ladies were in my head and singing their sweet, sweet song as the orgasm speared through my core and blossomed out in white starbursts through my body.

I shook on top of Tate's face as he continued to fuck me with that glorious tongue.

In and out, he never ceased; even through my panting and screaming, he just kept going. His thumb and finger twiddled and flicked my clit, pulling on it as it swelled and hardened with my release.

I filled his mouth with my climax, and he just lapped it up and hummed, moaning in satisfaction as I came down from the mountaintop.

I went to move off of him, but he held me in place with his hand on my ass and just continued to feast, to lick and fuck and plunder.

I mewled and tried to pull away. "No . . . no more. I can't."

"Yes, more. Always more, Parker. Come again for me, baby."

He ran his chin over my clit, and I let go one more time.

Moments later, once I found my head again, Tate lifted my hips up and slid out from beneath me. He was wearing a grin as wide as his cock was long, and his whole face glistened with my releases. He was about to lick his fingers but then thought better of it.

"Open your mouth and taste yourself."

I twirled my tongue around his fingers and sucked off my flavor.

I'd never been so wanton, so brazen, so . . . alive.

Closing my eyes, I let a whimper drift up from my throat as I sucked hard on his fingers, delivering a little bite before letting him go.

He groaned. "You're so fucking perfect, Parker. You know that, right? Incredible." Low and guttural, his tone dug down deep inside me and took hold.

No, I didn't know that. No one had ever paid me such compliments before. No one had ever called me incredible.

But from Tate, I wanted to believe it.

"What was it you wanted to do next?" he asked. His hands came up to cup my breasts. It felt good when he lifted them up, relieved the weight of their heavy need, ran the pads of his thumbs over my tender nipples.

I bowed my back slightly and pushed into his grasp.

"I want to fuck your cock with my tits and let you come all over my face," I said through ragged breaths.

Despite my two soul-shattering orgasms from moments ago, my body was still raring to go and wanted more.

"Is that what you want?"

"Mhmm."

"You're sure you don't want me to take you under the waterfall, slip my cock inside you and coax out one more sweet little orgasm?"

I bit my lip and closed my eyes. His thumbs and fingers were pulling and pinching my nipples, and fuck if I wasn't getting close again.

"Yes." I sighed. "That. I want that."

Removing one hand from my breast, he cupped the back of my head hard and pulled me toward him. His lips crushed mine, and his tongue swept inside, heated and insistent.

Tasting me, exploring me, cherishing me.

Slowly, carefully, without coming apart, we started to move.

He was backing me up. The gentle splatter and roar of the water thundering down into the basin along with the spray ricocheting off the pool filled my senses.

My heart beat just as fast as the falls pounded, perhaps faster.

Water fell all around us, and when I opened my eyes, I was blinded by the rushing stream. We were directly under the falls. Standing in the spray. My back was against the wall, and with a quick flick of his wrist, Tate hoisted me up on to his hips and pushed his cock inside me.

Hammering, plundering, pounding.

The man was a torrential and tireless driving force inside of me as the water poured down relentlessly around us, filling my eyes, my nose, my mouth.

Until all I could do was shut my eyes, let Tate's mouth claim mine and give in to the moment.

Harder and harder he drilled me against the wall, his pelvic bone grazing my clit in that oh-so-perfect way, until my climax was demanding to be freed once more. This one wasn't going to be nearly as mind-boggling as the last one, but it was still going to be a doozy.

"Come for me, Parker. One more time, then I'll give you what you want." He dipped his head low and latched on to a nipple, and when his tongue did that little flick thing back and forth, I was a goner.

When my climax finally subsided, Tate moved us out from under the falls and back over to the flat slate ledge. He helped me step down into the water, and he sat on the edge.

Both of our chests heaved, while my face was warm and my heart full.

I couldn't stop myself, and I looked down at his magnificent package.

It was so engorged, so hard, so big.

Upon further inspection, as I let my hand dart out and cup him, I found his sac to be even tighter than earlier, so full, and when I dipped my head to check, running my tongue along the velvety seam of his scrotum, it was indeed a very beautiful if not light shade of blue.

"You're sure about this?" Tate asked, making a fist around himself and giving his cock a couple of tugs.

"So sure," I panted. I spread his legs wide and stepped between them. Cupping each of my heavy breasts, I brought them together, sliding his cock between them. I moved them over his length, up and down, squeezing tight only to then lick and blow cool air on the tip when it emerged from between my pillowy breasts.

"Oh fuck, baby. The sight of your luscious tits fucking my cock, this is so hot."

His crown broke free of my tight grasp again, and I sucked on it hard, releasing it with an audible *pop* and then blowing cool air on the shiny head.

"So fucking sexy," he groaned. His hand came up, and he fisted my hair again. "Suck it again, Parker. Just for a sec. You give the best fucking head I've ever had. Your mouth is so hot, so soft. Let me fuck your mouth."

No one had ever talked so dirty, so bold, so direct to me before.

My entire life I hated it when a man ordered me around or told me what to do, but not Tate.

When Tate ordered my meals for me, demanded I tell him my fantasies, asked me to suck his cock, he wasn't coming from a demeaning place.

In fact, it was the complete opposite.

He was giving me all the power.

The power to let him into my mind, to know my dark desires and give my body to him.

And when he ordered dinner for me, well, that was just sweet, and he was taking a leap of faith that I'd like what he chose.

I could just as easily hate it and ask for something else.

No, Tate wasn't bossing me around, he was possessing me, cherishing me, and in the most intimate and intriguing way possible.

Licking my lips, I released him from my breasts and immediately deep-throated him.

Tears pricked and burned at the corners of my eyes, but I didn't care.

I wanted to take every single inch of him.

Every single millimeter.

I sucked hard when he reached the back of my throat, then I pulled him out to my lips and sucked on the crown.

"Baby, I'm going to come," Tate said with a grunt. "You're sure you . . ." But he didn't have time to finish. I felt his balls contract beneath my palm, and then I freed him from my lips.

He fisted himself and started to stroke as warm, salty jets of semen spurted from his rigid cock and out onto my face. I opened my mouth and stuck out my tongue, feeling the heat of his seed land on my lips; I greedily lapped up his release.

I watched him as he came.

Watched as he bared his teeth and shut his eyes.

An animal in its purest form.

Harsh and masculine, but also so incredibly beautiful.

When I knew he was finished, I used my fingers to wipe my face clean.

Then I sucked his cum off of my digits. He opened his eyes, they were full of awe and helpless fascination.

"That was . . ." he trailed off and he shook his head "That was the most incredible thing I've ever seen in my life. No woman has ever let me do that. No woman has ever . . ." he ran his hand through his hair and let out a sigh. "Fuck, Parker. You're incredible."

I couldn't hide the grin that erupted on my face.

I felt incredible.

This whole night, this whole experience had been incredible.

My body hummed alive and happy from all my orgasms, from having my fantasies come to life. I quickly splashed some water on my face, then took Tate's hand when he offered it to me, helping me climb back out onto the ledge.

I let out a sigh of both contentment and exhaustion. "I guess we need to put our suits back on and rejoin the real world. Head to bed. Accept the reality that sleep is necessary if we intend to be present and abled bodies tomorrow." I was about to bend down to pick up my suit, but Tate stopped me.

"We don't need to put them back on." He bent down and scooped up our wet suits then reclaimed my hand and led me over to the rock wall. Standing on practically his tiptoes, he fanned his fingers up and over a small outcropping of rocks and began to touch and prod them as if searching for something. "Ah, there we go."

A soft *click*, and a hidden door popped open. He led me through a pitch-black walkway, and then another soft *click* and a door right in front of us opened.

"Here." He handed me a towel. "Wrap this around yourself."

I watched as he haphazardly fixed a white towel around his waist. I did the same. Once he made sure all my bits were covered, he took my hand again, and out we walked into the warm night.

"So there *is* a way in besides through the pool," I said, keeping a firm hold on my towel to make sure it didn't slip off and show my breasts and freshly chafed thighs to the palm trees.

"Ah, well . . . I'm sorry I lied. But that's just the emergency door. I try not to use it. There's no sense making you put a wet bathing suit back on when I'm just going to tear that towel off you and fuck you one more time back in your bed the moment we get to your suite."

We came around the corner, and there sat our clothes and flip-flops. Tate snatched them up, took my hand again and pulled me along the path.

"You can go *again*?" I asked, more stunned with his prowess and insatiable appetite than anything else. If he wanted me again, I wouldn't say *no.*

A dark and wicked laugh rumbled low in his chest as my villa came into view. "Baby, I am pretty much constantly fucking hard when you're around. You are a walking, talking *Playboy* magazine. And unlike those sticky-paged two-dimensional tug books, you are the real deal, and I am going to soak up every bit of your sweetness for the short time I have you. I may die the moment you step back onto your plane, because you'll have drained me of all my electrolytes, but what a way to go."

I gaped at him.

He fished inside the pocket of my shorts that he clutched in his hand and finally retrieved my key card.

He flashed it in front of the panel, and a second later, it shone bright green in the darkness and my door clicked open.

"Now, any more filthy-as-fuck fantasies rattling around in that gorgeous brain of yours? And any of them involve a bed? My back is killing me from that slate floor."

Chapter Six

THE NEXT MORNING FOUND both Tate and I back at the pool.

We swam our laps, did the nasty in the shower this time, rather than the sauna, then dispersed to our rooms to change.

He said he wanted to take me on a hike up to The Belvedere lookout, but seeing as the day was unusually cloudy, we decided to hold off on the hike until tomorrow and instead head out fishing.

I'd never been fishing before.

Not even on the river, and I'd grown up right down the street from a Mississippi River offshoot. Not sure what to wear or what to pack, I tossed on a pair of khaki shorts and a black tank top over my bikini, slipped into flip-flops and wrestled my long red mane into a French braid down my back. And just to be safe, slathered on the SPF like there was no tomorrow.

A soft rap at my door had me jumping out of my skin as I dabbed on lip gloss in the mirror.

"Ready to go?" he asked, his eyes raking my body from head to toe and not hiding his appreciation for how I looked.

I nodded. "You bet." I glanced back into my room. "Do I need to pack anything?"

He shook his head. "Nope. Swimsuit, hat, sunscreen, sunglasses. If you've got all that in your bag, we're good to go." I opened up my bohemian shoulder bag to do a quick double check, gave him another nod, then followed him out the door.

"Where are the fishing boats?" I asked, struggling to keep up with his long strides as he made his way down the path toward the water. Just then, I noticed a couple of short blond strands of hair again. This time they were more on his back, closer to his left hip. My gut clenched at the same time as my jaw. Should I ask him?

Despite the fate of the cat, I couldn't control my curiosity, and I leaned forward and pulled the hairs off his back. "Care to explain?" I asked, feigning laissez-faire and plastering on a sassy grin.

He spun around. "What?"

"Whose hair is this?" I held up the blond strands and eyed him warily, removing my sunglasses for good measure.

He didn't bother to remove his sunglasses as he gave a sloppy shrug. "Huh? Oh, I dunno. No woman, if that's what you're wondering. Cat maybe?" His chuckle was awkward and a tad forced. But then he finally removed his shades and looked down into my eyes with the same sincerity as when he'd told me about his uncle's passing and how hard it was when his dad had left. "You're the only woman I'm having sex with right now, Parker. I promise."

Nibbling on my bottom lip, because I wasn't sure what else to do, I glanced down at my feet.

"Look at me."

My head snapped up.

"I swear."

I just nodded. The way he demanded my trust, my belief in him when we hardly knew each other, normally it would have sent alarm bells blaring, but it didn't.

It was comforting.

Trust wasn't something I was willing to give freely anymore, not after Xavier's betrayal, but Tate demanded it from me.

I had to trust him.

He wouldn't have it any other way.

His hand came up under my chin. "Okay?"

"Okay."

His face softened. "Now, to answer your earlier question about the boats, we keep the boats at the marina in the next bay because we're an eco-resort and there is a delicate reef right out front. I don't allow boats to moor too close to the beach. Also, it helps for privacy and security. If people want to come here off their yacht, they have to call in, make arrangements, then either bring their dinghy in via electric motor or row. Or, depending on the guest, we'll go out in our own electric-powered boat and get them."

And just like that, we were back to normal.

The tension from a moment ago gone.

Was it always this easy with Tate?

He wouldn't accept anything but order, trust and efficiency in his life, and when there was any threat of the peace being disrupted, he acted with lightning speed to calm the waters again as fast as he could.

I blinked a couple of times; the sun was trying desperately to burn my retinas.

Then I remembered my sunglasses were still up in my hair.

I pulled them back over my eyes. "Wow. So, then where are the boats?"

He grinned back at me and reached for my hand, giving it a gentle squeeze. "Not too far. Just around the bend is a marina where I keep five fishing boats moored. It's a ten-minute walk."

And sure enough, roughly ten minutes later, we emerged through the palm trees and foliage to find a small but very healthily populated marina.

Boats of every imaginable size and worth sat gently bobbing next to the dock, while various people milled around on top or inside.

Quiet, inoffensive music played from one big ship that wore a South Korean flag, and when the man on top saw Tate approach, his face split into a wide grin.

"Hello!"

Tate offered the man a small head bow. "Hello."

The two took off on a lengthy, animated and laughter-filled chat—all in Korean!

"You speak Korean?" I asked, after we said our goodbyes and carried along the dock in the direction of more boats.

He nodded. "Yeah. I lived there for a while. Did a year of my undergrad in Seoul, then went back and got my MBA there, as well. I also worked in Busan for a bit. I have a lot of connections in Korea, and we get quite a few Korean businessmen at the resort."

Shaking my head in wonder, I couldn't think of anything else to say besides, "Wow."

"I'm pretty good at Spanish, too. Know a fair bit of Arabic, though I can't read a word of it, and I'm learning Mandarin. But that's slow going. I can't seem to get the tone right."

"Wow," I repeated.

This man really was fucking my brains out because for an English major and photojournalist, my words were seriously lacking.

****

"That's it, baby, just like that," Tate said, after he'd shown me how to tie a reflector onto my line and cast it into the ocean.

My cast was not nearly as impressive as his, maybe half the distance, but it hadn't been a *plop* right next to the boat either.

"Now give it some line, maybe twenty or thirty tugs, set the bail and then put it in the holder."

"Like this?"

He nodded, a big, proud grin on his face, while the sides of his eyes crinkled beneath his sunglasses.

I smiled back, pleased as punch with myself for doing it right.

"Now what?" I asked, putting the rod in the rod holder.

"Now, we wait."

I looked back down at the rod, my lips pinching into a pout. "Well, that seems boring."

His chuckle made my belly stir and a warm tingle ignite even lower.

I couldn't control myself; when I was around Tate, I was on fire.

Constantly turned on and ready to be ravished.

He'd awakened a beast, and the beast was *starving*.

"Yes, well, sometimes it takes a while to *lure* the fish.

Some days we don't catch anything.

But I think today we're going to get lucky and land a *whopper*."

"A *whopper*," I mocked, eyeing him from beneath my lashes.

He came up behind me after setting his rod in the holder on the opposite side of the boat, his arms encircling my waist as he tugged me close, nuzzling my neck. "Mhmm, a *whopper*. I've got a *whopper* for you in my pants."

A snort rumbled from my nose before I could stop it. "Do you use that line on all the women you sleep with?"

"Mhmm," he hummed, setting us off to a sway.

Damn! Why did that sting?

"And does it work?"

"Mhmm."

Laughing, I spun around in his arms and draped my hands around his neck, playing with the soft hair at the nape.

Extending up on tiptoe, I pecked him on the lips.

He took my gesture as an opening and drew me closer, capturing my gasp with his mouth and driving his tongue inside.

"I like the beard," I said breathlessly, when we came up for air. "I've never been with a guy with a beard before. All my past boyfriends have kept their faces bare." The skin around my mouth tingled and burned slightly, and I lifted my fingers up to rub it. His grin made my bathing suit bottoms wet, and I could feel a trickle of need escaping the fabric and running down my inner thigh beneath my loose shorts.

"Beard-burn, baby. It's a thing."

"I'll say."

"Once you go beard, you'll never go back. My beard on your clit, on your tits, your thighs, the possibilities are endless."

"Hmm," I hummed, shifting on my feet and loving the light chafing on my inner thighs from said beard.

He'd given it to me good this morning, and I was rather glad it was just the two of us out on the boat.

My thighs were a tad red.

His eyes flicked to my fishing rod behind me. He released me from his embrace and took it from the holder for a second.

"Do I have something?" I asked, giddy with the thought of bringing in a trophy on my very first cast.

Tate held the rod still and watched, checking to see if it jerked again.

Finally, he shook his head and put it back in the holder. "Just a bite, I think. They took off."

"Can I ask you something?" I asked, taking a seat and sipping my water.

He fell into the seat across from me and tipped back his beer. "Shoot."

"You're so secretive about your resort and all the good you do; why is that? Don't you want the world to know, so that your cause can be more public and you can gain more support?" Even though I was having a marvelous time and it didn't feel like work at all, I still had a job to do and questions to ask. I wanted to find out more about Tate McAllister, billionaire philanthropist and sex god.

One dark brown winged eyebrow slowly arched upward, and the corner of his mouth lifted mildly in amusement. "Off the record?"

Letting out a huff, I nodded. Shit, there wasn't going to be anything *on the record* for me to write my article about.

"Some people have likened it to a concentration camp," he said, an evident chip on his shoulder. Meanwhile, my own eyebrows nearly flew clear off my head.

"If it's anything, it's a commune," he said with a nod. "But it's not even that. More like working on a cruise ship, where you live where you work, except it's on land instead. There are hundreds of resorts around the world where the staff live on site. This is nothing new. My staff are free to leave whenever they like. We have no religious affiliation. No binding contract—besides the standard employee/employer one. If they want to quit, I would appreciate two weeks notice, but it's not mandatory. They can live here or live off the property, eat here or eat off the property. Everyone has to work forty hours a week, they get two days off, and they all get holidays and benefits.

"The difference is, I mainly hire refugees and immigrants. I just want to give these people who have come from nothing . . . *something*. But it's hard to do that when half the world is rejecting them, telling them they're not welcome. A lot of my staff are refugees, nearly half. And when the rest of the world is calling them terrorists or accusing them of stealing the jobs of the locals, even if they *do* manage to escape their own country, they're not welcomed very warmly into another. I'll employ nearly any local that walks in with a resume and can prove their worth. And I do employ a lot of Tahitians, but I want to give others a chance, too."

I was still shaking my head at the concentration camp statement. Some people were so crass. "I think what you're doing here is marvelous. Saving people, saving the environment, and all from the pockets of those who could afford to give more."

He smiled, and his gaze turned avid. The chip seemed to have disappeared. "See, you get it. But if I advertise what I'm doing, and who I am, and what this place is, then the media will be all over it, all over me, all over my staff. And some bleeding heart without enough information but a penchant for stirring up shit will paint me as a slave driver or a cult leader or something, and then all that I'm trying to achieve will be for naught. And my hundreds of staff members will be jobless and homeless again. Or worse, sent home."

"I won't say a word," I said solemnly. "Not a word." This man was incredible. So giving, so   perfect.

His grin took my breath away. "I know you won't. I trust you, Parker."

I dropped to my knees and shuffled toward him until I was at his feet. Looking up into his eyes, I smiled while my hands made their merry way to the front of his shorts and worked the belt and zipper.

"You're an incredible man, Tate," I purred, plunging my hand into the hole of his boxers and pulling him free. He was already getting hard. "I've never met anyone like you. So powerful, so giving." Dipping my head forward, I flicked the shiny crown with my tongue.

"Parker . . ." he growled. He grabbed ahold of my braid, and tugged just a touch too hard, but I loved it. Every synapse in my brain fired at once as a surge of unbridled lust ran through me.

Yes, more! Pull my hair again, please!

Bowing my head, I took him in my mouth, running my tongue up and down his shaft in circles.

He inhaled as I pushed him deep so he hit the back of my throat, only to bring him all the way back out and swirl my tongue around the top. Precum glistened like a diamond when I brought him out again, oozing from the small hole. Using my finger, I pushed it around and around until the plum head glowed.

Only then did I let him bottom out again, savoring his salty flavor and the way he shamelessly bucked up into my face. I felt the exact same way when his head was between my legs, craving more, craving everything.

I loved that I could make Tate as crazy as he made me, loved that I could take him to the brink and beyond.

"Holy fucking Christ," he said breathlessly. "That is so fucking hot." His grip tightened in my hair, and he demanded his own rhythm, pulling up only to slam me back down, forcing himself even further down my throat until I was damn near gagging and tears pricked the corner of my eyes.

I worked him hard and fast, pumping and twisting my fist around, sucking on the head before ramming him back as deep as I could go, not caring that I was now crying and spit poured from my mouth. I wanted to please him, I wanted to please him so badly.

He moved his free hand to my cheek, caressing my face softly, feeling himself inside my mouth with his thumb. Making a fist with my braid, he rammed me down one last time, his cock jamming into the very back of my throat. His whole body stiffened, and then with a grunt and a sigh, warm thick spurts fell across my tongue as the man in front of me came undone.

His chest heaved while his cock pulsed inside my mouth, beautiful profanities tumbling past his lips and up into the sky as he found his release.

Gently, I slid him from my mouth, licking and kissing my way up his shaft before pushing myself back up to standing. I went to go grab a sip of water but wasn't even given the chance before strong hands grabbed me by the waist and hauled me back down so I was sitting on his lap.

"That was fucking incredible," he said with a whisper, his breath a burn against my ear. He nipped it, then licked the bite, tracing his tongue along the shell. "*You're* fucking incredible." He drove his hand into the top of my bathing suit and drew out a breast, pulling and pinching the nipple until it was a hard, red peak. His other hand was deftly making work of my shorts, and within seconds I was perched on his lap in nothing but my bikini.

I tried to spin around and straddle him, but he kept me firmly in position, facing outwards toward the horizon.

A pull of some strings, and my bottoms and top fluttered to the deck in front of me and I was naked, his one hand still torturing my breasts while the other one made its way down between my legs.

I was a sopping mess.

Taking Tate in my mouth had been such a huge turn on, and the way he'd come, so virile, so primal—I hadn't even been the one getting pleasure, but I had been close to coming.

My clit throbbed as he lightly ran a finger over it, dipping two into my heat, slipping them around with ease.

He pulled them free for a moment, and I could hear him sucking his fingers, moaning as he delighted in the taste of me. He was such a dirty bugger.

"You love it," he said, reading my mind, his voice dark and smooth like melted chocolate as those fingers made their way back down between my legs.

"I do," I panted. The hand on my breast came up and gently cradled my neck, keeping my head slightly tipped up but unable to turn.

Tate stood up, and I was forced to move with him.

The sound of his shorts falling to the ground filled my ears.

Seconds later, I was brought back down, his cock forcing its way into my body, splitting me open.

I moaned from the pleasure, how good it felt to have him inside me again. We'd made love last night and then again in the shower this morning, but I was becoming an addict. I wanted him more than I'd ever wanted anyone . . . anything, and each time he filled me I was becoming more and more dependent, obsessed with the need to be taken again.

The hand was back between my legs, rubbing rough and filthy circles around my clit, his other hand still cradling my throat, not letting me move or turn around to face him, to kiss him.

He bucked up into me, driving his cock further into my quivering pussy, the sound of our sweat-slicked bodies raging at each other, the only sound on the water.

I was lost.

Completely and utterly lost to the sensation of this gigantic force of nature inside my body and the way Tate possessed me.

I'd do anything for this man.

Willingly.

Down and up, down and up I rode him, my thighs cramping from the steady movement of having to bend and lift while my clit grew hard and swollen beneath his fingertips.

Teeth and rough stubble raked my shoulders and back as he snarled and groaned behind me, his release gaining ground, much like my own.

I was close, so close, I could practically taste my orgasm, and it tasted so sweet.

Lifting his hands from the juncture of my legs, he grabbed my arm and pulled it around behind me.

Then he reached for the other one, holding them behind my back with his one hand like shackles, the other hand still poised on my throat.

He was holding me in place, ramming up into me, taking what he wanted, using me.

"You're going to come hard, baby," he said, his breath like a gust of warm wind in my ear. "You're going to come so hard. Then I'm going to bend you over the side of this boat and fuck you again."

All I could do was close my eyes.

I couldn't even nod.

Words eluded me.

I was gone.

"The way your pussy grips my cock. So snug. I feel like it was fucking made for me. So perfect."

"Tate," I mewled. "Tate . . . please." I was ready, so very, very ready.

Using my neck and arms for leverage, he lifted me up until there was nothing but the tip inside. A quick erotic swirl of his hips had me seeing spots, then he slammed me back down. I came instantly.

Bright lights and stars flashed behind my eyes as the climax ripped through me, eviscerating everything in its path like a tropical storm. I moaned and gyrated into him, biting my lip to stifle my cries as I shook on his lap in the aftershocks, slowly coming down from the surge.

He granted me no moment of respite before we sprung up from the seat and he barreled us over to the side, his hands releasing me as he ordered me to bend over.

We hadn't even come apart, and without waiting for my hands to grip the railing, he began pounding into me again, my breasts jostling beneath me with each thrust. I squeezed my muscles around him tightly and then let go again.

I let the orgasm take control and do with me what it may. I was a slave to the pleasure, completely and utterly at its mercy . . . or was it at Tate's mercy?

I was too happy, too wrapped up in rhapsodic glee to know the difference.

Tate grunted behind me as he found his own release, but we were both suddenly jarred out of the moment when my fishing rod bounced and twanged beside us and the sound of line being pulled filled the air, drowning out our groans of ecstasy.

"Oh, shit!" he cried, pulling out of me mid-orgasm. Cum dripped and spurted from the head of his cock onto the deck of the boat as he lunged for the rod and started to crank the reel, making his erection *thwack* against his belly with his efforts.

A flash of yellowy-green skimmed the surface of the water, darting back and forth.

I had no idea what fish we were after, but whatever it was, it was big!

"Here!" he said, thrusting the rod into my hands. "This is your rod, your catch."

I shook my head. "No, I can't. What if I lose it?"

He shrugged as he came up behind me, helping me hold the rod as it vibrated and leaned toward the water, the fish desperate to pull it under.

My muscles ached from the strain, but I held on firm, the base of the rod jabbing me in the belly.

With my right hand I reeled in, sometimes grunting with the effort to turn it around even once.

All the while Tate was behind me, keeping the rod stable, his hand on mine.

"You're doing great, Parker. Oh, shit, it's a big one. Mahi-mahi, I think." More green and this time a bit of blue shone through the turquoise water, a big tail flipping back and forth, while the body shook like a ragdoll in the mouth of a big dog.

"Mahi-mahi?" I asked, not sure if I could remember what the fish looked like.

"Almost there, babe. Keep going."

I groaned with the effort.

It was getting harder.

Both the fish and I were tiring, but I wasn't fighting for my life, so I'm pretty sure the fish was fighting with everything it had.

Tate let go of me for a moment and went to reach for the big net.

He dipped it over the side of the boat as the big fish struggled with all its might to get away.

"All right now, Parker, keep reeling but swing the line this way if you can, toward the side of the boat. I'm going to try to scoop him up."

"Okay." Sweat beaded my forehead and chest as the sun beat down from above.

I did as I was told, maneuvering the line and fish as best I could into the net. It wasn't easy, but Tate managed to get the net over the fish's head.

Then, with a flick of his wrist, he scooped him up and heaved him into the boat.

"A beauty!" He grinned, reaching for the measuring tape from next to the steering wheel. He quickly measured the beast and then placed him on the scale. "Might be the biggest we've ever caught, at least this year, anyway."

It wasn't a pretty fish, that's for sure: big forehead, wide, almost beaklike mouth, and a fin that ran the length of its back like a sloping hill. But its color was magnificent, striking chartreuse and deep indigo. Without a second thought, I reached into my shoulder bag and grabbed my camera, snapping a few shots of my catch.

"Here," Tate offered, handing me the fish so I could hold it sideways. He took the camera from around my neck and started taking pictures. I grinned wide, feeling the cold, slippery scales beneath my fingers. But then I looked into the creature's eyes and saw nothing but fear, while its mouth opened and closed erratically.

It was drowning.

I let Tate take one final picture, and then I walked over to the side of the boat and let the fish go.

No dead fish!

Today had been so freeing.

I felt more alive than I had ever before when I was with Tate, more open to the possibility of anything, more open to fun and adventure.

Today was a day to be alive.

Even for the fishes, there would be no death on my watch.

And no *dead fish*, even more so.

I turned around and found Tate watching me.

He still hadn't put his shorts on.

We were both still completely naked.

Oh, shit!

I wouldn't be able to show those pictures to anyone now!

Drunk on orgasms and my big catch, I'd completely forgotten I wasn't wearing any clothes.

"Probably for the best," he said with a smile, watching the last glimpse of the fish disappear into the briny deep. "I wasn't looking forward to bonking it on the head and fileting it anyway. Takes time away from fucking you, and I'd much rather spend my time doing that." Then he pounced, and in seconds, I was beneath him on the back bench of the boat, full of Tate and blissfully happy.

Chapter Seven

WE WERE JUST COMING back down the path from the marina when Tate stopped short. I was behind him and not watching where I was going and bumped right into his back.

"What's wrong?" I asked, trying to peek around his big frame.

Did Moorea have bears?

"Justin?" he said.

"Hey, dude!"

Tate picked up speed, and before we knew it, we were standing in front of a gorgeous couple and their two little girls.

He was tall and dreamy with rosy cheeks and bright aqua blue eyes, while she was shorter than me by a few inches, had bright grass-green eyes and the same dark red hair as I did, only hers was pulled back into a ponytail, showing off her long neck.

"Long time no see, buddy. How's it going?" Tate asked, shaking the man's hand.

"Great. James told me how hospitable and welcoming you were when he and Emma were here last summer, so I thought I'd come check it out, bring the fam. You got my email?"

Tate nodded. "I did. I just couldn't remember what day you were showing up."

Justin wrapped his arm around his wife. "Ah, the weather back home is foul, so we thought we'd head out a few days early. If you can't take us yet, we have no problem heading to another resort for a few days."

"Nonsense," Tate said. "We'll fit you in. No worries."

Justin's smile drew wide and carefree across his handsome face. "Excellent. Well, I appreciate that. This is my wife, Kendra. And our daughters, Maggie and Chloe."

Tate shook Kendra's hand, and even though he and I were "technically" together and Kendra was Justin's wife, Tate was unable to hide his appreciation for the woman's beauty. How could you not? She was striking, like a sexy Pippi Longstocking.

"Well, welcome. It's so nice to meet everyone. This is . . ." His hand fell to the small of my back and he ushered me forward. "This is Parker."

"Oh, I didn't know you were seeing anyone. James never mentioned you had a girlfriend." Justin's eyes glittered with mischief as he raked my body from head to toe, much like Tate had done to his wife. I wasn't used to such blatant appraisal, or, by the way he smiled at me, adoration.

"It's new," Tate said with a grin. "How long are you guys here for?"

Justin shrugged. "A week maybe, or two. We brought the jet, so we'll see. But your prices . . . yeesh! Definitely trying to keep out the riff-raff millionaires with those rates, eh?"

Tate laughed. "Ah, my little millionaire friend, I'll let you in. But you better behave."

Justin chuckled. "That might be a problem. I've never been one to *behave*. You know that."

Tate smiled. "Even now that you're a dad?"

"Oh, he just has to get more creative with his mischief," Kendra put in.

Tate's eyes took on an almost wicked gleam as his gaze fell back to the beautiful mother of two. "I can upgrade you guys if you'd like? Beachfront, private veranda. It won't be as nice as Parker's, she's in the *presidential villa*, but it's just half a step down. Plus, it has its own pool. You only share it with one other villa, and I don't think it's occupied right now."

Maggie and Chloe's eyes went wide.

"Can we, Daddy?" the older one asked.

Justin's face split into another big grin. "If he's offering."

"All right, then, I'll go speak with Janessa and have you guys moved to The Sun Star post-haste."

Justin's eyes flicked back to me, then to his wife, and then to Tate. The three of them seemed to be having a conversation all their own. What were they talking about?

"Anyway, dude. We've got to get some food into these little bellies. So we'll catch up later, maybe go do a dive like old times."

Tate's hand fell back to my lower back, and we started to move.

"That sounds great, man. I'll come find you tomorrow. And hey, welcome to The Windward Hibiscus!"

"How do you know them?" I asked as we made our way back to my villa.

"Justin's an old friend from college. His best friend James was here with his new wife back in September."

"Ah," I nodded. "They have a beautiful family."

I used my key card to open the door, and we stepped inside my suite.

"Yeah. And apparently they used to swing."

My head whipped around. "As in sleep with other people?"

He nodded, prowling forward. "Mhmm."

Swallowing, I moved a step away from him.

The man was a sex machine, he'd already taken me numerous times that afternoon on the boat, and yet nothing seemed to satisfy his appetite.

I rolled my eyes at that, thought.

Who was I kidding?

I was just as hungry, just as desperate for him.

We only had ten days together, and if he wanted to fuck me ten times every day, I'd let him.

"A-and do you swing?"

My tank top was off before I even knew what was happening.

"I have, yes."

"Really?"

"Mhmm."

"Do you still?"

"Not much. It's hard to do here. There have been a few swingers' parties here that I've participated in, but not many. It's way easier to swing when you're single than when you're attached, and to be honest, I kind of got bored of the lifestyle. And way too many women offered to leave their husbands for me. I'm no homewrecker."

I snorted. "How gallant of you. Sleep with their wives, but you won't steal them."

His shorts fell to the floor in a thunk, belt, wallet and phone hitting the hardwood. "I'd like to think that's a gallant or chivalrous thing, no?"

His hands were making quick work of my shorts. We were still moving around the room.

I just kept backing up, and he just kept stalking forward, hunting me, undressing me, devouring me with his eyes.

"Maybe a little," I admitted. "Do you want to swing with them? With me?"

His lips drew up in a wolfish grin. "The thought did occur to me, and I *know* it occurred to them. You could see it on both their faces. But no, I would never ask that of you. And even though Kendra is beautiful, I only have you for a week and a half, and I don't want to share you with anyone."

Well, that hit me in the heart more than it should have.

****

I had invited Tate to stay the night, figuring we could have sex until the cows came home, pass out in each other's arms only to wake up bright and early and hit the pool. But after we'd made love, ordered dinner, made love again, which was followed by the customary twenty-minute post-coital cuddle, he pulled on his shorts and was out the door, leaving me pouty-faced and craving more orgasms.

We were finding ourselves in a bit of a routine each morning, or so it would seem.

Meet in the pool, swim laps, get our freak on in the sauna or shower, part ways to get dressed and then meet back up and go on an adventure.

Never having been a fan of routine, I found myself enjoying it and looking forward to each and every step.

I still wished we could mix it up and he'd sleep over one of these nights, but I chose not to dwell on the things I wasn't getting and instead focus on all the amazing things I *was*, like mind-blowing orgasms and the attention and devotion of a sexy man.

The last two days had been quite fun.

Tate had taken me on an orchard tour through the hundreds of sweet-smelling fruit trees in the interior of the island, full of oranges, lemons, limes, grapefruits, guavas and avocados.

We picked a basket for ourselves to bring back, but I also bought a few organic and locally made jams, made of all places at the local high school.

I couldn't wait to get back and try it on my morning toast.

From the orchard, we went to the juicing factory, where they take all the succulent fruit and turn it into delicious and healthy juice.

I bought six bottles and hoped to be able to pop back into the shop one more time before I left for good.

The next day we'd gone out with a local guide where we (I say *we* but really mean *I*) were taught how to paddle a long boat like a local and fish with a net. Then the local guide took us back to his home where he taught me how to prepare coconut milk and a traditional Polynesian grilled fish, raw fish and local vegetable lunch. It was just Tate, myself and the guide, so I was able to ask loads of questions, take tons of pictures and get the true experience from an actual Polynesian.

My hand was cramping from writing so much on my notepad, and my brain was sore by the time we got back to the hotel.

I couldn't wait to sit down at my laptop and put the day down in my own words.

This was the kind of thing I loved: meeting the people, experiencing the culture and learning new things. Between the fishing with Tate, the orchards and the "living like a local" experience, I knew I'd have enough for a story, but I just wasn't sure if it was the story I wanted; I was still frustrated that every time I asked Tate a question or interviewed a staff member, they prefaced their answer with "off the record."

It was day five and Tate had promised me a real treat today, but beyond the word "treat" he had remained evasive. So I had no idea how to dress or what to pack. I stood there in my robe after my shower, staring at a few outfits.

Shorts?

Tank top?

Skirt?

Dress?

Where were we going?

What was the plan?

I was just about to pick up the light gray tank top and black denim shorts when a knock at the door had me tightening my robe and removing the towel from my head.

"Breakfast!" Tate cheered, rolling the trolley into my room. I could smell the fresh coffee and what I could only assume was waffles.

Saliva flooded my mouth.

He was dressed in dark gray board shorts and a white linen t-shirt with only two of the buttons done up.

His sexy chest was visible and I licked my lips at the site of his defined pecs, wanting to sink my teeth into them and hear him hiss my name out on a slow breath.

He rolled the cart out on to the veranda and once again I noticed a blond hair hanging from one of the pearly buttons, waving like a golden flag.

But I pushed my worries out of my head.

He'd assured me I was the only woman he was sleeping with right now.

Not that we *slept;* he refused to stay over.

But I was the only woman he was having sex with.

I had to take him for his word.

Not all men were like Xavier Rollins.

Not all men were cheating scum.

"Such service," I said with a smile, joining him and popping a piece of mango into my mouth to fight the bitter taste of jealousy that was currently plaguing me. I moaned as the sweet and buttery flavor melted on my tongue.

"We aim to please." He grinned.

I sat down where he ordered me to. A plate of heavenly-looking waffles with fresh whipped cream and tropical fruit compote sat before me, beckoning me to dive in.

Tate sat down across from me and started to eat. But then his eyes flicked down to where I'd crossed my legs, my robe having slipped open just a tad.

"Are you naked under there?" he asked, licking his lips before taking a sip of his juice.

I lifted one eyebrow coyly and blew on my coffee. "Nope, got a full three-piece suit on under this bad boy. I just really like wearing robes." Brazenly I uncrossed and re-crossed my legs, flashing him my pussy, so he could see just how *dressed* I was.

"Miss Ryan," he purred with a grin. But then his face grew fierce and his brows narrowed. "Touch yourself."

Biting my lip, I let one hand travel down to the V of my legs.

Two fingers snaked their way between the lips to my slippery heat.

His eyes never left me, instead they caught fire.

Perhaps it was the glare from the sun overhead, or maybe it was just Tate, but when I looked into his eyes, all I saw was hunger, ravaged and true glittering back at me.

Lust, craving, desire, need.

I began rubbing my clit, back and forth, back and forth, enjoying the way the nub swelled beneath my fingertips and my slit grew wet. I let two fingers slide into my channel, and I started to fuck myself, enjoying the feeling of my own hand but also loving what it did to Tate, what *I* did to Tate.

"Smack it like you did before," he ordered, the bulge in his pants betraying the composure his voice still held.

I let the grin slowly drift across my face and closed my eyes as I began delivering light, tingly little smacks to my clit and lips with the tips of my fingers.

It felt good, a soft sting followed by a spreading heat, pleasure born of the pain.

"Fucking hell," he said with a snarl, sinking to his knees and shuffling over to my chair. He molded my body how he wanted it, lifting my legs onto the arms of the chair, spreading me wide. "My turn."

Swallowing, I leaned my head back and my eyes fluttered shut as overwhelming sensations claimed me.

I'd never done anything like this before, never pleasured myself in front of anyone, never let a man take me in so many ways, in so many places.

And yet Tate, Tate made me want to submit and let him have me as he pleased. I'd do anything for this man so long as he continued to make me feel the way I did now.

Alive.

Wanted.

On fire.

"Continue with your breakfast," he said as he blew cool air on to my wet, throbbing lips, denying me the touch I so desperately craved. "Eat, Parker, or else *I* won't." His eyes were all pupils now as he drew one sexy finger up between my folds. With his thumb and forefinger, he gave my clit a mighty pinch. I yelped, so he did it again. "Eat!"

I speared a piece of pineapple with my fork and put it to my lips; his eyebrows drew up in challenge.

My teeth clamped down around the sweet morsel, and I pulled it into my mouth with my tongue, nearly having a mouth-gasm from how incredible it was; it was the best pineapple I'd ever tasted.

I closed my eyes again, delighting in the burst of flavor on my tongue.

A rough scratch raked my slit.

The beard!

Yes!

"Oh, God!" I cried, my hands coming forward and burying into his hair, pulling him deeper into my cleft. I'd never witnessed anything quite so erotic before, his dark head bobbing between my trembling thighs, brows pinched in unwavering focus while his back muscles bunched and rippled beneath his tailored shirt as he perched there on his knees before me.

Letting out another moan of satisfaction, I pushed myself harder against his face. "Yes . . . more beard, more." He hadn't even touched me with his tongue yet. It was all chin, all stubble, and I was close to detonation. T-minus ten seconds, or sooner.

"Eat, Parker," he mumbled, flicking his tongue against my clit and making my whole body quiver. I was breathless, taking him in, the sight of him, the sensation of his mouth on me in such a wonderfully filthy way.

I didn't even bother with a fork this time and snatched another piece of pineapple off the plate and popped it into my mouth. Dear lord, it was almost too much, the delicious sensations between my legs and the delicious flavors in my mouth. It was a new level of erotica, mixing food and pleasure, and I couldn't get enough.

He slipped two fingers inside me and started to summon my release in that diabolical come-hither crook, rubbing against my anterior walls and making me quake. I clenched my muscles around him, wanting to pull him deeper inside.

I wanted all of Tate McAllister, even it was just for a moment; I wanted all of him.

Finally, after what felt like hours but I'm sure was only a few minutes, if not seconds, I blew my gasket.

Starbursts and flashes whizzed behind my closed eyelids as the sun shone down on us from above while Tate continued to feast on my flesh until I was slick with sweat and pushing his head away.

The pleasure was too much.

Too intense.

Too everything.

Sex with a man I'd just met shouldn't be this good, this soon.

Should it?

I'd been with Xavier for three years, and the sex had never left me speechless and so close to comatose I had trouble remembering what day it was, let alone where I was, or *who* I was.

When he finally relented and stood back up, his cheeks were a sexy, rosy pink and his eyes were glassy with his own arousal, while the whiskers on that wicked chin of his sparkled with the dampness of my release. He sat back in his seat, licked his fingers then popped a piece of pineapple into his mouth, chewing it sexily with a great big grin on his face.

"Hmm," he hummed, "you taste better."

****

Once I was dressed, I followed Tate outside. We wandered back down the trail and toward the marina, only this time, instead of jumping onto a fishing boat, we hopped into a sleek little white and black speedy-looking thing. It was all kinds of sexy, something you might expect to see in a rapper's music video with dozens of scantily clad women dancing on the bow, while the boat ran at Mach 1 out on the open water.

We piled in, and just when I thought we could visit déjà vu a little later and get naked and fuck on the bow, two other men, both with enormous smiles and straight white teeth, offered us big "hellos" and climbed down into the boat.

"Parker, this is Ifan and George. They're going to come with us today because we'll need a captain and spotter for our dive."

I licked my lips involuntarily while letting out a whimper of discontent.

It came out before I could stop it, and I clapped my hand over my mouth to halt any other inappropriate noise from emerging.

Catching on to my disappointment at not getting to be alone, he smirked, that impish crook at the corner of his mouth transforming into pure lust as his fern-green eyes grew dark and his lids sunk to half-mast.

Feigning innocence as our two boat-mates shuffled around us, he came over and wrapped an arm around me, planting a big smacking smooch to the side of my head. "Don't worry, baby, I'll do you up right tonight, how does that sound? Once, twice . . . *three* times?"

I couldn't stop the unladylike snort that rumbled up through my nose.

Once, twice, three times. Yes, please!

He started to laugh.

Was my horniness that obvious?

Was I *that* horny?

I'd never had a particularly high sex drive, two or three times a month was more than enough for me, but with Tate I wanted it all day every day, and more if he was willing.

Despite my job and the places I'd stayed, I'd neither been parasailing or scuba diving before.

Most of the hotels where *The Decadent Traveler* sent me were more interested in making sure I was given every single spa treatment on the three-page menu and inland tours such as wineries, silk factories, breweries, castles, temples, churches, museums, etc.

And even though I'd stayed at my fair share of tropical treasure troves, not once had I been high above the water being towed by a boat, or deep beneath the waves meeting clownfish after clownfish while turtles and rays looked on with mild interest.

Both experiences were life-changing—especially the diving.

I'd never been afraid of heights, per se, but I couldn't say I went out of my way to look over a ledge or down into a ravine. So as safe and exhilarated as I felt with the wind in my hair and nothing but air and sea beneath my toes as I was tugged behind the speedboat at warp speed, donning the mask, regulator and tank and then bailing over the side of the boat into the cerulean sea was much more my cup of tea.

Weightless, refreshingly cool and with a whole new world to explore, I was in awe. Although Tate had said he had planned to take *Mr.* Parker Ryan spearfishing, I had politely declined after giving it great thought. Much as with the mahi-mahi, I did not want to be responsible for any lives lost on my trip.

No dead fish.

I wanted to see life, wanted to experience the intensity of a school of ten thousand fish swarm around me in a tornado of silver scales and wary eyes, darting around as a united mass the moment a barracuda or reef shark came skulking by.

No, I wasn't a vegetarian, and yes, I would probably order the mahi-mahi later that night, but I had never felt more alive on this trip in all my life.

I'd never been so adventurous, so brazen, so . . . uninhibited, so like hell was I going to be responsible for taking another life when I was in the process of reinventing mine.

Chapter Eight

It was day six, and we'd finally managed to get out for that hike he'd been promising me. Hopping in his Jeep after another glorious morning of swimming, sex and breakfast cunnilingus, we parked at the base of the mountain, tossed on our sunglasses, SPF and backpacks and set forth up the trail.

We'd reached the top of The Belvedere Lookout, having made good time, and even though I was slightly out of breath from the trek, had I not been, the view alone would have done the job.

It was stunning. You could see everything from the viewpoint, the entire island, in all its heart-shaped beauty.

It was busy at the top, loads of eager-beaver vacationers trying to snap that perfect shot, while at the same time avoid having an unknown person photo-bomb their attempt at a postcard-worthy photo (weren't we all?).

Sunset was the best time to come, Tate had said as we meandered around the top, dodging other weary but bright-eyed hikers, as it painted the sky into a rainbow of reds, oranges, pinks, yellows and purples. But if you wanted to hike (which we did), that was best done in the daylight.

He promised that another night we'd drive up and enjoy the sunset.

I didn't really care either way; I was on top of the world and feeling amazing.

The hike had been exhilarating, awakening muscles and challenging my lungs in ways I just didn't experience doing the front crawl every morning in the pool.

And the reward at the end was totally worth it.

We were at the pinnacle of paradise, and I couldn't imagine experiencing it with anyone else.

My heart felt light and my mind clear as I swept my hair off my neck and dabbed a towel on my chest to mop up the thin layer of sweat that had accumulated.

"Tell me about your family," Tate asked, handing me a water bottle out of his backpack.

"Thanks," I replied, taking a healthy swig from the bottle, running the back of my wrist over my mouth.

We wandered over to the edge and elbowed our way to the front. The din of marveling and awestruck tourists along with the snap and click of cameras filled the warm breeze, while the unfettered view of the Opunohu Valley left many others in introspective silence.

I was one of the quieter ones.

"So? Your family?" he asked again.

At this point, I'd pulled out my own camera and was adjusting the lens and specs to account for how bright it was. "What's there to say?" I finally said, moving to the left just a smidge and out of the shadow of a big tall blond man behind me. He looked part mountain, part man. "Mom was sixteen when she had me. Never met my dad."

Obviously that was *not* the answer Tate had been anticipating, because his eyebrows nearly shot clear off his tanned forehead. "Oh."

I couldn't hide the wry smirk that tugged at my lips as I continued to take pictures.

That was most people's response.

They were left stunned silent, unsure of what to say next.

"It's okay," I said, checking the last couple of my shots on the screen. "It's not that big of a deal. She did the best she could."

"Like you don't *know* who your dad is? Or he never wanted anything to do with you or your mother?"

Slanting him a side-eye, I moved over to another spot at the lookout, closer to the little souvenir stand, and started taking a few snapshots of the stand itself.

"As in she doesn't know who he is. He could be one of three or four guys. My mother was . . . *generous* with her affections as a teenager, beautiful and a wild child. My grandparents both worked long hours and weren't really around much to keep her on a clean and even path. Depending when I ask, I was either conceived at a pep rally, in the projection room of a movie theater or the back of a Ford pickup. Or *my* favorite, in a hot tub where there was nothing but hand stuff, but apparently his seed was just that potent."

Tate snorted beside me, and I just rolled my eyes.

"But either way, my mother never told any of the men. I'm not sure she was able to find them after their night of reckless *coupling*, and so I was raised without a dad."

"What about your grandparents? Did they step up?"

"Kind of, after the shock of it all wore off. They'd initially kicked my mother out, but after I was born and they found us living in pretty much squalor, they took us in. Though they were quick to point out that they would not be used as a babysitting service and my mother had to get a job and pay rent—which she did."

Tate motioned for us to start heading back down the trail, and I nodded, stowing my camera in its bag and then slinging it over my shoulder.

"I'm sorry," he said, his voice softer than I thought I'd ever heard it, full of remorse and pity.

Shaking my head, I gave him a stern look. "I don't need your pity. She tried her best, my mother. She worked three jobs, finally just got her GED a few years ago. And as much as she's a bit of a partier *now* because she spent her twenties holed up with a kid, she was a good mother. She tried. She didn't do drugs, didn't drink. I was never hungry, never without a roof over my head or clean clothes. I graduated high school and then college. I was a lot better off than a lot of teenage-pregnancy babies. Apparently the year I was born was one of the worst years for teenage pregnancies. Something like twelve girls in my mother's school became mothers before they turned eighteen."

"Where did you say you were from again?" he asked, awe and disbelief in his tone.

"*Bumpkinville,* Mississippi," I said sarcastically. The real name of the town was irrelevant. There were so many of them along Route 61 that they didn't even make it onto most maps. We had one high school, one grocery store and one bar. That was it.

"Really? I can't hear any accent."

"Good." I grinned back at him. "Then the thousands I spent on a speech coach paid off."

"Running from your past, eh?"

"You pretty much left wherever in Canada you're from and set up camp in a remote part of the world. Obviously your past wasn't that rosy, either." I knitted my brows together into a scowl. How dare he say I was *running* from my past? He didn't know me at all.

"I never told you I was Canadian." There was humor in his tone but not in his eyes. He was trying to get me to crack my shell, let him in, tear down my walls.

Never.

"The fact that you end nearly every question with an upward inflected *eh?* betrayed your origin," I said dryly.

"I'm from Victoria. It's on an island close to Vancouver and Seattle. Beautiful city, and I'd live there again in a heartbeat. I'm not running from anything. I had a fantastic childhood. My mother and uncle were incredible role models. But I can do more good on a global scale here. But enough about me, we're talking about you."

"Not anymore we're not."

"Come on, Parker. Just because this *arrangement* is only a ten-day fling doesn't mean I don't care about you or want to get to know the woman I'm sleeping with. You're more than just a piece of ass, to *me* anyway. I might be just a piece of ass to you, but to me you're more than that."

I stopped in my tracks and spun around to stare at him while my breath jammed up in my lungs, and I'm sure that stab to my abdomen was the bottom of my stomach giving way.

He moved into me.

"I like you, Parker." His arms encircled my waist, and he pulled me tight against his hardness, the heat and draw of his body making me dizzy.

I was a moth to a flame.

Despite the risk of being singed and rendered flightless, I was drawn to him.

Drawn to the heat of his body, his intensity, his fire and passion.

He wasn't just a piece of ass to me, he was a breath of fresh air, he was . . . *mine.*

"And admit it." His eyes held a seriousness to them, fathomless pools of sage that seemed to glow almost gold in the late morning light, but he also looked like he was trying to hide a smile. "You like me, too. I'm more than just a piece of ass . . . although I do have a *great* ass."

I made a noise in my throat that was somewhere between a snort and a giggle.

But nothing else was able to come out, because his mouth slanted over mine, and that was the end of the conversation.

Before I knew what was happening, he was running off the trail, through the thick green brush and into the jungle, with me in a front piggyback, my legs wrapped around his hips and arms around his neck.

We were both out of breath by the time he stopped, even though I hadn't been the one exercising.

Tate rammed my back up against a tree and then went to work on my clothes, shucking my sky-blue tank top, followed by my sports bra, which wasn't easy to remove.

My shorts were next.

Then it was his turn.

We were frantic, much like the first time we'd done it, desperate for skin-to-skin and each other, wanting nothing more than to have a connection to another person, to feel the rhapsodic glee that comes with orgasms and the feeling of being needed, claimed, possessed. And if there was anything Tate McAllister did well, besides run a hotel, make oodles of money, save refugees and fuck like it was his last day on earth, it was possessing me, mind, body and soul.

I let out a gasp followed by a mewl as he sheathed himself inside me, pushing my thong to the side, not even bothering to check if I was wet or not.

He knew my body.

He knew I would be.

I was a walking slip and slide when the man was around.

"You're more than just a piece of ass to me, Parker," he grunted, his teeth and stubble raking their way across my collarbone as his fingers dug deep wells into the plump flesh of my ass, holding me up and pounding me against the tree. "Say it."

Say what?

My head tilted back, and I noticed gray clouds rolling in with ominous intent, dark and foreboding, threatening rain of the torrential kind and possibly some thunder and lightning too.

"Say it!" he demanded again. "Say I'm more than just a piece of ass to you. Say I'm more than a fling."

"God, Tate . . ."

"Say it, Parker, or I'll pull out right now. I know you feel it, too."

"Tate . . ." His name was but a whisper past my lips as his body coaxed me to the brink but left me teetering on the edge. He knew exactly what he was doing.

The man was a master, and he was going to tease me until I said what he wanted to hear or I passed out from sheer exhaustion.

"Say it, Parker!"

Every cell in my body felt it.

It was more than just a fling, of course it was. I'd never been with a man like Tate McAllister, a man who made me excited to start every day and treat each moment like an adventure.

But the fact of the matter was, this *was* just a fling. I was only here for ten days; after that I would be leaving and going back to reality, and he'd have his tropical haven and the next heartbroken guest to breathe new life into.

"Yes," I finally sighed, deciding to give him what he wanted. It wasn't a lie. I felt it all, too. But the way he kept his own walls up, his unwillingness to stay the night, to invite me to his place . . . it was all just as temporary to him, too, even if he didn't want to admit it.

"That's right!" A snarl of satisfaction had him picking up speed and hammering into me harder, measured thrusts born of the triumph that shone in his eyes.

His pelvic bone rubbed against my clit while his cock massaged that sweet spot deep inside me until I was a quivering mess, ready to let go and drift off up into the ether, hoping, wishing that Tate would come with me.

He bent his head low and latched onto a nipple, drawing the bud into the wet heat of his mouth, while letting his stubble prickle and torture my pale areolas.

They were already hard and tender, so the soft bite of pain and deliberate tug were all I needed to shoot me clear over the edge.

I gripped his cock like a fist and tumbled backward over the cliff, freefalling, holding on tight to Tate and encouraging him to join me.

Pleasure surged through me as the orgasm took hold, ripping around my body, taking no prisoners and giving no quarter.

There would be no mercy shown this afternoon.

This climax was out to destroy.

My hands dove into his hair and I tugged on the ends, wanting to cause him just a touch of pain. I knew I'd succeeded when he inhaled harsh and quick and delivered a saucy pinch to the bottom of my left butt cheek. Even mid-orgasm, I couldn't help but laugh.

"You're going to be the end of me, Parker. I lose my head when I'm with you." His cadence was waning. He was getting close. I felt a quake pass through him, followed by a shudder, and then he stilled. His entire body went rigid, muscles flexed, body taut.

He grunted and let his head fall to the crook of my neck while sharp teeth nipped and grazed my skin and made me mewl and beg for more. I milked him, squeezing myself tight around his pulsing shaft, feeling every rush of his seed as he filled me. The pressure of his release against my sensitive walls was enough, and with the toss of my head and a low groan, I leaped off the cliff one more time.

"I'm going to book you an appointment later today, okay?" Tate said when we'd spiraled back down to earth and claimed our clothes, dodging golf-ball-size raindrops as we hightailed it back to his Jeep.

"What kind of an appointment?" I asked. The rain was picking up, and I was starting to fear for my camera, even though the case was waterproof.

"You'll know once you get there," he said solemnly. "I think it could help you. Sort out some of your issues."

He was being evasive again, and it irked me. What kind of *issues* did I have, exactly?

"If when you get there you don't want to do it, you can walk right out and come punch me."

I barked out a laugh, and he just flashed me a smile that made me want to tear off his clothes and ride him again. But then his brows met in the middle again.

"I want to help you, Parker, and I think this *appointment* might be able to do just that."

We reached the Jeep and piled inside. It was a soft-top, so Tate hastily unrolled the canvas before the rain soaked the interior too badly, and then we were off, rosy-cheeked, drenched and ready for our next adventure.
****

I changed out of my wet hiking clothes and into something a little more comfortable and beachy. It was still raining pretty hard, so the inside of the hotel was buzzing like a sunscreen-scented beehive with people in every imaginable corner. It made me quickly realize how busy and populated the resort really was. When it was sunny and warm, people were much more scattered, and the property seemed less full. I walked down the hallway past the pool and the soundproof room, around the corner where I waved at Janessa behind the desk and then to the left where a door marked "Allison Sheffield" had me coming to an abrupt halt and getting ready to knock.

All sorts of "help with my issues" scenarios raced through my head.

Was she some special massage therapist?

Reiki?

Hypnotist?

I had no clue.

I hadn't even knocked when the door swung open and a woman wearing light linen pants and an understated short-sleeved pink blouse smiled widely at me. She was probably no more than three or four years older than me, with wavy brown hair that fell just below her shoulders, a classically symmetrical round face with peachy cheeks and naturally long lashes that encased dark chocolate eyes.

"You must be Parker?" she said, a delightfully soft British lilt flowing at me like a melodic hum.

I nodded. "Yes, I am." I stuck my hand out. She took it with a knowing smile. Her hands were soft and delicate, with long fingers and beautifully shaped nails.

"Well, welcome. Come on in, won't you? Have a seat, and we'll get started."

I followed her inside the room, which at first glance appeared to be an office, but upon further inspection looked more like a therapy room, with two mirror image couches facing each other, a couple of other chairs and a bookshelf that housed works by Freud, Jung, Erickson, Morgan, Skinner, Chapman and Joannides. She took a seat on one of the cream-colored couches and motioned for me to do the same. But I'd stopped mid-stride and was just gaping around the room. Diplomas and certificates, one from Cambridge, another Oxford. I think she'd gone to Brown and done something as well; it was too far down the wall for me to know.

She was a shrink.

Tate had sent me to see a shrink!

Shaking my head, I started to back up. "Uh, I think both you and Mr. McAllister may have been mistaken here. I don't need a shrink." My hand was on the doorknob now.

She shrugged. "Okay."

"Okay?"

"Yeah, okay. You don't *have* to sit and talk with me. We could just stare at each other for an hour. Or we could talk about whatever you want to talk about, work, your life, nail polish, your favorite food or cooking show. Or you can go. Totally up to you."

I cocked my head at her like the curious kitten I felt like, unsure what I'd just gotten myself into but not altogether terrified. "Why does Ta— Mr. McAllister think I need a shrink?"

"I'm not a *shrink*," she said with an amused eye roll. "I'm a clinical counselor who happens to specialize in family, relationship, sex and meta-psychotherapy. I also teach yoga. We're all multi-taskers here. One of the doctors on site is also a personal trainer, and I think the other one is a lifeguard. My husband is the executive chef in the Tiki Lounge."

I'm not sure why she said that last bit. Perhaps it was to quell the subconscious worry that perhaps Dr. Sheffield and Tate were lovers, or at the very least, *itch scratchers.* It wasn't until she said anything that I realized that had been precisely what I'd been thinking. And why wouldn't I? She was gorgeous.

My fingers left the knob, and I took a couple of steps deeper into the room. She held out her hand, offering the couch again, like one might offer up a scrap of food to a mangy and snarling dog, with equal parts kindness and hesitation. If she was too forceful, I'd bite off her hand and run away; too gentle, and I wouldn't take her seriously. This woman knew exactly what she was doing. With a resigned sigh, I ate up the rest of the distance and slumped into the couch cushions.

"I'm not sure what Tate thinks I need help with. I'm perfectly fine. Unless he thinks I'm *crazy?*"

Dr. Sheffield smiled a small smile and jotted something down on her notepad.

"I'm not crazy, you know? At least I don't think I am. Heartbroken? Yes. Lost? Yeah, probably. Contemplating a career change? You betcha. Unhappy? Well, up until recently, that too had been a big ol' yes."

"Oh?" Her eyes lit up, and for the first time since I'd arrived, I noticed a hint of copper glimmering just around the pupil. I'd never seen such interesting or beautiful brown eyes. They were like shimmering cocoa truffles with flecks of gold leaf. "And why are you all of sudden *happy?* What has changed?"

"Don't get carried away with that admission there, doc."

"All right, then, so why don't we talk about why you're heartbroken and lost, rather than why you're happy. It seems you'd prefer *not* to focus on the good things."

Well, that was like a cold slap in the face.

I toed at a piece of fluff on the harsh white tile, deliberately avoiding her gaze. "My mom was sixteen when she had me. She did her best. But as soon as I turned eighteen, I got the hell out of there and only go back twice a year. I hired a speech coach to help me lose the drawl and have spent the last fourteen years trying to reinvent myself, distance myself from that town, that life, that . . . *stigma*. I don't know my father, and you *mind-meddlers* would probably say I have daddy issues. I might in fact. Xavier seems to think I do."

"Who is Xavier?"

"My ex. He dumped me about three weeks ago, in a room full of people with his mistress sitting on his lap." I couldn't stop the derisive snort that burst through my nose.

Dr. Sheffield lifted one perfectly spa-threaded eyebrow. "And how did that make you feel?"

"Do you provide counseling for all the staff too?" I asked.

Her lip twitched. "Yes."

"Figures."

The eyebrow ascended again. "Figures?"

"He's fucking perfect, isn't he? A modern-day Robin Hood. Only he's not *stealing* from the rich, he's just giving them something highly prized for an exorbitant price. Then turning around and giving back to the less fortunate, those that need it the most. Does the man have a flaw?"

"Mr. McAllister?"

"Of course, *Mr. McAllister*. Do you call him Tate?"

She shook her head. "Not very often, no."

"Why?"

"Because as staff we've drawn a clear line—"

"Yeah, yeah, I've heard that spiel before. Don't want to muddy the water. So does Tate . . . Mr. McAllister have *any* friends?"

"I can't answer that."

"Can't or won't?"

Her lips pursed into a perfect little pale pink rosebud.

"Does he come to see you for sessions?"

"I can't answer that, either."

I exhaled through my nose and eyed her with building frustration. "So, what's wrong with me?"

A sculpted shoulder bobbed ever so slightly, making the waves of her hair glimmer and shine in the light that burst through the big north-facing window. It would appear the rains had fled and the clouds had parted, because outside it was beautifully bright. The sun was peeking in through gauzy drapes, while a fan in the corner made them move ever so slightly. I suppose an open window would defeat the privacy aspect of this session, even though at that moment I was feeling rather suffocated and would have liked some fresh air.

"Let me ask you something, Miss Ryan. Think of a time when you were most happy. When was the time you were at your happiest? Close your eyes." I did as I was told. "All right now, focus."

"Okay." Still skeptical but willing to give it a whirl.

"Do you have that moment?"

As soon as I closed my eyes, Tate's face popped up. We were out on the boat, hiking, wandering through the orchard picking fruit, sitting at the Tiki Lounge eating dinner, on my veranda laughing and clinking our breakfast mimosa glasses. Every moment that had any kind of happiness in it was full of Tate. I couldn't find a moment in the last week, month . . . *year* where I had felt even as remotely happy as I did in these last few days.

"Do you have that moment?" she asked again.

I nodded. "Yes."

"Good. Now hold on to it. You don't have to tell me when it was, but just think. How can you get back to that moment, that feeling? Who were you with? What were you doing? If being happy is what you're after, do the things that *make* you happy, be with people that *make* you happy."

I swallowed, and the feeling of a warm tear trickling down my cheek made my whole chest shake. The thought of having to leave all this happiness in just a few days made my heart hurt.

I wanted to feel this way forever.

"You can open your eyes, Miss Ryan."

Licking my lips and trying to discreetly sweep my finger beneath my eye to catch the stray drop, I fixed her with a look that was equal parts confusion and frustration. How dare she make me identify what made me happy when that happiness was fleeting? When there wasn't anything I could do to hang on to it? I couldn't afford to stay here more than the week and a half I was slotted, and even though Tate had said I was more than just a piece of ass, he sure as hell wasn't in love with me and about to ask me to stay. That was pure insanity.

"Now, how do you feel?"

"Pissed!" I said, trying hard to pop her head off with my mind power.

"Wonderful," she cheered, uncrossing and re-crossing her legs. "Let's explore that, shall we?"

****

Since the good doctor's time was fixed into the price of the hotel stay and she didn't have any appointments or a yoga session after me, we ended up talking for nearly two hours.

I spilled my guts.

All about Xavier, my seemingly endless stream of Mr. Wrongs before him, all crappy guys who treated me like an afterthought or not a thought at all, and my aloofness toward it all.

My *dead fish* exterior that bored men and inevitably caused them to break it off in search of someone more *adventurous* and *alive*.

Because when I dug down deep, really, really deep, Xavier wasn't the first man to call me boring or *dull*. An *ice queen* or *dead fish* or some variation of the insult.

Of course, this all stemmed from my lack of a father figure, or so the good doctor had me deduce.

Apparently, I'd put up these giant walls around myself and donned this "I don't need a man" attitude that could be seen from space. And that wall, inevitably, pushed all the men in my life away. They felt neither needed nor wanted, because I was too afraid of getting attached to someone only to have them leave me later on.

For so long I'd tried to leave the life I'd been brought up in behind, and I'd ultimately succeeded. No more drawl. My driver's license said "Resident of New York." And when I HAD to go home, no one recognized me anymore when I walked through the lone and rundown grocery store.

I'd achieved what I set out to do, and that was exorcise Mississippi from my veins, my soul, my life.

I lost the glasses, grew my hair out, lost twenty pounds, started using top-shelf moisturizers and wrinkle creams. I had a standing appointment at the salon every eight weeks for a trim and every five weeks with my eye-brow threader. I'd dabbled with Botox and fillers for a while but realized I didn't need them, though Xavier seemed to think I needed to start getting them again.

But I wasn't a fan.

I changed everything about myself thinking that it would make me happy. Make me whole.

When instead it had turned me into this sad, empty, emotionless robot. Prim and cold and incapable of forging warm and serious relationships because I was terrified that the "true" me, the "real" me, the Parker Ryan from *Bumpkinville*, Mississippi, would be found out and be looked down on.

I'd gone and taken up with the likes of Xavier Rollins, a man so snobby, so conceited, with his head so far and so firmly embedded up his own ass, that I'd forsaken and forgotten all the good parts of myself in the process. I had become a snob just like Xavier, looking down on my past life, on my mother, on my family, and in turn, on myself; forsaking fun, adventure and excitement because it wasn't "cool."

By the end of the session I was a sobbing mess, clutching tissues in both hands as I cried through my explanations, rehashing every single relationship I'd ever had—down to my eighth-grade boyfriend, Beau, and how he'd humiliated me at our school dance by sneaking off with my best friend, Shelly, to go and make out behind the stage. It may have even been as early on as that moment that I removed my emotions from the equation and went into a relationship guarded. I'd cried for hours over Beau, but after seeing the mascara stains on my pillowcase, I'd vowed never to let a man make me feel that way again.

I didn't need their love or attention to be whole, to be successful, to be happy. What I'd needed was to get the hell out of Mississippi, and start a new life. And I'd done just that. Only I'd done so at the cost of my own soul. Because as successful as I was, as far as I'd come in the last fourteen years, I was neither whole nor happy, and none of that had been because of a man.

I left Dr. Sheffield's office feeling better.

I still didn't think it was possible to obtain the happiness I felt with Tate and hold on to it for more than my allotted time on the island, but during our discussion, without giving away the identity of the man I was smitten with, I decided that I was going to take this time as the respite from seriousness that I needed. I was going to go with the flow (something I'd *never* done) and live each day on its own and to its fullest, with zero expectation or plan. Besides, Tate had everything planned; he expected me to just submit, sit back and enjoy. I could do that. I *would* do that.

A quick stop in the lobby washroom had me splashing cold water on my face and regaining my composure. It had been a very revealing two hours, but a good two hours. I hadn't expected to see a therapist while on vacation, but Tate seemed to know exactly what I needed; he'd been on the money every day so far.

"Do you know where Mr. McAllister is?" I asked Janessa at the front desk, after making sure my eyes no longer looked like two red-rimmed orbs of sadness.

"I believe he is upstairs in his office, Miss Ryan." She smiled. "Would you like me to call and check?"

I nodded. "Yes, please."

The queen of discretion and poise, Janessa called upstairs and spoke with

Tate, and whether she knew of more than just a professional relationship she didn't let on, but she also didn't disclose as to why she was calling.

My arrival at his door would be a secret.

How had she known that's what I'd wanted but was too afraid to ask for?

"He's up there, Miss Ryan." Her face didn't give away anything. If I lived here, I'd try my damndest to befriend that woman. She was spectacular.

I gave her a quick nod of my own, then pushed the button for the elevator. "Thanks, Janessa. I'm going to head on up then."

"You're welcome, Miss." Then finally, after she'd made sure no other staff member, guest or otherwise saw her, she gave me the most indiscernible wink. But I caught it. She put her head back down and started to tap away on the keyboard.

Son of a gun, she knew!

In no time, I was standing in front of his office door. Feelings of nostalgia ran through me without restraint as thoughts from the last time I'd prepared myself to tap my knuckles to the smooth teak took my whole body by storm. It'd only been a few days, but already so much had changed. I knocked quickly and then waited.

"Come in," he called from inside, the shuffling of papers muffled through the door.

Hesitantly, I opened it, poking my head around the corner. "You busy?"

At the sound of my voice, his head snapped up from where he'd been glowering at a document on his desk. The smile on his face made my skin tingle.

Even the ends of my hair felt the spark.

He was up and out of his chair and, in less than six strides, across the room and pulling me into the depths of his office.

"So, how was it?"

I gave him a sideways look. "You mean my *therapy* session? You shanghaied me into seeing a shrink while I'm on vacation!" But I couldn't hide my smile, and my need for his touch wouldn't allow me to pull away from his embrace.

"You're not on vacation, you're working," he said with a wily grin, tugging me against his warm, hard frame. My whole body ignited. A needy heat pooled between my legs, want amplified by emotion, and right now I was a rollercoaster of emotions.

"You know what I mean," I finally said, letting him tug me over to the couch, but I resisted that and instead steered him back over to his desk chair, pushing him into the body-hugging leather, hearing it *whoosh* out air and the springs slightly groan as they took his weight.

"Are you mad at me?" he asked, his eyes wary as he attempted to figure out what I was up to.

"I was," I started, sinking to my knees in front of him and wedging my way between his thighs. I began to unbutton his dress shirt, letting each morsel of sun-kissed skin reveal itself.

Faint threads of dark hair came into view as I released each opalescent button, defining the valley that led to his taut stomach and down into the waist of his slacks. "But in the end I gave in and we talked."

"Good. And how do you feel now?"

"I still have some thinking to do, lots and lots of thinking, but I also feel better. Dr. Sheffield offered for me to come back again before I leave. If I have the time, I might take her up on it. Otherwise maybe I'll look into counseling when I get back to New York."

"Wha—" His Adam's apple heaved thick and heavy in his throat as I snaked my hand into the front of his trousers. "What did you guys discuss?"

I fished around inside his pants and pulled out his erection. A delicious bead of pre-cum glistened on the head like a pearl.

"Unless you're willing to tell me what *you* and the good doctor talk about, my lips are sealed . . . besides when I do this, of course." I dipped my head low and let him bottom out in my throat.

"Sh-she told you I go to see her?" he stammered, his hands making their way into my hair.

I popped up and off his cock and gave him a sinister grin of triumph. "No, but you just did." Then I bent my head again and went to task, making the most of my time on Moorea, of the moment, of paradise . . . of Tate.

Chapter Nine

The following day we went for an afternoon-long bike ride around the island.

Not one to just jump on a ten-speed and zip in and out of traffic like a New York messenger boy, I was quickly sucking wind on the first big hill.

It was nearly dinnertime, and although we'd stopped and grabbed lunch at a cute little restaurant in one of the many quaint villages, all the activity of the day and the sun overhead had drained me of my energy.

But it'd also left me with a ravenous hunger, and my belly grumbled loud and demanding with each pedal of the bike.

"How much further back to the hotel?" I wheezed, feeling the heat from the afternoon on my shoulders and kicking myself I hadn't packed my sunscreen to slather on another layer. I'd never been very good with directions, and my bearings were completely off. I knew we'd cycled almost completely full-circle, or at least I thought we had, so I figured we'd be coming up on the hotel any moment.

My rumbling stomach certainly hoped so.

"We're not going back to the hotel just yet," Tate said with a grin over his shoulder, having pedaled around the island with the ease and familiarity of a seasoned cyclist.

I'm not even sure the man had broken a sweat.

Did he swim a hundred laps every morning and then head out and bike around the island every day, too?

I mean, you can't be a slouch to get a body like that, but come on!

My expression betrayed me, and he started to laugh. "It's not much further, babe. We're meeting Justin, Kendra and the girls for dinner at a restaurant up ahead in another little village."

I perked right up and put the pedal to the metal to catch up with him. "Oh, that sounds like fun."

He nodded. "Yeah, it should be. They do traditional Polynesian dances as dinner entertainment here."

I caught up to him and fell in line, the two of us pedaling side by side down the road. I resisted the urge to reach out and hold his hand. It would have been cute, and made one heck of a picture if there was anyone behind us with a camera, but undoubtedly awkward as hell.

"So, what's Kendra and Justin's deal?" I asked, bending down to grab my water bottle from the holder on the frame of my bike.

Tate shrugged. "I've known James since high school. He's a year or two older than me, and he introduced me to Justin. The three of us hung out in college. But then James and I had a falling out one year when he caught me sneaking out of his sister's bedroom one night when we were all home for Christmas. Amy was eighteen, and I was twenty-one. She came on to me. Called me up and invited—nay *demanded*—I come over. But James only saw red, not that fact that Amy and I were both adults, or that she had her own life. So, he hauled off and decked me. We lost touch, but Justin and I always remained friendly, although he sided with James, as the two are as close as brothers."

"But James forgave you, I take it? If you met up with him and his wife last fall?"

He nodded. "Yeah. The guy has a temper, but it seems Emma has really mellowed him out. And Justin has always been a really easygoing guy. He retired at thirty-five. Now he's a stay-at-home dad to their two girls, and Kendra runs a wellness center."

I was about to say something about how beautiful their family was when, speak of the devils themselves, they came into view as we rounded the corner, jumping out of a Jeep. A flurry of flowy dresses and matching pigtails, the girls were dressed the same, but they couldn't have been more different. Where Chloe, the little one, was fair and round-faced like her dad, with the same bright blue eyes and unruly sun-streaked light brown hair, Maggie was dark, with black hair and chocolate eyes. Tate had said the day we'd met them that Justin and Kendra had adopted Maggie from Haiti when she was three. But it didn't matter that the little girls weren't blood. The way they interacted and behaved, and how Chloe looked at Maggie as though she was neater than candy, showed the girls were sisters through and through.

I parked my bike next to Tate's and slipped off, my butt aching from having sat on the hard and narrow seat all day.

"How was the ride?" Kendra asked, brushing a stray tendril of dark red hair out of her eyes and tucking it behind her ear.

"Long, tough . . . and wonderful," I said with a sigh and a smile. "I can't remember the last time my muscles felt so good and tired or my mind felt so clear." I was talking to Kendra, but my eyes fell to Tate. He was taking a sip of his water bottle and chatting with Justin. The evening sun glinted off his hair and made it shine, bringing out the copper highlights in the dark brown while his beard appeared to almost sparkle.

"Yeah?" Kendra asked, a twinkle of something in her eye when I finally turned back to face her. "Wonderful?"

I bit my lip. "This has been a great trip so far."

"Seems like it," she sung, hoisting Chloe up on to her hip with one hand while running her free hand over and down the back of Maggie's head.

"Shall we, ladies?" Tate asked, coming up behind me, his hand falling to the small of my back and urging me to move with the rest of them.

I melted into his warmth and moved into the crook of his arm. He grinned at me and looped his arm over my shoulder. "You had fun on the bike?"

I beamed up at him. "I did. Though, I'm not looking forward to riding back. My butt's a little sore."

"Don't worry, baby. I've got a couple of staff members bringing me my Jeep. They're taking the bikes back. It'll be dark by the time we get back, and I'd rather spend that time doing other *things* than riding a bike in the dark."

A moan rumbled deep in my throat as he turned his head and nipped my earlobe. "Me too."

The night ended up being a whole lot of fun. The authentic Polynesian dancers were spectacular, complete with grass skirts, headdresses and body paint. Most of the men had the traditional tattoos, much like Tate, while the way the women's hips swiveled and gyrated as if independent from their bodies was hypnotizing.

Kendra and Justin were sweet as could be.

Both of them, along with Tate and the girls, kept me in stitches most of the night, telling stories about their days in college and the highlights (and lowlights) of being parents.

When Maggie and Chloe were off wandering through the small fairy garden the restaurant had designed, the exhausted parents confided in Tate and I that they had yet to have sex here on Moorea or at the resort since they'd arrived. The girls kept them busy all day, so they were exhausted come nighttime, barely able to keep their eyes open through dinner. And even if they had the energy, it seemed either one or both girls ended up in their bed by morning.

Half the time, Kendra said, she didn't even know when the girls would crawl in. Suddenly she'd just wake up and find a tiny arm draped around her, or warm toddler morning breath would be wafting in her face.

They sounded exhausted and slightly overwhelmed, and despite being on holiday, they also looked it. I thought it all sounded idyllic. In a masochistic kind of way, of course.

I seemed to like a bit of pain with my pleasure, I was finding out.

My mind quickly zipped to Tate's beard between my legs, and I squeezed my thighs together for a moment. But then I got back to the topic at hand.

Jesus, I was horny.

What was this man doing to me?

I knew parenting wasn't easy. I

knew it was the hardest job in the entire world.

Shaping and raising another person.

Providing for them and trying your damnedest to make sure they didn't grow up to be a serial killer, or worse, a douchebag.

But seeing this beautiful family and hearing such heartwarming stories about hugs and trips to the park and pool and endless cuddle time made the other tales of tantrums and diaper explosions seem trivial.

I wanted a family.

And now more than ever, I knew I wanted it in the worst way.

"So how long have y'all been together then?" I asked, taking a sip of my Tahitian sunrise.

Three sets of adult eyes went wide and stared at me.

"Whoa, hey! Where'd that sexy twang come from?" Justin joked. "Are you a Southern belle? A Georgia peach?"

Shit. I hadn't even realized I'd said it. It'd just slipped out.

For years I'd been so conscientious about controlling my drawl, making sure

I didn't drink too much and it didn't sneak out.

But I felt comfortable with these people and I'd let my hair down, and apparently that damn accent just refused to go away.

I swallowed and nodded, a building heat worming its way up into my hairline. "I am . . . well, not Georgia. But I'm from Mississippi."

Were they judging me?

Did they think I was just some country hodydo or a swamp kid?

"I think a Southern accent is sexy as hell," Kendra crooned.

Justin's head swiveled to face his wife. "Do you, now?"

"Mhmm." Her perfectly sculpted eyebrows bobbed on her forehead.

Justin's Adam's apple lifted and fell thick in this throat, and he licked his lips. He only had eyes for his wife.

We could all be on fire or fighting zombies, and the man wouldn't have noticed. "Well, we may just have to explore this new *interest* of yours, *darlin'*. Would you like this here cowpoke to do you up right in the hay bales?"

Tate snorted next to me, and Kendra giggled.

"Darn tootin'." She beamed.

"We made sure that those double-wide hammocks on the verandas of the villas can accommodate the weight of two grown adults . . . just saying," Tate added with a wry smirk. "In case you find yourselves *not* alone in your own bed this evening."

"What, no hay bales?" Justin asked with a chuckle, tipping back his beer.

"I'd much rather you just *speak* like a cowboy and *bang* me like a cowboy than cause me to get hay crammed and lodged in some *delicate* places." Kendra laughed.

"Done and done!" Justin said. Just then the girls ran back, both of them holding what appeared to be "wands" made of carved wood.

"Look, Daddy," Maggie said. "There's a lady over there who makes these. Can we buy them? They're *real* fairy wands."

Justin dug into his pocket and pulled out his wallet but then hesitated and looked down sternly at his two smiling pixies. "Do you two promise to sleep in your own bed tonight?"

Pigtails bounced and bobbed frantically as they nodded their tiny heads.

"All right then, here. Go pay for them. But I want my change. And you two better keep your promise." The girls took off skipping and running back to where the Polynesian woman was manning a small table of souvenirs.

"You know they're going to be in our bed tonight by midnight, right?" Kendra said with a chuckle, taking a sip of her virgin Bellini.

She hadn't said anything, but just based on a few observations, I was starting to wonder if she might be pregnant. She was cautious with her movements and made sure she only ordered cooked fish, turned her nose up at the smell of Justin's beer and had been very direct with the waiter that her drink be non-alcoholic. I wasn't about to pry, but when she'd gotten up to use the washroom earlier, I caught myself studying her belly just to see if I could detect a bump. Her loose and flowy dress left oodles to the imagination, and I couldn't quite tell.

"I know," Justin murmured, stuffing his wallet back into his pocket. "Looks like this cowboy is going to be getting lucky under the stars tonight."

"It won't be the first time," his wife said wistfully.

He flashed her a smile that made even me swoon. "No, my love, it won't be."

Tate's hand reached under the table for mine and gave it a tender squeeze, the same thought flowing through both our boozy brains. Maybe tonight we could take advantage of *my* hammock on the veranda.

Have sex under the stars and let the night air kiss our skin.

He leaned down until I could feel his warm and faintly beer-scented breath on my neck. I thought he was going to kiss me, but instead he paused for a moment and brushed a strand of hair off my face, tucking it sweetly behind my ear. The gesture was so minimal, so gentle, but the way it made my whole body burn, I was sure there was going to be a puddle in my panties.

His nose pressed into the side of my head, and he inhaled. My pulse quickened and my breath stopped.

"Yes, Parker. Yes, I will fuck you in the hammock tonight."

****

"Did you have fun tonight?" Tate asked as we wandered through the gardens back at The Windward Hibiscus toward my villa.

"I had so much fun today, thank you. Justin and Kendra and the girls are wonderful."

He nodded, and a look passed across his face, I couldn't quite place it, but it seemed almost reflective with perhaps a dash of envy.

Do you want a family too, Tate?

But I shook that thought from my head almost as quickly as it came.

He'd been upfront about how busy he was, how he had no time for family or children or relationships.

He said I was more than a "piece of ass" but he never once gave me any hope that this could be more than just a ten-day fling. I guess it just helped that in addition to our sexual chemistry and being genuinely attracted to each other, we also liked and cared about each other as well. Not being one to have too many "flings," I wasn't sure if those things made the relationship better or worse. But one thing I knew for sure, it was certainly going to make leaving a hell of a lot harder.

"Can I ask you a question?" I asked, fishing my key card out of my purse.

"Off the record?"

I stopped in my tracks and spun around to face him. "This *off the record* bullshit is really starting to piss me off. You agreed to have me come here and interview you and review the resort, but you're treating this all like a fucking game. What do you think an interview consists of? Your favorite color, food and animal? I'm a journalist. I write the truth. Did you do any research on me before I arrived?"

He went to say something, but I cut him off.

"What am I saying? Of course you didn't, otherwise you would have *known* I wasn't a man. You've got to be the only person in the world who doesn't Google the shit out of someone before they meet them. I would expect this from Mr. Tate McAllister if he were, say, seventy-five or eighty, but not you."

I let out a huff and then swiped the key card. The light flashed green, my door clicked, and I pushed my way inside. I don't know why I was suddenly so angry. We'd had a terrific day, full of laughs, adventures and new friends, but somehow his "off the record" comment really pissed me off. Maybe it was just a reminder of why I was here. That this was all just part of the job, and no matter how close we got, he was always going to be on guard and watching what he said in case it was ever "*not* on the record" and I wound up putting it in the article.

Well, that just made my blood boil even more.

The man didn't trust me.

But, he insisted that I trust him.

I spun around to face him. "I think you should leave."

Green eyes flared wide at me, and his hands reached out to my shoulders, but I spun away from him and stalked farther into my suite.

I wanted space.

I needed space.

"Parker, what the hell just happened? What did I say? Why are you so mad all of a sudden?"

I ground my teeth. "Because you don't trust me. You *say* you trust me, but you don't. You feel like you have to say 'off the record' before you even answer me. How do you know that what I was going to ask you was even going to be work-related? Maybe I was going to ask you to stay the night. Maybe I was going to ask you if you have any allergies, or what your favorite childhood comfort food is. Maybe I was going to ask you if I could 'friend' Kendra and Justin on Facebook; they seem like great people, and I'm kind of lacking in the friend department right now. But you didn't even let me get my question out before you put up this giant wall between us."

Here I'd been working on tearing down my walls and starting fresh, and he was just putting up his own.

We were quite the pair.

He let out an exasperated huff, and his arms fell to his sides with a light *slap*. "What do you want from me? I value my privacy."

"And I'm just another *guest* you're shtupping. Got it. Well, this *shtupted* guest would prefer not to be *schtupted* tonight, so you can get out." I pointed at the door.

"Parker." He took a step toward me.

I backed up a step.

"Parker." He took another step.

So did I.

"Parker, come on. I *do* trust you. And no, I didn't Google you, because . . . well, I don't know why. I Googled your magazine, and I read a few of your articles. You write beautifully, which is why I accepted your offer. But you also don't give any indication in your articles as to your gender. You write sexually ambiguous, if not a little blunt, like a man. Your articles are well written and captivating, but they are incredibly fact-based. Not a lot of flowery words or superfluous adjectives."

I blinked for a second.

He *had* read my work.

And everything he'd just said was true.

He also wasn't the first person to say I wrote like a man.

My boss liked to say, and I must admit it irked me, that when you want emotion left at the door, get Parker to write your story. It'd bothered me, but I'd never let it eat away at me, until now that is.

"And there was no picture and a very vague biography," Tate went on. "I just *assumed* you were a dude. Just like you *assumed* I was wrinkled and arthritic with one foot in the grave."

My lip twitched.

I had totally been expecting some Warren Buffet-looking guy, not the sex beast with the most diabolical beard and tongue of a god standing in front of me.

"See, we were both wrong. I'm happy I was wrong. Aren't you?" His lip twitched this time.

"Of course," I finally said. "I don't think the sex would be half as good if you were constantly worried about your bad hip."

He barked out a rich and throaty laugh that sent a shiver racing across my flushed skin. He started to close in the gap between us, and this time I didn't back away. His arms came up on either side of me before resting on my hips. "What were you going to ask me? And it can be *on the record*."

I sighed heavily. "I was *going* to ask you if you'd mind if I 'befriended' Justin and Kendra on Facebook. I deleted my account when I left New York, so I'm having to build my friends list from scratch again."

"Oh."

"See, not everything I ask you is going to go into the article. In fact, none of the questions I've asked you will be going into the article, because you . . ." I trailed off and looked down between us at my feet.

One hand came up, and he placed a knuckle lightly under my chin. He applied just enough pressure that I had to lift my head and my eyes to look at him.

"Everything I've told you can be *on the record* if you need it to be. I trust you. I trust that you won't betray my privacy or my desire for anonymity. Use what you need to make your story shine." Hesitantly, but not without need, he leaned in and brushed his lips across mine.

"Stay the night?" I whispered.

"I can't. But I'll stay for a bit."

My heart hit the bottom of my stomach, and a wash of dread, loss and longing filled every crevice and dark corner inside me as he backed me up toward the bed, his lips continuing to travel across mine, then down my cheek and neck while his hands made quick work of my tank top and shorts.

I was on my back and in nothing but my underwear in a matter of seconds.

"I do trust you, Parker. I don't want to fight. I only have a few days left with you, and I'd like to spend as much of that time *inside* you as I can."

Swallowing the harsh lump in my throat, I blinked up at him, determined not to let a tear slip through. He quickly undressed in front of me as I lay there quietly on the bed, watching in open awe as the Adonis revealed himself.

Once he was completely naked, he scooped me up and carried me outside to the veranda. I

wrapped my arms around his neck and glanced behind him, and when I knew he wasn't looking at my face, I finally let that persistent tear fall.

Chapter Ten

After our morning routine, Tate and I parted ways for the day.

He said we would catch up later that evening and have dinner, but Justin had invited him to go out on a dive, and they would be gone for the better part of the afternoon.

I needed to go over my notes and the photos I'd taken from the last few days, so it seemed like the perfect plan.

Kendra and the girls found me later in the day, after I made my way to the buffet for lunch, and they asked if I would like to join them down at the beach.

I jumped at the chance

Any extra time I got to spend with that sweet family was fine by me.

The girls were adorable and so quirky, and Kendra was a breath of fresh air.

Living in New York for so long and hobnobbing with Xavier's social circle, I'd come to believe that self-righteousness and snobbery were the norm, and as much as I hated to admit it, I'd fallen into the trap as well. I hadn't realized that was who I'd become until my sit-down with Alejandro. And my session with Dr. Sheffield had all but confirmed it.

But that was all going to change.

I was going to change.

To meet a millionaire who was as down-to-earth and easygoing as Kendra was such a welcome change, if not a tad weird at first. I kept expecting her to talk down to the wait staff or make a comment about the beach towels not being soft enough. Had I been with Xavier and his crew, complaints would have filled the air within our first five minutes of arriving on Moorea.

We were just wandering through the lobby toward the restaurant—the girls had said they were hungry and wanted smoothies—when the sight of an all-too-familiar back and hair, and the indignant voice of a man I once loved stopped me in my tracks. My bottom lip nearly hit my toes and I had to peel my sunglasses off to make sure it was the real deal, that I wasn't suddenly wearing virtual reality shades and seeing my worst nightmare.

I wasn't.

It was him.

"I don't understand why I can't just stay in Miss Ryan's room," he said, sneering at Janessa behind the desk. "She's in the presidential suite, I'm her boyfriend, put me in her room. God, the staff here is absolutely insufferable. Where's the manager? Where is Mr. McAllister?"

Janessa's eyes flicked up to me, and Xavier caught where she was looking.

He spun around, his ugly snarl quickly morphing into a big but palpably fake smile.

"Parker, darling, there you are!" He took a few steps toward me, but I backed away.

"What are you doing here?" I asked.

He gave me a dubious look, like I should know exactly why he was here and should have expected him to show up at some point. "I'm here for you, darling. Why else? Though this *bitch* behind the desk won't put me in your room. Talk to her."

I shook my head. "She's not a *bitch.* That is incredibly rude and cruel. You need to apologize, now! And no. You dumped me, remember? On New Year's Eve, no less. You are not my boyfriend anymore. You need to go." I pointed at the door, and that's when I noticed my hand was trembling.

Kendra's hand fell to my back. "Everything okay?"

"Mummy, we want *smoothies*," Chloe said with a whine, pulling on the hem of her mother's beach wrap.

"Yes, baby. Just a moment. Parker, are you okay?"

With a curt nod, I gave her a forced smile, my eyes not leaving Xavier. "I'm fine. Go. Take the girls."

Kendra's eyes took in Xavier for a moment, wariness on her tanned face. But Chloe was threatening a tantrum, so she grabbed both the girls' hands and whisked them off toward the restaurant.

"What are you doing here?" I asked again.

He took another step forward. "Oh come now, darling. Let's not play games. I'm here for you. And what a wonderful place to make up, don't you think?" He reached for my waist, but I backed away another step and put my hands up.

"You dumped me."

Rolling his eyes, he made a derisive snort. "Yes, well. I realized that I was wrong. Felicity was . . . a lapse in judgment, albeit a *fun* lapse in judgement. But she's not who I want. I came here, to this *billionaire's* haven, to win you back." Amusement filled his eyes.

He was enjoying this.

Dear lord, the man was sick.

"You told me I bored you. You called me a dead *fish*. You broke up with me in a restaurant full of your friends," I enunciated.

Another eye roll. "You're being rather dramatic right now, darling."

"No, actually I'm not," I said, shaking my head. "Xavier, you dumped me in a room full of over a hundred people, celebrities and socialites, people willing to ruin someone else just to get themselves ahead even if for a moment. I don't even want to think about how many memes I was turned into."

His mouth jerked ever so slightly. Thank God I'd deleted my Twitter, Facebook and Instagram accounts. I just couldn't handle getting constant messages and seeing my face pop up with some snide text overtop.

"You told me I was cold and unadventurous." I brought my voice down. "In *bed.* In front of everyone. While your mistress sat perched on your knee like a smoky-eyed ventriloquist dummy. What on earth makes you think I'll take you back after you humiliated me like that?"

He lifted one shoulder. "Because you love me."

Shaking my head, I gnashed my molars together until an ache ran up the length of my jaw. "*Loved*," I said coldly. "Emphasis on the past tense." He rolled his eyes again. Apparently, I was boring him . . . again. "We'll see. Have dinner with me tonight."

"No.

"It's just dinner, Parker. Unless you have *other* plans." He chuckled as if the idea of me having things to do and friends to spend time with was a ludicrous notion. If we'd been back in New York, he would have been right. I kept people at arm's length and didn't have a lot of friends. If I wasn't working, I was with Xavier. But things were different now. *I* was different, and I did have other plans. I had plans with Tate. But like hell was I going to stand there and argue with Xavier or give up Tate's identity. It was none of Xavier's business who I was spending time with.

I nodded, but just barely. "Fine. Dinner. Seven o'clock at the Terrace Bistro on the far right of the property." It was the last thing I wanted to do, but I knew he would hound me around the property until I gave in. This was the only way to state my case, get my closure and be rid of him once and for all.

Giving him the best I-want-to-pop-your-head-off-with-my-mind-power glare, I walked past him to go and find Kendra.

****

Tate still hadn't gotten back from being out on the boat with Justin.

He'd mentioned that they were going a ways away to a deep wreck located just off a reef and might not be back until late. So I spent the remainder of the afternoon hashing out the horror story of my love life with Kendra over smoothies as we watched the girls make sandcastles.

She wasn't sure me agreeing to have dinner with Xavier was such a good idea, but she also understood my desire for closure. I hadn't seen him since the night he'd humiliated me.

Although I had no desire to get back together with him, I couldn't deny the pull I had toward the man.

We'd been together for over three years, and I had loved him.

Checking myself out in the mirror back in my villa, with a pointed toe and half-twist, I took in my appearance. I was wearing a simple but flattering turquoise halter maxi-dress. I let my hair do its thing, falling down just past my shoulders in waves of fire, and because I'd spent all day in the sun, I didn't need any makeup besides a dab of lip gloss. I wasn't trying to *dress up* for Xavier, but I also didn't want to show up looking like a train wreck and just reconfirm his decision to dump me.

I arrived at the restaurant at 7:12, deliberately late. He was sitting on the patio with a rye and tonic in his hand and bowl of half-eaten bread in front of him. He never was one to wait for me, for anything.

Despite his New England aristocracy upbringing, he didn't bother standing up when I approached the table, didn't pull my chair out for me, hardly even smiled.

I thanked the waiter and ordered a glass of chardonnay before fixing Xavier with my steely glare. "So, how's your *room*?"

His nostrils flared. "Not as nice as yours, I'm sure."

"No, probably not," I said with a thin-lipped smile.

The waiter returned, and we placed our orders.

I'd actually begun to enjoy Tate ordering for me. It wasn't that he was controlling, he just knew the best dishes on the menu and wanted to make sure I enjoyed my meal to its fullest. I knew that if at any point I wanted to order for myself, he'd have no qualms. So when I had to actually open the menu and pick something, I was slightly disappointed.

"Let's stop this charade, shall we, darling?" Xavier said, taking a sip of his rye. "You'll come back to me, you know you want to. It was all Felicity, she wanted me to end it with you." Of course, typical Xavier, never taking responsibility for his own actions. He was forty-seven and had never accepted responsibility for a thing in his life.

Even his eight-year-old son was more mature.

"You mean the woman you were *cheating* on me with. One of the many."

I saw the waiter's eyes bug just slightly as he poured my chardonnay for me, but his trained discretion had him tossing on the mask of indifference in a flash. Xavier rolled his eyes again. "We never had the conversation about whether or not this was an *exclusive* relationship, darling."

"I never realized we'd had to. I thought that after over three years, and the fact that when I was home, I practically lived with you, exclusivity was implied. My bad."

"Come now, you can't honestly say you haven't indulged in an international *delight* over the years on all your travels?"

I shook my head. "Actually, I *can* say that."

He didn't believe me, and the look on his face said as much.

"How'd you get a room here anyway?" I asked. "I know how much a night costs." I couldn't stop the smug smile that coasted across my face. "And, well . . ."

Xavier stiffened. The man *hated* being reminded of his "status"—how although, yes, he had money, he didn't have as much as some. His lack of maturity and responsibility over the years had resulted in his younger brother, Rufus, assuming all control of the family company and slowly selling off Xavier's shares right out from under him. Xavier was so bad with money; he hadn't even noticed. And by the time it was done, there wasn't much he could do. From there it had been easy for the board of directors to vote him out. If I were to guess, I'd say he *maybe* had five or six million to his name. Pocket change to the guests that frequented The Windward Hibiscus.

To all the guests here, and a man like Tate, Xavier would be small potatoes. A pauper.

"Billy Winters over at *The Decadent Traveler* hooked me up. I called him, made a 'sizeable' donation to his kid's school or art camp or something, and he pulled some strings. Made some calls. And *voila*, here I am. Ready to kiss and make up and go and enjoy that glorious *presidential* suite of yours."

Fucking Billy Winters. Xavier had always held their friendship over my head. Said the only reason I got the job was because he and Billy were frat brothers. Of course, he'd "made a call."

Fucking Billy Winters.

Fucking Xavier.

Just another reason why I no longer wanted to work there. I hated their buddy-buddy friendship and the power they thought they wielded over me.

I shook my head. "You're not stepping foot in my *suite*. I could have you removed from the property this minute if I wanted to. I've interviewed and spent time with Mr. McAllister. He knows me, he likes me."

He rolled his eyes. "Really, Parker, I'm growing tired of this little song and dance. You're taking me back. Now let's just agree that I messed up, I shouldn't have ended it, and then we can go and alert the front desk about my room change."

I was about to open my mouth when a deep and delicious voice behind me cut off my words at the knees.

"And how is everything tonight, folks?"

I glanced up to find Tate standing there, query and hurt in his eyes.

Xavier shot him a bored look. "Just fine, thanks."

My bottom lip was between my teeth as my eyes darted between the two men. One curious and the other oblivious.

"Actually, man, could you do me a solid and run and tell the front desk woman to move my room to Miss Ryan's room? Have a bellhop or something pack my bags, would ya?"

Tate swallowed and then stuck his hand out. "I'm sorry, and you are, sir?"

Xavier stared at Tate's outstretched hand. He was wondering why on earth a manager was offering to shake his hand. He had no idea who Tate was. Finally, with Tate not backing down, Xavier clasped his hand.

"Xavier Rollins, Miss Ryan's boyfriend. Now please, run along. We're getting back together and have much to discuss."

Crimson filled Tate's cheeks, only to continue traveling up into his hairline and down his neck and into the collar of his shirt.

But he didn't say anything.

He also didn't take his eyes off me.

"Is that so?" he finally gritted. I could hear his teeth grinding together from where I sat.

Xavier gave him a dubious look. "Yeah. Why are you asking me that? And why aren't you doing as I asked? Do I need to speak to your supervisor?"

I went to cut Xavier off. The way he was speaking to Tate was inexcusable. But he held up his hand. "Parker, please. I'm talking." Tate's face filled with rage and I had to wring my hands together to keep from decking Xavier right then and there. The oblivious moron turned back to Tate with a smug smile. "Perhaps Mr. McAllister would like to come meet me?"

A muscle ticked strong and thick against Tate's jaw. "No, I think *Mr. McAllister* is busy at the moment. Right away, Mr. Rollins, no need to *speak* with my supervisor. I'll *take care* of you. My apologies." He gave me one last look. "Miss Ryan."

I mouthed the words "I'm sorry." But his face was an unreadable mask. He nodded once more to Xavier but didn't smile, then spun on his heel and took off.

"You were incredibly rude," I snapped back. "There is no need to treat people like that, service industry or not. He's still a person. They're all still people."

He rolled his eyes for the umpteenth time. "Since when did you care about the ninety-nine percenters?"

"I've always cared. I was one, don't forget. And I've since realized that being with you, living with you and hanging out with all your snob friends has turned me into a snob as well. I don't like it. I'm not getting back together with you, Xavier. I know you only came here because you wanted to *experience* a place you could never actually afford to come on your own. You'd use me, then dump me again the moment we got back to New York. Was this whole ruse Felicity's idea? Tell me something, Xavier, if I'd been at some really nice but not nearly as elite hotel in Spain or Greece, would you have come for me?"

His eyes grew fierce, and he bared his teeth at me in a sneer. "I made you what you are, don't forget. Before me, you were living paycheck to paycheck, waiting tables in Brooklyn and trying to get your career going by writing articles for that shitty little online magazine. You owe me."

"You're right." I nodded. "I do. I owe you thanks. So, thank you. Thank you for using your contacts to hook me up with an interview with *The Decadent Traveler*, thank you for loving me . . . if you ever did, though I'm skeptical on that one. Thank you for letting me use your pool, and thank you for dumping me and helping me realize how fucking toxic you and your lifestyle are. I want nothing to do with either anymore, and I'm not sure I even want to work for *The Decadent Traveler* anymore. This may be my last piece. So, thank you, Xavier. I can honestly say I have never been happier than I am now."

His mouth hung open for just a moment, but then like the asshole he was, he had to have the last word. "I could ruin you, you know? Make you a social pariah. You'd be the laughingstock of the Upper East Side. No magazine will hire you when I get through making phone calls. What are you going to do? Go back to waitressing?" He scoffed as he sat back in his seat, tipping his drink back and draining it.

"Maybe I'll write a book," I said with a shrug. "Maybe I'll move home, so that I don't have to deal with *your* people on the *Upper East Side* anymore. Maybe I'll just start over somewhere where no one knows me. I've done it before. I can do it again. But one thing's for damn sure . . ." I stood up and pushed my seat away with a screech. A few eyes around the restaurant took in my sudden movement. People had been eavesdropping anyway, you could always tell. "I'm done with you, Xavier. Done for good. Goodbye, *Bubbles.*" Then I took off through the restaurant in search of Tate.

I didn't have to look far. He was standing behind a palm tree, just out view, but well within earshot.

A giant smile was plastered on his face.

His eyes snagged mine, and without saying a word, we fell in line at a brisk pace, his hand falling to the small of my back as we made to leave the restaurant.

"You're schlepping it with hotel staff?"

Oh, fuck!

We stopped in our tracks to find Xavier behind us, a tad out of breath.

Had he actually run to catch up?

"Wow, you really have changed. Best way to get over a millionaire is under a . . ." he paused. "Sorry, *how* much do you make?" Snide laughter filled his tone as his eyes raked Tate from head to toe. Tate was dressed down after his day of diving in a white hotel logoed polo shirt and khaki shorts, and when I scrutinized him closer, he had the outline of the scuba mask still around his eyes. He looked like a sexy beach bum with chin scruff, wild salt-filled and windswept hair and a righteous tan. Not the enigmatic billionaire real estate mogul who owned this resort and nearly a dozen others.

A wide grin flashed across the planes of Tate's handsome face as he shoved out his hand again. Xavier glared at it in disdain but also building confusion. He took it because prep school had trained him to do so. His quick inhale told me Tate was gripping his hand just a *tad* too hard.

"I'm Ta—"

But I cut him off; he was just about to blow his cover, and as much it meant to me that he would do that, I wouldn't let him. Xavier didn't deserve to meet Tate McAllister.

"This is *Taylor Wilson*," I said. "And so what if he *is* a manager? I'm not slumming. He's ten times the man you could ever be. Money or no money. And . . ." I looked back up at Tate and rested my hand on his chest, "and he's made me realize that the only *dead fish* in yours and my relationship, Xavier, was *you*. I'm crazy *adventurous*, you just didn't bother to ask."

I reached for Tate's hand and turned us both around. His smile was a mile wide. I caught him nodding at an enormous man in the corner dressed all in black with Morpheus shades and a FBI ear-thingy.

"Come on, baby," I said, tugging harder on Tate's hand, "let's go."

I didn't bother to look back, even though I would have loved to. But the sound of Xavier's protestations as security accompanied him out of the restaurant and eventually out of the hotel was music to my ears.

We practically sprinted back to my villa. Tate tackled me before we even got to the entranceway and started peeling my clothes off like a starved dog might go at a steak bone, before the door was even fully shut.

He ravished me. Brought my body to orgasm after orgasm until I was afraid I'd black out from the pleasure and not wake up until the following week.

A short while later I woke up from a doze. The cool night breeze wafted in through the gauze drapes and across my body.

I ached in all the right places, while a fresh chafe on my inner thighs reminded me of his beard and the wonders it had wielded.

Stretching like a satisfied cat who'd just downed a quart of warm milk and then slept the day away, rather than the hour or so I'd been out, I looked to my right.

Tate was next to me—he'd decided to stay over.

I fought the urge to fist pump and instead just smiled and took in his beauty. I rolled over and watched him sleep. A little creepy, I know, but I couldn't help it.

It was the first time I'd ever slept next to him, and I just felt as though I was finally peeling away the layers of Tate McAllister; this was yet another side of him. In the dim light of the bedroom, with nothing but the last hints of twilight filtering in through sheer drapes, I had trouble making out his expression, even being only inches apart.

He took my breath away.

The angles of his face, so chiseled and manly; his skin, tanned and perhaps slightly weathered from being out in the sun all the time; and faint lines around his eyes, mouth and on his forehead, barely discernible unless you were inspecting him up close and personal like I was.

But those lines just made him more refined, added to the allure and maturity.

He was no spring chicken, and I liked that.

Long dark lashes lay flat against his high cheekbones, while his sculpted chest rose and fell in deep and even breaths. He had been designed by the gods, and when they were in an incredibly good mood, it would seem; even the freckles on his strong forearms were sexy.

He looked peaceful. Probably more peaceful than I had ever seen him. So far, I'd seen the playful Tate, the seductive Tate, the businessman Tate, the angry Tate and the jealous Tate. But this was an entirely new look. It was as if he walked around all day every day with tension in his jaw, a constant worry or problem sitting like a boulder of stress on his broad shoulders, and only in sleep was he able to let go of it all and just be and find some peace.

My chest grew tight as I continued to take him in, wishing this wasn't just a *quick and dirty* fling anymore and that I could live here, with Tate—forever. I wanted to feel this content, this happy, this *at peace* every day, and I knew that with Tate I could, I would.

But we'd only known each other for a week. I certainly couldn't go making such proclamations and asking to stay.

That's what crazy women did.

And besides, I was sure he had women constantly asking to live here with him.

He probably had a full spiel prepared for letting them down easy.

No.

I would not be one of those women.

I would not beg.

This was ten days of fun.

Ten days of strangers humping like bunnies, and that was it.

So then why did I feel like when I stepped onto that tarmac in a few days, my heart was going to break more than it ever had before?

He must have felt me staring at him.

I almost always knew when someone was watching me.

Long camel lashes fluttered open, followed by an enormous grin spreading on those sensuous and talented lips of his.

"Hello, beautiful."

I swallowed down the lump of emotion in my throat and flashed him the biggest smile I could muster. "Hi."

"What time is it?"

I lifted myself up just an inch or so and peered at the clock on his nightstand. "Just past eleven, why?"

"Oh, shit!" His eyes opened wide, and he bolted up to a sitting position.

"Stay the night?" I asked, waves of melancholy swamping me like a tsunami, replacing all those feelings of peace and tranquility and dreams of living here with Tate, happily ever after with little ruddy-haired children half-naked, tanned and happy running around.

"I can't," he said, swiveling his legs over the side to pull on his boxers. I couldn't tell if there was remorse in his voice or not. "Sorry, babe." He went on the hunt for his clothes, finding his shirt on one of the sconces and his shorts hanging down the back of my vanity.

I'd been just as wild for him, too, tearing off his clothes and tossing them away like confetti.

"C-can I come stay the night with you, then?" I regretted immediately that I'd asked such a thing.

I sounded like a desperate, needy, whiny woman.

Three things I had promised I would NEVER be.

Tate just shook his head.

Had he heard me, or was he ignoring my question on purpose? "Pool tomorrow, then I have one final surprise for you, and I must say, I think this one is going to be the best."

I gave him a half-hearted smile as I sat there in the bed, watching him dress, willing him to shuck the clothes and climb back into bed with me.

I had one last full day on Moorea, then I'd be leaving.

I wanted to spend as much time with him as I could, including the time we were asleep.

He pulled his shirt on over his head before he bent down to kiss me. "I'm so proud of you, Parker. That had to feel good. Telling off your ex and hearing him get hauled away by security. We can watch the camera footage of it tomorrow if you want."

I bit the inside of my cheek until I tasted blood as I nodded, a lump the size of a pineapple forming in my gut while tears stung the back of my eyes. Even though I knew we had one more day, for some reason *this*, here and now, felt like "goodbye."

I wanted him to stay.

I wanted to grab him by the hem of his shirt and pull him on top of me.

Show him what he would be missing when I left.

I wanted to communicate, somehow, even just half of what was going on in my mind, my body, my heart.

I wanted him to know what he meant to me and how in just ten short days he'd changed my whole world.

He kissed me again, but this time it was no more than a peck. "I'll see you in the morning. Sweet dreams." And with a final tweak to my nipple, he was out the door, leaving me heartbroken and horny and alone.

Chapter Eleven

The next day was my last full day on Moorea. I was set to head home in the late morning the following day, so Tate said he had something extra special planned. We were going to take a ride in a helicopter and fly over all the surrounding islands.

He would point out the other resorts he owned, and we would touch down near the small set of bungalows on stilts in which he owned shares on Bora Bora and have lunch.

I was used to living the life of Riley when I was with Xavier.

The man lived a lavish and opulent lifestyle, throwing money around like it was no big deal and letting everyone within a ten-mile radius know he was loaded.

But there was something so much more down-to-earth and refreshing about Tate. Sure, he had more money than I or anyone I knew could shake a stick at, but he didn't act like he did. He was humble and sweet, and even though I knew we only had one last day together, I couldn't control or quell the feelings that stirred inside.

I was falling for the billionaire, falling hard, and if I wasn't careful, I was going to crash and burn.

And unlike the Phoenix, I wasn't sure if I had the strength to rise from the ashes.

"And that's Huahine down there," he said, pointing across me and down at a small island loaded with hills and vegetation. "I own a bed and breakfast and a small set of eight bungalows down there."

I had thought that we were going to use a pilot and Tate would sit in the back with me and play tour guide, but oh, no. In addition to being a top-notch fishing guide, a dive instructor, a hotel owner, a French Polynesian real estate mogul, fluent in multiple languages and a sex god, he was also, of course, a helicopter pilot.

We sat in the front seat with sunglasses and the headgear on, and over the course of an hour, he careened us over sparkling blue water, white sand and lush, hilly islands.

My face hurt as I looked out the window, high above the world with such an amazing man at the helm. I hadn't smiled like this in ages, and it was all because of Tate.

He'd brought me back from a dark place, saved me and shown me what it

was like to have fun and not take life too seriously. And now I was getting ready to head back to reality, where life was serious and demanding and . . . boring.
****

Lunch on Bora Bora had been spectacular: fresh fish with Tahitian vanilla sauce and the most incredible *poe,* which is a decadent dessert made from banana and pumpkin starch, mixed with other fresh fruits like papaya, mango and pineapple, all cooked in banana leaves inside a Tahitian oven.

We borrowed masks and snorkels and floated around the bay just off the restaurant where we'd dined. And as one last surprise, or gift, Tate let me "fly" the helicopter.

I was terribly nervous, but this trip was about living and adventure, so when he asked me if I wanted to try steering, I'd swallowed my fear and gripped the cyclic stick and boldly traversed us around the sky. It was invigorating, it was life-changing, it was absolutely terrifying, and I loved every minute of it.

By the time we got back to the hotel, I was exhausted.

We were having a quick drink with Justin and Kendra at their private villa, watching the girls splash in the pool, when Tate's phone vibrated on the table and one of his managers ran up behind us out of breath and with a look of sheer panic on his face.

Tate snatched his phone, checked the message and stood up just as Quincy approached.

Tate and his manager shared a quick look, and then Quincy nodded. Justin, noticing the building tension, stood up too.

"Is it what we feared?" he asked.

Tate nodded.

What the hell?

What had they *feared?*

Dread settled in my belly like a lead balloon.

It had to be something involving Xavier, I just knew it.

Tate turned to face me. "Xavier has gone to the press in retaliation for being kicked out of here yesterday. Somehow, we're not entirely sure *how* yet, he figured out who I am and has gone to the tabloids bashing the hotel. Spreading rumors and lies about me, my employees and you. A huge front page spread is on the magazine slated to go out to newsstands tomorrow. It's already online." He handed me his phone where quotes like "Tate McAllister, billionaire philanthropist or petty dictator?" and "Parker Ryan, the billionaire's arm candy . . . for a price" graced the cover.

Bile burned the back of my throat.

He was calling me a prostitute.

Fucking Bubbles, when I got back to New York I was going to kill him myself.

"Want me to get James on it back home?" Justin asked, grabbing his phone out of his back pocket. "He's got a guy, a couple guys who can go *talk* to him."

Tate shook his head. "Not yet."

I pushed myself to my feet. "Do we even know if Xavier is back in the states yet?"

Tate shook his head. "He's not. Quincy just told me that he's booked at a four-star hotel on the other side of the island."

"Should we go?" Justin asked, bouncing on his heels with excitement, but then he caught his wife's eye, and the two exchanged a quick look.

"You're on vacation, my Dark Knight," she said blandly. "Leave the crime-fighting to the men *on* duty."

He nodded solemnly, then immediately started to backpedal. "I mean, should we send one of your big security guards to go and *speak* to him." The disappointment in his eyes was plain as day.

Tate was still studying his phone and whispering with Quincy, not really paying attention to what Justin was saying and behaving as if I no longer existed.

Did I exist anymore?

I was the reason his cover was blown.

The anonymity, the privacy he'd worked hard to keep for all these years was gone in seconds, and all because of me.

He looked up at me, his eyes fierce. "We have to go."

"Where?"

"We're going to talk to Xavier."

"*We?*"

He nodded.

"You need help?" Justin asked. Kendra made a noise in her throat from where she sat. "I mean, I can drive if you guys need someone in the getaway car or something."

Tate shook his head and slapped his friend on the shoulder. "Nah, man, I think we're good here. We'll take Mako, my biggest security guard. Should be enough." He bit the inside of his lip for moment in thought before turning to Quincy. "Want to go and grab Michael as well? Won't hurt to have my attorney there too."

Quincy nodded. "He's already in his office printing up the cease and desist papers."

Tate nodded. "I only hire the best."

Quincy made a face. "We're also working on figuring out who revealed your identity, sir. As well as how Mr. Rollins obtained photos of you and Miss Ryan. We won't let them get away with it." Quincy was making a face similar to the one Alejandro had made a few days ago when he'd talked about "getting rid of" subpar employees, or ones who didn't toe the line.

Tate's face softened. "I'm sure it was a mistake. Or he may have just figured it out on his own. As for the photos, who knows?"

But Quincy's eyes were hard. He was taking this violation personally.

Tate's hand fell to the small of my back. "Ready to go?"

I swallowed and nodded. Not at all, but it had to be done.

Fucking Bubbles needed to be dealt with.

Moments later we were climbing into the Jeep, with an enormous Polynesian man behind the wheel whose biceps were the same size as my waist and whose neck was as thick as his thighs. Michael, a scrawny little white guy with Coke-bottle glasses, sat in the front seat while Tate and I sat in the back.

I was shaking.

Freezing, despite the warm evening breeze that coasted across my skin as we raced down the road to the other side of the island. Fear and anger comingled inside of me into an icy froth that settled heavy in my stomach and slowly seeped out like a toxic wound into the rest of my body. I'd forgotten a cardigan, so I just wrapped my arms around myself and rocked back and forth. Tate glanced down at me and then, without even batting an eye, removed his T-shirt and pulled it over my head.

"It'll be okay," he said, pulling me close and rubbing my shoulder, planting a kiss on the top of my head.

I continued to shake. "I'm so sorry."

"It's not your fault."

Mako slowed down the Jeep as the lights of a resort up ahead came into view. He rolled up to the security gate and spoke with the man at the front. The gate swung open seconds later, and we pulled through. He parked, and when we clambered out, we were greeted by a friendly-looking man in a crisp white dress shirt and tan pants, wringing his hands. He had the name of the resort emblazoned on the top corner of his shirt, *The Moorean Sunrise Resort and Bungalows.*

Tate stepped forward and shook his hand. "Thanks for doing this, Arturo. I really appreciate it."

The gray-haired man with soft brown eyes nodded. "I'm so sorry, Mr. McAllister, if I'd had any idea who he was, I would have turned him away."

Tate shook his head. "I keep telling you to call me Tate. You're old enough to be my father. I should be calling *you* Mr. Mendez."

Arturo blushed.

Tate went on. "No need to apologize. You didn't know. No harm, no foul. But if you could show us to Mr. Rollins' room, we can take it from here."

Arturo nodded and motioned for us to follow him, with Tate behind him, me behind Tate, followed by Michael and then finally Mako. I looked behind me—jeepers, the guy had to be at least seven feet tall, three hundred pounds. And I was guessing most of that weight was pure muscle. Yeah, if Michael's papers didn't do the trick, Mako's size and half-tattooed face certainly would.

We came up to a small bungalow right on the beach. Xavier could step out and be in the surf in a matter of seconds. It was no presidential suite at The Windward Hibiscus, but it wasn't too shabby, either.

Tate stepped forward and went to knock, but I stopped him, pulled his shirt over my head and handed it back to him. He tugged it on and gave me a brief smile of thanks before lifting his fist and knocking.

Seconds later, the door opened. A woman wearing nothing but a peach thong and matching bra was standing there with a dubious expression on her face. "You're not room service," she said stupidly in her little breathy baby-doll voice.

"Lani, babe, is that room service? I'm starving." Xavier came around the corner towel-drying his hair, wearing nothing but a confused look on his dumb face. He lifted his head up, and his eyes went buggy as he took us all in. The towel dropped from his head, and he immediately draped it around his waist. "What the fuck is the meaning of this?" he asked, indignation in his voice. But a quaver of unease was there as well. Mako stepped out of the shadows and loomed behind me. All the blood drained from Xavier's face.

Lani's eyes drifted back and forth between Xavier and Tate. "Babe, what's going on?"

Arturo pushed past Tate and looked at Lani. Now it was time for her face to pale.

"M-Mr. Mendez, wh-what are you doing here?"

Arturo lifted an eyebrow. "That's my line, Lani."

The woman started to scramble around the room collecting her things. She tossed on a pair of khaki pants and then pulled a hotel logo-emblazoned navy polo shirt over her head. "P-please, sir," she stammered, tears welling up in her dark brown eyes. "I'm sorry."

Arturo gripped her by the elbow and led her past us down the path. "Let's go have a *chat*, Lani. I'm sure we can sort something out. After all, you didn't see anything, right, now did you? Not a soul knocked on the door; nobody by the name of Xavier was staying at this hotel, right? You've been working in the dining room on a double-shift all night, right?"

Her breath caught in her throat as she shuffled along with him. "N-no, sir. Nobody. Nothing. Whatever you say."

Xavier's eyes were still wide as dinner plates as he watched his little paramour stumble down the path with her boss. When they disappeared around the corner, his gaze whipped back to Tate, but instead of the fear that should have been there, he sneered smugly and turned to face me. "So you saw my little *post* in *America's Scoop*, did you? Here I thought you were slumming it, Parker, but in fact you're an even bigger gold-digger than I thought. What, my millions not enough for you anymore? You too *good* for me?"

"I'd say she is," Tate snapped back. "Especially since you don't have a fucking million to your name anymore."

My head whipped around, and I gaped at Tate. What the hell was he talking about?

Xavier's mouth mimicked my own. "Fuck you," he said with a snarl.

Tate just smiled. "See, one of the *many* advantages to being a billionaire is the resources you're able to afford. It took my team no time at all to realize you are fucking bankrupt. Like the ponies, eh?" Tate clucked his tongue disapprovingly.

Shit.

I'd thought Xavier had stopped going to the track, at least that's what he'd told me last time I'd asked him. He'd had a bit of a problem before we'd met, but when his ex-wife threatened to sue him for full custody of their son, he'd stopped. Apparently, though, even having his kid in his life wasn't enough to quit the addiction or thrill.

Tate crossed his arms in front of his chest. "You thought selling your story to *America's Scoop* was going to be your big score, get you back into the black. Well . . . I just *bought America's Scoop*. Have already issued a story to recant yours, painting you as an idiot, desperate to reclaim his fame, blah, blah, blah. You can read the whole article tomorrow on your flight home. Secondly, I've threatened to sue any other tabloid that publishes your story or any photos surrounding either Parker, my staff, my resort or myself. They're all aware and have agreed to back off and not print your story. You won't be getting a dime."

Blood flooded Xavier's face. "You can't do that!" he spat.

Tate made a bored face. "I can do whatever the fuck I want, and don't you forget that. Thirdly, this here is a cease-and-desist order for you. If you remember, when you 'checked in' to The Windward Hibiscus, you signed a bunch of non-disclosure agreements. Do you remember that?" He waited a half-second for Xavier to respond, but the man just stood there like a slaw-jawed guppy. Tate went on. "I didn't think so. See, you're not the first prick I've had to deal with, so I've covered my ass quite well. I can afford the best attorneys, and they've written up a pretty wicked iron-clad non-disclosure agreement into the forms you sign when you first arrive. Most people don't even bother to read them, like you. But they say very clearly that if anyone shows my picture or prints anything about me without my permission, they will be sued."

Michael stepped forward and thrust a manila envelope into Xavier's hand. "You've been served."

Xavier started to shake.

"Furthermore," Tate went on, "I'm in the process of procuring your family's *soap* business as well. Your brother seems like a reasonable enough man, and I'm sure he'll convince the board members to sell to me, with the caveat you receive none of the buyout." Did Tate know Rufus had sold off all of Xavier's shares years ago?

Was he bluffing?

Or did he know something I didn't?

Xavier's knees wobbled as the realization of his actions and everything he was losing finally started to sink in.

Tate smiled. "Now, this can *all* go away if you sign the top form inside that envelope there. I won't buy your family's company, I won't sue you, and I won't have Mako here take you out on a boat and feed you to the sharks."

Xavier took a step to the left and rested his hand on the desk to support his weight.

The man looked like he was going to pass out.

"The form on top there." Tate waited for Xavier to open the envelope and pull out the paper. "It's you admitting to spreading falsehoods and rumors about me, The Windward Hibiscus and Miss Ryan. It states that you accept full responsibility for your libel and any and all repercussions that may be the fallout of the mess you've created. There is a gag order, however, and you are not allowed to speak of any of this. All you are allowed to speak of is the fact that you lied."

Michael stepped forward again and poked a bony finger into the center of the paper. "This here tells you *exactly* what to say."

"I'm a liar. I have never met Mr. McAllister, I do not know what he looks like, and I have never even been to The Windward Hibiscus. In a desperate attempt to make money, after making one too many poor business decisions, I took the opportunity of my ex-girlfriend being at the resort to spread rumors and make accusations. I was wrong, and I'm sorry." Xavier's Adam's apple struggled to make it down his throat as he swallowed.

"Deviate so much as one word from this script, and we will come after you," Michael said, claws out.

For a tiny bespectacled man who weighed as much as one of Mako's legs, his voice held the venom and strength of a man ten times his size. No doubt this wasn't the first jugular he'd gone after and successfully drained.

"You will be leaving tomorrow morning at five," Tate said. "Mako here will escort you. And if we so much as hear a whisper of your time on Moorea, or my name or Parker's name in a tabloid, we won't even bother with suing you. Do I make myself clear?"

Xavier nodded slowly, his eyes scanning the paper.

Michael stepped forward and handed him a pen.

Xavier put the paper down and started to sign and initial where Michael instructed.

I lifted my head and just stared at Tate.

I had never been more turned on or afraid at the same time. Would he really "dispose" of Xavier?

Michael pulled the paper away and stuffed it back into the envelope.

Then he snatched his pen from Xavier's sweaty palm and, with a glare at my frightened ex, tucked the ballpoint back into his breast pocket.

Tate let out a heavy sigh. "All right then, now that that's been settled ..." and out of nowhere he hauled off and punched Xavier in the nose, causing the man to stumble back and fall flat on his ass. The towel came loose, and he was suddenly laying there in a heap on the ground, his penis having turtled in fear and barely visible while blood poured from his nose and his beady eyes darted around the room in horror. "And that's for calling Parker a gold-digger." Tate grabbed me by the elbow and motioned for us to leave.

"You really should read what you sign," Michael lectured Xavier as we left the bungalow. "You can't even sue him for assault. You signed that right away, too." The little attorney clucked his tongue as Tate had earlier. "Moron." Then he closed the door, and he and Mako followed us back down the path toward the Jeep.

"You're shaking again," Tate said, stopping us on the path and removing his shirt for the second time. He pulled it over my head and tugged me close. "It's okay, Parker. It's over."

A half-sob, half-chuckle caught in my throat as I leaned into him, letting the warmth of his big body wash over me. "Would you really have him killed?" I finally asked.

Mako chuckled behind me.

Tate and Michael joined in on the laughter.

I looked back at the two men behind me, then back up at Tate. "What?"

We all stopped on the path, and Tate took my hand. "I've never had anyone killed or killed anyone, Parker. The implied threat seems to be enough, combined with Mako."

The big Polynesian man grinned, showing off a gorgeous row of straight, bright white teeth. "Something about the tattoos on the face seems to scare 'em straight." He laughed.

"And Michael's ruthlessness, too," Tate replied, continuing to laugh. "Nothing has ever gone further than a threat. Come to think of it, I'm not sure what we'd do if someone ignored our threat."

"Shark food," Mako said, sobering.

Tate just chuckled. "Remind me not to piss *you* off."

I gazed up into Tate's face. "You honestly think we're done with him?"

He nodded and pulled me close, and we resumed our walking. "We're done with him. The man doesn't have a pot to piss in. By the time he gets back to

New York, he won't have a friend left to turn to, and unless his brother takes pity on him, no job, either. In the last three weeks, he's been foreclosed on, gone into receivership, had to declare bankruptcy and closed all his restaurants and clubs. The man has ruined himself. We're just making sure he doesn't ruin us as well."

I shook my head and snuggled into him.

I had had no idea any of this was going on.

None.

Then again, we'd been broken up for three weeks, and Xavier never really discussed his businesses with me. Even when I'd ask, he'd dismiss my questions or change the subject.

I was relieved that I wasn't having to go through this with him right now.

He'd dumped me just in the nick of time.

Tate opened up the Jeep door for me, and I climbed in.

Four doors slammed, and seconds later we were on the road heading back to The Windward Hibiscus, the wind in our hair as the pinkish-purple sky drew us toward the horizon. Crisis averted.

"I think that went rather well." Michael sounded chipper, bouncing in his seat next to Mako.

Tate brought his hand up and checked his knuckles. They were red and swollen. One had busted open, and a thin trickle of blood ran down his middle finger.

I took his fist in my palm and wiped the blood away with my finger, then brought his hand to my lips, planting a soft, gracious kiss on his skin.

"I couldn't let him get away with calling you a gold-digger," he said softly.

I looked up into his eyes, and the rush of love I had for this man inundated me.

My chest tightened.

But I had to be realistic.

As much as I felt for him, this was day nine of a ten-day thing.

We'd agreed to it. Letting the lump in my throat settle and shrink, I smiled shyly and ran my hand over his bloody one. "I hope you broke his nose."

I giggled to hide my true feelings and instead just cuddled back into his side. He wrapped his arm around me and pulled me into him.

Kissing the top of my head, he looked out into the trees whizzing past. "Me too."

Chapter Twelve

When we returned to the resort, we stopped in briefly to see Justin and Kendra. Kendra was busy putting the girls to bed, and Justin was sitting outside on his phone.

We waited until he signed off, then approached.

"That was James," he said. "He's sending Heath to go and collect Xavier from the airport in New York."

Tate nodded. "Good idea. Just drive the threat home a little longer. Make him think that he's being watched back home too."

Justin grinned. "He doesn't need to know Heath is from Canada or just going to hang out for a couple days and follow him. We just need to scare the shit out of him. Keep him thinking he's being followed."

"Exactly," Tate said with a tired smile. "Thanks for doing that."

"Of course." Justin tipped his beer back. I was in slight awe of how nonchalant both men were behaving, as if we hadn't just gone and threatened Xavier's life if he so much as breathed a word about anything that had happened in the last two days. But then again, maybe this was just the way it went with high-powered men. I'd thought Xavier had been powerful and with influence; I couldn't have been more wrong.

At least not compared with the two men in front of me.

Justin's eyes fell to Tate's injured hand. "You slam your hand in the door of the Jeep or something?"

Tate just grinned and wrapped his arm around my shoulder. "Or something."

A second later, Kendra emerged like an angel through the sheer gauzy drapes, shutting the French doors with the kind of silent care and attention only a mother of slumbering babes could do.

"Everything okay?" she asked with a big yawn, walking up beside her husband.

He reached for her and brought her down onto his lap.

"Just peachy," Tate replied. "But if you don't mind, guys, we have somewhere to be. We'll come find you tomorrow morning so Parker can say goodbye, k?"

They both nodded, already seeming to be off in their own married person world. They were eyeing up the hammock, but I couldn't tell if it was because they wanted to go have sex on it or fall asleep.

Tate and I headed off down the beach hand-in-hand. It was getting dark, and the beach was clearing out for the night. Not too many people speckled the lily-white sand past dinnertime. They were all just as tired from the sun as we were and heading inside to answer the call of their growling bellies.

"I can't believe you leave tomorrow," Tate said quietly, his hand linked so tightly with mine I was feeling a cramp make its way up my wrist toward my elbow.

I let out a lengthy sigh, determined not to let the loss I was feeling in my heart come through in my tone. "I know. The days just flew by."

"They certainly did."

We rounded a corner, and the flicker and dance of candles low in the sand drew my eyes, playing tricks and making my brain wonder if they were indeed candles or small pixies or fireflies dancing among the shells. When we approached, I realized it was a picnic. A blanket was spread out over the soft sand, and candles aplenty lined the spot, while a basket perched in the middle and a bucket of ice with a bottle of chilled champagne sat next to it.

"Tate . . ." was all I could say as he flicked his wrist and spun me into his arms, my chest smashing hard against his.

"I wanted to say *goodbye* properly," he said softly, his lips brushing across mine.

I swallowed. "Well . . . this is certainly a good start."

Releasing me, he motioned for us to sit down. "That's right, this is just the beginning. When we get back to the villa, I'm going to fuck you silly, woman."

I grinned at him. "I can't wait!"

He deployed the cork on the champagne like a pro and poured us each a flute, and as I sat there taking in my surroundings, I couldn't stop the lone tear that trickled down my cheek.

I was in paradise with a gorgeous billionaire, and I was happier than I'd ever been in my life.

And that was all going to end tomorrow.

By this time tomorrow, I'd be on a plane headed back to New York, back to my apartment, back to my job, back to . . . no one.

There was but a sliver left of orange on the horizon as the sun slipped off onto the other side of the world, leaving us bathed in the glow of stars above and a crescent moon hanging high and fierce in the cloudless sky, like a bright yellow sickle. I never wanted this day, this night, this moment to end.

"Here you go," Tate said. He laid out the bounty of the picnic basket on the blanket.

I hastily wiped away another vexatious tear before I turned to face him, plastering on a huge grin and bringing my hand up to take a cracker from him. It appeared to be laden with caviar.

"Uh-uh, I'll do it," he tutted, playfully swatting my hand away and encouraging me to part my lips.

I did so, and he gently placed the cracker on my tongue.

I took a bite, fumbling with my hands to catch a few rogue crumbs, but the flavors that overwhelmed my palate had me swooning where I sat. Salty and savory and fishy and oh, so wonderful.

I'd eaten my fair share of caviar with Xavier, but nothing as rich or spectacular as this.

"Do you like it?" he asked, his eyes hopeful.

"It's wonderful."

"More?"

"Please."

He proceeded to feed me my entire meal. More caviar on crackers, pieces of mango with salty chili flakes, grilled pineapple, savory prosciutto wrapped around perfectly ripe and juicy melon, and papaya. It was all to die for, and I ate every bite.

I tried to allow him to let me feed him in return, but he wouldn't hear of it. "I want to spoil you, Parker. Savor you. Worship you. Don't say *no* to me tonight, please?"

My bottom lip damn near hit the sand as his words wrapped around my heart and squeezed. When we'd finally finished, both of us full and content and just a touch lightheaded from the champagne, I thought for sure we'd head back up to the villa, but Tate had other things in mind.

"The beach is empty. Let's go skinny-dipping."

"Are you sure?" I asked, my head swiveling side to side to check each direction of the beach. He was right, the beach was empty. It was night now, and nothing but a few hungry sand crabs skittering across the ground seemed to be our companions.

"Don't say *no* to me tonight."

He removed his shirt, his smile widening when he heard my gasp. It'd been over a week now, and still the sight of this man shirtless made me lose my ever-loving mind. I wanted to lick each and every one of those abs, then his pecs, and then his biceps, finishing off with that luscious line that ran around his hip and beneath his shorts. That line, I wanted to lick *all* the way down.

He ditched his shorts, and within seconds his beauty stood before me, his hand outstretched, waiting for mine so he could help me to my feet. I gave in. I always gave in. For Tate, I always would. I would yield to Tate every day for the rest of my life. Let him order my meals for me, bring me breakfast, take me on adventures. The man had managed to make me want to start over, love life and love myself, and all in just ten short days. I'd do anything for him, if he'd let me.

I went to peel off my tank top, but Tate stopped me, his eyes fierce in the candlelight. "Let me. I want to undress you."

My throat bobbed, and I nodded. A breathy "Okay" floated past my lips as I let my arms hang by my sides, my eyes taking in the exquisite man before me.

Slowly, ever so slowly, almost painfully, he lifted the hem of my tank top. The fabric, although only cotton, felt like a soft brush of silk against my sun-heated skin as he languidly brought it up and over my head, tossing it to the blanket. My shorts were next. His fingers were precise and sure as he unsnapped the button, lightly grazing my hips until a moan built dark and deep at the back of my throat. He pulled them down over my thighs, and I stepped out. Last was my bathing suit. A pull here, a tug there, and the scraps of Lycra drifted down to join the rest of my clothes.

He reached for me again, and I took his hand. We turned to face the darkness of the water, the sea reflecting the sky with its multitude of stars, while the moon lay long and bright, rippling slightly in the calm waves. We stopped for a second and just admired where we were. The wide open ocean in front of us.

Paradise. Then hand-in-hand, naked as jaybirds, and me hopelessly in love and trying my damnedest not to think about having to say "goodbye," we walked into the water.

****

"I hope there are towels in that picnic basket," I said with a laugh as we trudged out of the surf and ran the dozen or so steps up the sand to our waiting blanket. The majority of the candles had burned down or been snuffed out by the warm evening breeze, so the only real light we had was the moon overhead, and the justice it was doing to Tate's body was the kind of image dreams were made of.

"But of course," he teased. "I've planned the entire night."

"Including the skinny dipping?"

"But of course." He opened up the big basket and pulled out two plush white towels. He wrapped one around my shoulders and pulled it tight in front of me; his hands ran up and down my arms to help warm me up, not that I was cold.

He hurriedly dried his own body and then gave a quick pass of the towel over his hair before tying it provocatively around his waist so that it slung low and inviting. His eyes caught mine and where they were staring.

"I want to lick that line," I said huskily, running my tongue between my lips and enjoying the salty tang from the sea water.

"Whatever you want, baby," he purred. "But first . . . what I want. No saying *no*, right? I want to fulfill as many of your fantasies as I can, Parker. I think I know more of what you want than you do. Trust me, okay?"

I nodded. "W-what do you want to do?"

A wily grin flashed across his face before he whipped the towel off of me and scooped me up, laying me down gently on the soft blanket. He reached for his shorts and fumbled for a moment in the pocket, then he pulled something out.

"I want to brand you."

"What?" I moved to sit up, but he quickly swung a leg over my waist and straddled me, his cock lying thick and ready along his taut belly. An opalescent bead of pre-cum sat on the tip, and I licked my lips again at the thought of tasting him.

"Not *actually* brand you. But I want to mark you . . . for a bit. It's not permanent, even though Sharpie says so. But I want you to remember me for the next few days when you strip and look at yourself in the mirror. I don't just want my bruises and bite marks to be the only reminder. I want . . ." He trailed off for a second, and his Adam's apple jogged thick in his throat. "I want you to remember *me*. My name. I want you to look down at your body when you touch yourself in the shower, when you're in bed and using your fingers or vibrator. I want you to grab your tits and read my name as you come, picture me inside you, fucking you hard. Say my name as you climax. Because you're mine, Parker."

My chest heaved, and all I could do was nod again. I would never say "no" to this man.

He popped off the cap of the Sharpie and brought the tip down to the creamy swell of my breast, and then in big, bold, but beautiful cursive script, he wrote his name. *Tate William McAllister*. He did it again to the other breast, signing his name, branding me just like he'd said. The cool felt tip of the marker was weird at first, it didn't hurt, but as he slowly wrote his name, dragging the damp ink across my flesh, I started to feel a deep pooling in my belly and between my legs. It tickled, then it started to feel good. Down across my ribs he continued to scrawl, to mark, to own.

Writing his name, over and over again, making me his.

Laying claim.

And with each gentle stroke of the marker, my pussy grew wetter, and the ache in my belly grew stronger.

My nipples pulsed from the pain of needing to be touched, to be licked and pulled and bitten.

I wanted his chin to scrape across the sensitive buds until I writhed and squirmed on the blanket and begged him to stop, because if he didn't, I'd come.

He did one final sweep, then sat up.

"And now here," he said, moving off my torso and slinking down onto his belly, where he spread me wide and proceeded to write TATE on the top of my pubic bone. He wrote his full name again on each of my inner thighs. While he was writing, I brought my hands up and started to caress my breasts.

I needed to ease the dull ache.

I pinched my diamond-hard nubs and pulled them away from my body, feeling them pulse hot and quick between my fingers.

Tate looked up from what he was doing, and a big smile wandered across his face. He loved it when I took my pleasure into my own hands.

"How does that feel?" he asked, blowing cool air on my throbbing cleft.

My hips jerked off the blanket, and I moaned. "So good. Especially because it's you."

"Do you want more?"

I nodded. "Yes."

Always more.

"On your stomach, woman. Stick that gorgeous ass up in the air for me then."

I swallowed hard, then did as he demanded. He helped me, positioning and molding my knees and legs just how he wanted, so my pussy and ass were on display for his inspection.

A curious finger ran up my cleft, and he groaned.

"You're so wet for me, Parker. And I haven't even touched you, not really. Are you always this easy to turn on?"

"No," I sighed. "Never. It's all you."

"Would you like me to eat your pussy, or would you like me to finish signing my name, and *then* eat your pussy?"

"Decisions, decisions," I murmured, not actually knowing which one I wanted more.

A hard and silence-piercing slap landed on my backside, and I yelped. I craned my head around to look at him.

He grinned back at me. "Any more sass like that, and I'll tan your ass until you won't be able to sit down on your flight tomorrow without wincing. Got it?"

Holy sweet baby Jesus!

Yes, I got it. And I wanted more of it.

Now! Forever.

No man had ever spanked me.

No man had ever expressed interest.

I'd never expressed interest, and yet one slap from Tate and I wanted to open up the dialogue and let him spank my ass until it was good and red.

"Got it?" he asked again.

"Yes," I said quietly.

"Now, what would you rather, Parker?"

"Um."

Whack!

"That one was because you're taking too long to decide. And because I think you're enjoying the spanking."

A trickle of wetness dripped down my inner thigh and onto the blanket, and at that moment, all I wanted was for Tate to stick his fingers inside me and make me come.

But I also wanted his name.

I wanted his brand.

I wanted it all.

"Y-your name first. Make me yours first, please."

A primal growl behind me made my pussy clench and my nipples tighten even harder.

And then, just because I think we both needed it, both craved it, he rammed his cock inside me and fucked me hard for thirty seconds.

Not enough for either of us to get off, but just enough to satisfy the want, the desire for the intimate contact.

I whimpered when he withdrew from my body, but the way his hands kneaded and caressed my backside had me mewling and pushing my ass into him, begging for more.

"I'm going to write my full name on each of your perfect cheeks," he said, as he began to slowly drag the pen across the meatiest park of my left buttock.

I had to really stop myself from pushing into his ministrations; I didn't want to ruin his art.

But it was torture.

Even the simplicity of the act, the Sharpie being gently raked across my tender flesh, the sweeping movements of the pen, had me damn near close to orgasm.

A final *dot* of the *i* in McAllister, and he was done, and suddenly I wished for more. I wanted him to cover every square inch of my body in his name.

Tattoo me, brand me, claim me, mark me as his.

But I hardly had a moment to be verklempt before a velvety softness swept up between my folds from behind, swirling and twirling around my clit, while two fingers spread me wide, then plunged inside. I couldn't stop myself, and I bucked into his face, eager for him to drink me down and push me off the cliff.

He hummed softly before his mouth left my skin.

A sob escaped me.

The man was torturing me.

Slowly, softly, erotically, he drew his fingers from my channel and slid them up between my cheeks, his fingers circling my tender rosette.

"Tell me, Parker. Have you ever had a man take you here?"

I thought for sure he was going to push a finger inside, but instead I felt something softer, something warm.

Holy mother of God, it was his tongue!

He poked, once, twice, three times, before pulling away and replacing it with his finger again.

He swirled his slick digit around my forbidden hole, but he didn't push. He was waiting for my answer.

"Hmm, Parker? Have you?"

My throat was thick, and my heart was beating a million beats a second. "N-no. I haven't."

"Never?" He seemed almost shocked. "You've never even tried? Not even a finger?"

I shook my head. "N-no. No man has ever asked. I've never brought it up."

"Hmm," he hummed again. "It's a shame you're leaving tomorrow. I'd love to claim your ass. Work you over, stretch you out, get you primed, prepped and ready for my cock." He let out a weighted sigh, one that mimicked the loss in my own heart. "Pleasure, orgasms like you've only ever dreamed of, Parker. That's what I would do for you."

Yes! Yes, please, I wanted to say.

Take me there. Stretch me out.

Prep me, prime me.

Make me ready.

Make me yours.

I want to try it.

I want to try it all with you.

The man had already ruined me for other men.

Never again would I be able to be with a man who routinely shaved.

No, I had to have the beard.

And now, I wanted a man with tattoos.

I wanted a man who was philanthropic and modest, whose staff adored him, who could deep-sea fish, scuba dive and fly a helicopter.

I didn't want to settle for a man who had only ticked one or two things off this list.

I wanted a man who ticked everything off on this list.

I wanted Tate.

Another soft wet poke, and my whole body shook. "Is it one of your *dark* and secret fantasies, Parker? To be taken here. To be touched . . . here?" His tongue swept up my crevice, then swirled around my rosette before being replaced again with an inquisitive finger.

"It is now." I sighed.

"You would like that, wouldn't you? For me to claim your ass, make it mine? Show you a new level of pleasure you've only ever dreamed of?"

"Yes," I whispered. "Yes, Tate."

I could practically hear the lump bob in his throat. "Parker," he finally breathed. His fingers resumed their slow and evocative journey around my slick flesh, in and around my anus and then back down to gather more of my wetness. He'd graze my clit periodically, sending a zing of pleasure and need flying through me up to the crown of my head, then right back down to my toes.

"Take me, Tate," I practically pleaded. "I can't say *no*. Take me . . . please."

Another growl, this time deeper; so deep, so raspy, it sounded more like a snarl. The kind of noise a beastly creature might make right before it devoured its prey . . . or claimed its mate.

"I—I can't. There's not enough time. I don't want to hurt you."

I swallowed. "You won't. I can take it."

He was quiet again for a moment, but this time his fingers didn't stop. I felt the push of his erection at the juncture of my thighs, and I spread my legs wider so he could enter me. Gently, languidly he embedded himself inside me, stilling for just a moment before picking up the pace and starting to thrust. I moaned from how good it felt, from how good he felt, his hands roaming my skin while his cock pumped hard and true inside me.

But I wanted more.

I wanted what he'd offered.

I wanted to try new things, experience and explore new possibilities.

He'd opened up this door and I'd only just walked through it, into a whole new exciting and sexual world.

I wasn't ready to close it.

Not now.

Not ever.

"Stick a . . . stick a finger . . . " I trailed off.

"Tell me, Parker," he grunted. "Ask for it. Tell me your fantasy. Tell me what you want."

"Stick a finger in my ass, Tate!" I finally cried, perhaps a tad too loudly as well.

But I didn't care.

I wanted it.

Now!

"Fuck," he groaned, his slippery digits moved around and around my tight hole. "You're sure?"

"NOW!"

Pressure—foreign, weird, divine pressure unlike anything I'd ever experienced before—had me inhaling and then puckering on instinct.

"Relax," he cooed. "Relax."

His other hand came down and around in front of me, and he started working rough and effective circles mixed with light smacks on my clit, until my whole body felt nothing but good. My muscles relaxed, and I let out a sigh.

I pushed my backside further into him, eager for more of his cock inside me, for more of his finger.

"Push out," he whispered. "Relax and push out, Parker. That's it. Good girl. Holy fuck, you're tight. My cock would destroy you, baby." He pushed in a little further, and I felt my eyes threaten to disappear into the back of my head. Then he moved that curious finger back and forth a few times, in and out of my body. His cock followed the rhythm and did the same. "How does that feel?"

"So . . . so good," I moaned.

"You like that?"

"Mhmm."

"You want more, baby?"

"Yes . . . please."

He pulled his finger out of me, and there was more pressure. This time I immediately relaxed my muscles and pushed out.

Pressure again, followed by a mild bit of stretching and discomfort, a small bite of pain, and then holy frickin' hell. Two fingers were so much better than one.

In and out he pumped, fucking my ass with his fingers while his cock drove hard and swift into my quivering center.

I was so close.

"Tate," I said with a sigh. "Tate." I bent down onto my elbows and pressed my cheek into the blanket, the smell of sand and salt filling my nostrils as a sudden gust of wind swept over my damp body, sending a rush of gooseflesh chasing across my skin.

"Parker," he growled.

"Tate, I'm so close."

Those devious fingers started to smack my clit, just like he knew I loved, while those *other* fingers pumped deep and dirty into my secret place and his cock fucked me hard and swift.

My whole body shook with the need to let go.

The orgasm was there, brewing and building and threatening to unleash.

"I . . . I can't hold on," I said, choking out the words as if his hands were on my throat just like they had been on the boat.

"Don't hold on, Parker. Let go. Come for me, baby. Come hard."

His finger and thumb pulled my swollen clit until I thought I was going to pass out. Then he pinched, pulled again and delivered one hard smack, and I was done.

Gone.

Lost.

Falling.

Over the precipice I tumbled, head-first, eyes closed, not caring where I landed, because the free-fall was just that glorious.

Waves and surges of pleasure coursed through me, radiating out from new and never-before-touched erogenous zones while my clit pulsed and my pussy trembled with each unrelenting buck of his hips.

"Tate!" was all I could say.

Over and over again, his name spilled from my lips as I let the climax unfold, shredding my very soul, until there was nothing left.

I was not the Parker Ryan that had shown up at The Windward Hibiscus ten days ago.

I was a completely new woman.

New outlook, new desires, new interests; a whole new person.

And it was all because of Tate.

I'd been so caught up in my own pleasure that, much like our first time, I wasn't even sure if Tate had come. I hadn't heard him, and I hadn't felt him. Had my orgasm been so intense, had I been calling out his name so loudly I didn't hear him come?

Once my body stopped quivering, he slowly withdrew and spun me over on to my back.

"You okay?" he asked.

I blinked up at him and nodded. All the candles around us had gone out now. There was nothing but the stars and moon left to shed us any light. Shadows cut deep into his chiseled cheeks, while harsh lines and edgy angles made him look all the more masculine and menacing. My mysterious, handsome billionaire. A breath caught in my throat as I took in this beautiful man, who was, at least for the next several hours, all mine.

"Did you come?" I asked, my hand traveled up to cup his cheek and I encouraged him to bring his lips down to mine.

He grazed them across gently but then pulled away.

A deep, rumbling chuckle started in his chest and shook his whole body. "Yes. Were you too caught up in your own euphoria again to notice?"

I nibbled on my bottom lip before answering. "Perhaps."

"Well, good." He stood up and offered me his hand. "Let's get dressed, clean up and head back to your room, where I can fuck you properly in a bed. I'm not saying this wasn't fun, because it was. But I'd like to do you up right in a bed. A *lady* should be fucked in a bed."

I snorted. "You just licked my ass and fucked me on a beach blanket. What does that make me right now?"

He tossed me my tank top. "A fucking filthy *lady*."

Chapter Thirteen

We fell into bed that night like savages, tearing off each other's clothes as if they were on fire, desperate for skin-to-skin, skin *in* skin. I needed to feel his flesh beneath my fingertips as I clawed up his back and bit his pectoral until he hissed out from the divine pain.

It didn't matter that we'd just screwed like horny cavemen on the beach in the dark.

Once was not enough.

I needed more.

We both did.

I needed Tate to fuck me like there was no tomorrow, because for *us*, there wasn't one.

I'd be gone by lunchtime.

My room would be cleaned and cleared out of my dirty towels and garbage, and by two o'clock, someone new would take up residence.

Would it be the same with Tate?

Would someone else take up residence in his heart by this time tomorrow?

"Stay the night?" I asked, hating how needy I sounded but hoping that it drove my point, my hope, my wish, home. "Please." It was my last night on the island; I left tomorrow, and after all this time, we'd never spent the night together.

Sitting up and pulling his boxers on, he shook his head. "I can't, babe. I'm sorry. But I'll meet you tomorrow morning at the pool, then we'll have breakfast, come back here, screw one more time, and I'll drive you to the airport, okay?" His back was to me, and I watched as his muscles flexed and strained when he reached for his shirt off the floor and pulled it over his head.

Quickly wiping away the tear that was threatening to make a break for it down my cheek, I put my head down, allowing my hair to cover my face. I was desperate not to let him see me cry. "Oh. Okay. Tomorrow, then. Sure."

He stood up from the bed and pulled on his shorts. His pecs were still visible, as he hadn't bothered to button up his shirt, my bite mark from just a few moments ago was red and possibly even a little puffy. Just like he'd done with me, with his bruises and bites, his scruff chafing me, and the Sharpie—I'd branded him.

He was mine.

But like the bruises and the chafing and the Sharpie, it was all just temporary.

"I've gotta run," he said, sliding his feet into his flip-flops, then coming around to peck me on the cheek. "Sweet dreams. I'll see you tomorrow." He grabbed his wallet, watch and cell phone off my vanity and was off, leaving me sitting there in bed, staring at the closed door, tears running down my face as I willed him to come back and spend the night.

To come back to me.

To love me.

It was almost one o'clock in the morning when I finally decided to do something. I'd been lying there tossing and turning for nearly two hours, unable to get comfortable or settled after the way Tate had turned me down and left.

No, he hadn't been rude or mean.

And yes, he had been apologetic.

But over the last week and a bit, we'd made love in my room every single night, and every single night he'd stick around to cuddle for an hour or so, look at the clock on my nightstand and then hastily get up and leave.

As if he were keeping someone waiting and he had to go and meet them for a date.

Did he have a *date*?

I tossed back the covers with a huff, threw on my dressing gown as I stalked over to the desk and turned on my laptop. I read through all the notes I'd typed up over the last ten days. The pieces of my article, facts and interviews, things I'd done and people I'd met.

Only after reading through it three times, I realized it was complete garbage.

I scrunched my nose up, selected "all" and then hit "delete."

That wasn't me anymore.

Those words might have been mine, but they were no longer who I was.

They were no longer the words I felt in my heart.

Because now my heart was full, my heart was open, and my heart was on my sleeve.

I unplugged my computer and opened up the door to the veranda, and with the sea ahead of me and the wind at my back, I wandered down to the beach, nestled down into the cool sand and began writing.

I was leaving tomorrow, this was our last night together, and if he didn't want to stay at my place, maybe, just maybe, he'd want me to stay at his. Perhaps he had a special bed or pillow or wore a night-guard because he ground his teeth.

That I could handle; I used to wear one, too.

But what I couldn't handle was if he had *someone* back in his house.

That he wasn't as "unattached" as he had professed.

I made my way back from the beach to my villa, quickly printed what I wrote with the complimentary printer, slid into my flip-flops, grabbed my key card and headed off into the gardens and up the path.

Although I'd never been to his homestead, as we'd always wound up back at mine, I knew where it was.

And thanks to my presidential villa all-access pass, I had no issues making my way through the locked gates and down the garden path that led to Tate's bungalow.

I had thought he would have wanted to claim one of the oceanfront villas as his own, but then he lived on the ocean, owned the whole resort and his office overlooked the water, so in the end it was probably more financially lucrative for him to rent out an ocean view unit than keep it for himself.

The lights were on inside, but the blinds were drawn, and as I approached, I heard his voice murmuring through the door, followed by his rich and hearty laugh. It wrapped around me like a mantle as a wave of melancholy washed through me. This might be the last time I ever heard such a wonderful laugh.

And then I heard a woman's voice.

A woman's laugh.

Oh, no, he *did* have someone in there.

I turned to go, embarrassed and furious at my own stupidity.

I'd come here ready to do something I'd never done before, and that was show a man my true feelings.

Let my emotions, my heart, take the wheel rather than my fear.

But in my haste as I spun around, I managed to bash my elbow into a tin watering can, sending the empty vessel to the ground in a noisy clatter.

"Fuck!"

I didn't even have a chance to flee before the door opened and bright light from inside pierced the night. "Parker?"

I shook my head, fresh tears burning my eyes. "I'm sorry, I didn't . . . I didn't mean to bother you and . . . your *guest*. I'll just go." I turned to leave but was stopped by a soft, fluffy thing wending its way between my legs. I looked down to find a cat. A huge cat. A sandy-blond, long-haired cat. A Maine Coon. My mother had two gray ones, Ruckus and Mayhem.

"Grab her, please," he said, panic in his voice. "She's an indoor cat and doesn't go outside."

I picked up the furry beast and cradled her against my chest. "Hello, baby," I cooed, letting her sniff me a bit before I began to stroke her back. Instantly she closed her eyes and gentle purr rumbled through her.

"Everything okay, honey?" I heard a woman's voice call out from inside the house.

I froze.

Tate's eyes went wide when he saw my face.

Then the realization dawned on him.

"Wait here," he said as he ducked back in the house only to emerge seconds later carrying his tablet. "Parker Ryan, I'd like you to meet my mother, Helen McAllister. Mum, this is Parker, the girl I've been telling you about."

A woman in pink scrubs and hair the same color as Tate's, but pulled into a bun, smiled back at me on the screen. "Hello, Parker. It's so nice to finally meet you." She wrinkled her nose and chuckled softly. "Sort of. Though, in person would be better."

I swallowed. "Um . . . hi, Mrs. McAllister, it's nice to meet you, too." Tate's eyes caught mine and he invited me inside, his kitty still safely nuzzled against my chest.

We sat down on his couch and chatted with his mother for around ten minutes. Even though it was roughly five in the morning back in Victoria, Tate's mother, a nurse, was on a quick break at work and wide awake. Apparently she and Tate chatted several times a week, often at weird hours. Both were so busy, it was the only opportunity they had to connect.

When we finally signed off, I'd been extended a sincere invitation to go and visit her in Victoria. When she went to New York in the fall with a couple of other nurses, she was going to look me up, and I was to play "tour guide."

"So, that's my mother," Tate said with a sigh, flipping the cover closed on his tablet, his eyes traveling down to a sleeping and purring cat in my lap. "And this . . . this is Rosie." He reached out and stroked her soft fur. She opened one eye just a fraction but when she realized who was petting her, closed it again.

"Is . . . is she why you won't spend the night?" I asked, hoping that the butterflies zooming around in my belly were all for naught.

He nodded. "Yeah. Even though I live where I work, I'm gone all day. When I come home at night, this is our time. I feed her, we play for a bit, she sleeps on my bed." He made a noise in his throat and looked up at me. Wariness clouded his eyes. "She's my family. My mother won't move here. The one brother I know lives in New York and isn't willing to move here yet, so Rosie's my companion. My best friend. And even though I'd love to spend the night with you, I can't do that to her. It sounds stupid and corny, but she's family. And I keep my family private. I keep my life private."

Love streamed warmly through my veins like the buzz of a fine wine, and I felt my heart swell inside my chest as I continued to run my hands lightly over her back, her sweet face turned in toward my belly.

He owned a cat.

He was a devoted cat-dad.

A chuckle bubbled up inside my chest, and though I fought to keep it down, I couldn't, and I started to giggle.

"Are you laughing at me?"

I shook my head. "No, I'm laughing at me. I was jealous of a *cat*."

Rolling his eyes, he draped one arm around my shoulders and let out a contented sigh, the tension in his shoulders dissolving much like my butterflies. "You have nothing to be jealous over. I'm sorry I didn't tell you sooner. Didn't invite you over or ask you to spend the night. It's just . . . well . . . I don't *ever* invite women over. This is my home, *our* home, and inviting in the flavor of the week just . . ." His lips twisted in thought. "Somehow it doesn't feel right to me."

I swallowed and pulled away slightly. So, that's what I was, then, "the flavor of the week," only for a new delicacy to show up tomorrow and he could start the whole seduction routine over again. I motioned to get up, but he put a hand on my thigh. Meanwhile Rosie stirred on my lap and made a mewl of discontent.

"But you're different. You're special. None of the women I've ever hooked up with here knew I was the owner. They all thought I was a manager, an accountant or guest or something. You're the first guest I've ever revealed my true identity to, Parker. I'm sorry I didn't invite you over. I should have. It's just, well . . . the last time I got attached and invited a woman to spend the night, she broke my heart and made fun of me for having a cat. So now I'm wary and I keep Rosie a secret. Ridiculous, I know. But it's worked well . . . until now."

My heart did a flip flop in my chest. He was a wounded heart just like me.

He swallowed and looked up into my eyes. "Would you . . . would you like to spend the night?"

I let out a weighty sigh. "What makes you happy?"

"What?"

"That therapist you sent me to, she asked me to think about what makes me happy. To think about the last time that I was truly happy. What was I doing? Who was I with? So, I'm going to ask you the same thing: What makes *you* happy?"

Eyes as green as the lush tropical mountains we'd hiked through and flown over stared back at me. They were so full of whirling emotions I was having a hard time figuring out how he felt or what he was going to say next.

"You," he finally said, reaching for my hand. "You make me happy, Parker. I haven't felt like this in ages. Excited to start the day, to spend it with you. Being with you makes me happy." His throat undulated with a hard swallow as he continued to look at me. "So, I guess the other reason I didn't invite you to spend the night was because I was protecting myself. I've fallen for you, and you're leaving tomorrow."

If it were possible, I'd be floating.

My heart felt light, the butterflies were back but this time having a righteous dance party, and my body all but shook with excitement.

I thrust the pieces of paper I'd folded up and put in my robe into his hand. "Read. Please."

He gave me a quizzical look. "What is this?"

"It's my article."

He started to unfold it. "You could have just emailed it to me," he said with a chuckle.

"Says the man who doesn't know how to Google people."

All he did was snort, then his eyes began to shift across the page.

Life-Changing. Soul-Saving. Heart-Mending. My Time at The Windward Hibiscus on Moorea
By: Parker Ryan

The breeze, the salty air, the fragrant perfume of frangipanis and hibiscus. Green peaks, rolling hills, plantations and orchards. A turquoise sea so clear, so pure you can see your shadow on the bottom. Sand so white, so soft, so warm you want to pull it around you like a cashmere throw and sink in deep while sipping on decadent Tahitian sunrises from the beachside bar. This only just scratches the surface of the magic of Moorea, of the magic of The Windward Hibiscus Hotel. Of the magic of paradise.

A hotel for the elite, for the one percent, for those with more money than most of us could ever dream. And yet somehow I found myself here. I am not elite. I am not of the one percent. What many of you may not know about me is that I grew up in a very small town in Mississippi. Although never without food, a home or clothes on my back, I did not come from money. My mother had me when she was but a child herself, and together we struggled to make ends meet. So, to spend a day, let alone ten at the place I am dubbing "Paradise for Plutocrats," was positively life-changing. I've been to my fair share of nice places, thanks to my job, but I've never been to anything or anywhere like this before, and I'm not sure I ever will be again. And I'm absolutely CERTAIN nothing will ever come close.

Welcomed with open arms and a genuine smile by the reclusive and mysterious Tate McAllister, I spent ten days touring the island and experiencing everything Moorea and The Windward Hibiscus have to offer. When I stepped off the plane onto the steaming black tarmac, it was unlike any feeling I'd ever had before. Yes, it was tropical; yes, the balmy breeze whipped my hair up into a frenzy of fire in front of my face; and yes, it was as lush and beautiful as they say. But that wasn't it. A place I'd never been before, and only just recently even heard of, and for some reason I felt like I was coming home. The breeze, the casual island vibe, the beauty, they were all eclipsed by an overwhelming moment of complete and total serenity. Weight from a rough couple of weeks slipped off my shoulders and was caught up in a sudden gust of warm wind, where it was pulled up into the ether, only to be replaced with the benign heat of the sun and an all-encompassing feeling of peace. It's like when you walk into your childhood home after being away for far too long and smell that pot roast your mom made every Sunday. A feeling of familiarity, a feeling of calm, a feeling of being right where you should be. Where you're meant to be. Home.

It was nothing but smiles and friendly chit-chat the whole way to the resort. Rico, my shuttle driver, was animated and jovial, speaking fondly of his family (wife Anila and two girls, eight and five, Yola and Kindi) and how he loves working at The Windward Hibiscus. He finds himself waking up with a smile on his face, excited to go to work. I don't know very many New Yorkers who wake up smiling or who are excited to go to work. Maybe on that first day, maybe that first week, but eventually the stress and monotony set in, and when Monday rolls around, you're hitting snooze far too many times before schlepping your way to the bathroom and then rushing to get out the door on time. But not Rico, not any of the staff at The Windward Hibiscus. They all love where they work and enjoy what they do, and it shows. When you are at The Windward Hibiscus, you are immediately enveloped into the low-key, carefree island mentality. It's a stress-free zone, and nothing but love, happiness and a chill outlook on life will be tolerated. Only pure relaxation and contentment are allowed.

The most egregious voicemail message took those immediate feelings of peace that I had embraced as I'd stepped off the plane and destroyed them. It sent me into a foul mood, a funk. (Note to self, leave phone at home on next holiday.) So when I walked into the gorgeous hotel lobby, a smile could not have been further from my face. I was instantly greeted by a handsome man alarmed by my scowl. No, sorry, handsome does not do this man justice. Let's just say his smile alone has ruined me for all other men. His eyes were the same color as the hills around us, and his hair was a deep, dark brown with flecks of gold from time spent in the sun. He didn't know who I was, nor I him, but without hesitation, because no staff member at The Windward Hibiscus ever wants to see you with anything but a smile on your face, he asked me if there was anything he could do for me. I told him what I needed, and he saw to my every whim, instantly making me feel like I was the most important guest there and my pleasure was of the utmost priority.

I was given the presidential suite, with my own private veranda, beach view and fruit trees, ripe with decadence which I indulged in multiple times a day (mangoes have become a staple in my diet, and pineapples are my new favorite fruit). After a quick change, I went to go meet with Mr. McAllister. I wasn't sure what to expect. Would he be crotchety and crass? Sweet and gentile like an old Southern gent? Handsy and overly flirtatious? I think you get where I'm going *here—I thought he was old. I was wrong! So wrong. So wrong that when the man who greeted me at the door turned out to be the green-eyed man from the lobby, I asked him where his father was. *Insert foot in mouth here**

Wanting to maintain the enigma and anonymity he has fought so hard to maintain, Mr. McAllister has asked that I not post any photos of him, and of course, given that I was his guest and put up in the presidential suite, no less, I have obliged. We toured the grounds, where I was left slack-jawed and humbled again and again by such overwhelming beauty. Modern architecture blended perfectly with traditional French Polynesian, all with nature harmoniously intertwined. It's an eco-resort—The Windward Hibiscus has solar panels on nearly every roof and flat sky-facing structure, as well an innovative recycling and composting program and its own garden, where some of the food for both the staff and guests is grown.

Four communal guest pools, three outdoor, one indoor cover the grounds, while a tennis court, basketball court and volleyball court offer plenty of opportunity for the guests to keep up with their fitness regimes. Not to mention the gym inside that could rival any Planet Fitness, the yoga and dance studios and grand ballroom, complete with stage and wall-to-wall windows overlooking the ocean.

My first day in paradise finished off with the most mouth-watering barracuda steak on my plate and a snazzy boozy umbrella-coiffed drink. I still have no idea of the ingredients, and I am just fine maintaining my ignorance. It was delicious. I had three that night and many more on the nights to follow, and that's all that matters (I think it was a twist on a pina colada, though).

From there, my days just kept getting better, and I felt myself falling harder and faster in love with The Windward Hibiscus, Moorea and French Polynesia as I consumed each breakfast waffle and my tan grew darker. From scuba diving on the neon-colored reef, plentiful in fish and corals and sea creatures you'd only expect to find in a Pixar film, to morning hikes, parasailing and a visit to orchards and the local juice factory, every day was full of adventure and fun, and before I knew it, my ten days were up.

As amazing as all those excursions and experiences were, the cake was delivered and devoured by my first-ever fishing trip. Mr. McAllister, who is not only a real estate mogul, scuba diving instructor, helicopter pilot and philanthropist, also happens to be a top-notch fishing guide, and he helped me reel in my very first fish, an enormous DayGlo yellow and blue mahi-mahi.

I let the scaly beast go, though, and before I was able to get any pictures of myself or my catch. So, unfortunately, you're just going to have to take my word for it. But I will tell you, the thing was a monster. Easily mistaken for a Kraken or Moby Dick by many a fisherman, I'm sure of it. And he put up a good fight, which is why I didn't take him home and make him my dinner. The experience was enough.

This entire trip has been an experience like no other. The far corners of the globe, faraway mountaintop lodges and hotels with spa packages a mile long—I've visited them all. But nothing, and I mean nothing even remotely compares to the way I feel being on Moorea. To the way I feel staying at The Windward Hibiscus. I started this trip off in a bad state of mind, but now I end it with more clarity, more hope, more zest for life than I've ever had before.

Much like my fish, I have been given a second chance, found a new lease on my life, and it's not one I will take for granted. I now know what I want, who I am and who I want to be. I love life, I love myself, and I love that my possibilities are endless. And it's all thanks to Moorea and The Windward Hibiscus.

Regretfully, this will be my last article for The Decadent Traveler. *As much as I have enjoyed my time writing and traveling the world, I now realize what my true passion is, and I intend to pursue it.*

I would like to thank everyone at The Decadent Traveler *for their support, the staff and Mr. McAllister at The Windward Hibiscus for their over-the-top, gracious hospitality and, of course, you, my loyal readers, whose letters I have so very much enjoyed receiving over these past three years. I will miss those most of all.*

I will leave you all with this, whether it's just a visit to the next town over, a road trip in the car or a flight to a faraway land, never stop exploring. Never stop having fun, never stop having adventures and never stop living the life you want to live. Because we only have one, so make the most of it.

Happy trails, and don't forget to tip housekeeping,

Parker Ryan

Pink filled his cheeks as he got to the last page, while his nostrils flared and his pupils grew dark, black invading the bright green until there was hardly any color left.

"Is this . . . is this true?" he finally asked, a croak in his voice.

"I've never written a lie in my life," I said quietly.

"Am I . . . am I . . .?"

"Moorea? The Windward Hibiscus? Of course."

"But you've always been so upfront about this being a ten-day fling. I didn't think you felt the same about me as I did you. God, Parker . . . this . . . this is unlike anything you've written before. It's so . . . full of *heart*. So full of passion. These last ten days, when I came home from your bed, I would read your articles. I've read everything you've written, even from your old online magazines and your college and high school newspapers."

My mouth hung open. *All the way back to high school?*

"You've never written with such conviction or . . ." he trailed off.

Love. I wrote the article with love because I love you, Tate.

But I couldn't say that to him, could I?

I glanced down at my knotted fingers. "I've never felt this way before, and I decided to write what I feel. I wasn't sure you felt the same, but I . . . I didn't want to leave here without telling you."

"I figured if you wanted more, you would have asked for it."

"That's not who I am, though."

"But you asked me to fuck you in a broom closet. You asked me to stick a finger in your ass earlier on the beach. The amount of times I've teased you and you've begged and then *demanded* that I take you . . ." He was shaking his head, trying to figure out my words, my feelings. His words, his feelings and what they all meant. "You're more forthright and willing to ask for what you want than you think."

I looked him in those soulful green eyes, ready to put my heart on my sleeve.

I was forthright and honest because of Tate.

He'd transformed me.

Swallowing my fear, my pride, my old self, I set my jaw firm and held his gaze. "Fine, if you want me to ask, I'll ask. I'll ask for everything I want from now on. Ask me to stay, Tate!" I blurted out. "Ask me to stay! Let me stay with you. Let me live here. Let me be with you. I want you. I want to be with you. Not for just ten days, but for forever."

His head snapped up from where he'd been studying the pages of my article again.

"You make me happy, too," I said softly, bringing my voice down again. "When Dr. Sheffield asked me what made me happy? When was my happiest moment? Immediately you popped into my head. Every happy moment I've had this past month, hell, this past *year*, has been with you. I emailed my boss and quit my job. I don't want to work there anymore. I don't want to live in New York anymore. I want to fulfill my lifelong dream and write a book. Ask me to stay."

He blinked at least a dozen times, his head still shaking with what could only be described as disbelief. And then the shake quickly turned into an emphatic nod, and a smile so wide, so true erupted on his face. "Stay, Parker. Stay here with me, live here with me. Be with me."

I nodded. "Okay!"

Suddenly poor Rosie found herself knocked to the couch as Tate pulled me up to my feet, his hands on either side of my face, holding my head steady as he looked into my eyes. "I love you, Parker. You are who I've been waiting for."

I blinked back at him. "I love you, too." Biting my lip, I looked away for a second. "But . . ."

"But what?"

"But I think I want children. I've done a lot of soul-searching on this trip, and I realized that I want to be a mother. I want a family. I never really had one growing up. I was an only child to a teenage mom. I want a nuclear family. One with two parents and lots of kids. I never had it, and I want it."

"How many kids do you want?"

My eyes whipped back up to his. "What?"

"How many kids do you want? I'm thinking two or four. One of each, or two boys and two girls."

Holy shit.

His eyes were glowing, crinkling at the corners as his smile just continued to get bigger and bigger. "I want them, too. I—I was afraid of turning into my dad, but with you as the mother, I'm willing to take the risk. I want it all, Parker, and I want it all with you."

I scanned his handsome face while my head just shook in awe.

Tears of pure joy pricked the corners of my eyes, and I choked on a sob.

"Seeing my friend James and his beautiful wife, Emma, and then Justin and Kendra and their gorgeous family . . ." A warm and content smile tugged at the corner of his mouth. "I didn't know how badly I wanted that, too, until I saw it. Until I met the person I wanted it with. I've been lonely and bored—sad, for a while—but meeting you has changed all of that."

Now I was nodding like there was no tomorrow while tears streamed down my cheeks.

He used his big thumbs to wipe them away.

"I like the idea of four," I blubbered, the words getting strangled by my joy on the way out. "A house full of children. Busy and noisy and full of love. That's the perfect life for me."

He smiled. "So full of love. So perfect."

I laughed and hiccupped at the same time.

This was insane. I'd known this man for all of ten days, and here we were saying we loved each other and planning to have four children.

This didn't happen in real life, and certainly not in *my* life . . . did it?

"What are you going to write your book about?" he asked, his fingers weaving their way into my hair as his palms cupped my cheeks and he held my head in place, his eyes boring into mine. Claiming my soul as his.

I chewed on my bottom lip. "I dunno yet. Maybe about my life and growing up back in Mississippi. Or maybe . . . maybe I'll write about a lost thirty-something woman who finds herself on a tropical island and in bed with a sexy billionaire. Only what starts out as just a lust-fueled fling blossoms into a love like none other. She finds herself, she finds true love and her happily ever after. What do you think? Thoughts on a title?"

He scooped me up and headed off down a hallway. "I've got the perfect title for you," he said.

I wrapped my arm around his neck and kissed his chin, the beard tickling my lips. "Yeah? And what's that?"

"*Quick and Dirty*." He kicked open a door like a Viking and tossed me on to the bed in the dimly lit and very manly but homey bedroom.

I bounced twice, staring up at him with wide eyes.

He growled. "But enough about the book." He removed his shirt then covered me with his big body. His long, strong index finger lightly traced the letters of his name on the tops of my breasts and a small but cocky smile spread across his lips.

He'd marked me.

Claimed me.

The Sharpie would fade but my love for him wouldn't.

I was Tate's forever.

"Do you still have the Sharpie in your pocket?" I asked, loving the weight of him on me.

He fished around in the deep pocket of his cargo shorts and handed it to me. "Here."

I pulled the cap off with my teeth and brought the felt tip of the pen up to his hard, sculpted chest. Right over his heart I wrote my name: *Parker Elizabeth Ryan*.

His eyes were glassy as he looked down at my marking and then back up into my eyes. "And now I'm yours," he said, his voice thick with emotion.

"Always."

Sobering he flashed me another dazzling smile and rotated his hips against mine.

A rush of pleasure crashed into me from how good the friction felt.

Even clothed the man knew exactly how to drive me wild.

"Let's start now!" he said doing another hip swirl. I let my nails rake down the length of his back, feeling his warm skin and chiseled muscles bunch beneath my fingertips.

"Start what?" I asked breathlessly, inhaling and then squeaking when his hand made its way into my robe and up my shirt. Fingers pinched and pulled on a hard nipple, and a moan fled from my lips.

"A family." He quickly sprung to his knees and shucked the rest of his clothes. Once he was completely naked he went to work relieving me of my robe and skimpy night dress.

"Seriously?" I propped myself up on my elbows to look at him. The man was crazy.

"Yeah. Let's start a family now. The kid'll take nine months to cook anyway."

To cook? I snorted a most unladylike laugh as he pinned me back down to the mattress. That decadent and manly scent of him all but poured inside me, warming the breath in my lungs and wrapping around my heart.

"But I'm on the pill."

He paused for a second, but then his mouth started trailing its way down my chin and neck until he found a needy nipple and sucked it into his hot mouth. I wilted into his touch and brought my hand up to his chin. I wanted the beard. Always the beard. Forever the beard.

"Oh, yeah," he murmured, tugging on the bud. He shrugged. "Okay, well, then, we'll just practice. Get *really* good at the 'making' before we actually try for real. You can go off the pill next month."

"You're really serious, aren't you?"

His mouth was still bouncing back and forth between my breasts, but two devious fingers had made their way down my body and between my legs. A gasp escaped me when he plunged them inside.

My body ached.

Desire edged with a sharp blade of pain pulsed fiercely inside me as he crooked his fingers against my sensitive walls.

"Like a heart attack," he said. His head popped up. "I'll do it right if you want me to, but nothing about our start has been conventional." Where was he going with this? His eyes grew even darker for a moment, the lids dropping to half-mast while his nostrils flared and his fingers inside me pumped. "Marry me, Parker."

Another gasp, and not because he'd slipped in another finger.

"Marry me. Have babies with me. Make me as happy as I am now, and I'll spend the rest of my life trying to make you just as happy."

Oh fuck, new tears.

I couldn't remember the last time I'd cried this much.

Grabbing him by the ears, I pulled him back up to me.

His fingers slipped out, but I didn't care.

We were nose to nose.

All I could see were his eyes, but of course, I saw so much more.

I saw all the way to the depths of his soul and what a truly wonderful man he really was. He was excellence marbled with flaws.

Intensity sheathed in elegance.

Powerful and fierce and yet, at the very same time, so kind and gentle.

The perfect paradox.

My perfect paradox.

"Yes." I nodded, brushing my lips across his. "Yes, I'll marry you."

His scruff scratched me as he smashed his lips against mine in a need-driven kiss. When we finally came up for air, his smile took my breath away. "I love you, Parker."

I looped one arm around his neck while the other one fell to my name over his heart. I shimmied my hips until he was nestled between them, his cock notched at my core.

"I love you, too." I lunged at his bottom lip and tugged on it, releasing it a second later. "Besides, I pretty much have to stay here forever and marry you and have your babies. You've ruined me for other men anyway. I'm not sure I could ever be with a clean-shaven man again, let alone one who doesn't fly his own helicopter, have tattoos, spear fish or scuba dive or try to make the world a better place for *everyone*, including the other ninety-nine percent."

His hips lifted up, and he swirled himself around my entrance. My eyes threatened to roll into the back of my head. "I told you before, baby, once you go beard, you never go back." And with that he took me, all of me, forever.

EPILOGUE

7 years later...

"Look Mommy, look! Heidi and I made a sand mermaid." I arduously prop myself up on my elbows with a grunt to take a peek at what Ellie is pointing at. She and her sister are standing proudly over top of what appears to be a mermaid built out of sand, with shells for a bathing suit and eyes, and palm frond pieces for her hair, tail and smile.

Both girls beam proudly.

"It's beautiful," I say, wincing slightly as I awkwardly adjust myself on the blanket.

"You okay?" Tate asks. His hand lands on my plump belly. "Whoa!"

I snort. "He's a feisty one. Takes after his father. Hasn't stopped kicking me all morning. I'm pretty sure he's punishing me for that spicy chicken salad I had last night. He hates spice."

"I *don't* kick you," Tate chuckles. "Now spank you, flog you, whip you, tie you up, that's the kind of punishment *I* can get on board with. But I've never kicked you."

I roll my eyes and give him a gentle nudge with my shoulder.

"Dadda."

We both look down at the toddler in his lap, his chubby little limbs stretching as he groggily wakes up from an impromptu cat-nap.

Oh, man, what I would give to be able to just conk out at any given moment, but getting comfortable these days is proving to be a challenge.

Tate plants a kiss on Garon's forehead and brushes his ruddy bangs off his face. "Hey, buddy. You feeling better after your snooze?"

Garon reaches up and grabs his father's nose. "Daddy's nose."

I snicker as Tate tries to crane his neck away and dodge the curious fingers.

For some reason, the child is obsessed with sticking his fingers up everyone's nose. If they're not up his nose, they're trying to explore someone else's.

Two pairs of tanned, spindly legs run forward kicking up sand, both dripping wet.

I look up and shield my eyes from the sun to find the girls, six and four, staring back at me with big smiles and bright eyes. They're perfect. Ellie, the oldest, is just like Tate. Same green eyes, same dark brown hair colored with streaks of sunshine; same dominating, bossy personality. Your typical firstborn, I'm told.

But she has his heart as well, and it's so full and so beautiful, and the way she cares for her siblings and loves them unconditionally makes my own heart melt. Then there's Heidi, our sweet and quiet little gem. With my hair and Tate's eyes, she's the perfect blend. The peacekeeper and quintessential middle child. She idolizes her big sister and has already decided that she's a vegetarian. Heidi wouldn't hurt a fly, let alone eat a chicken nugget. And at almost two, Garon is my doppelganger. Blue eyes, red hair and a stubborn streak that makes me want to pull my hair out at least once a day. But he's so full of life and such a quirky little thing that you can't help but ruffle his hair and smile when he sticks his finger up his nose and gives you that look, before he starts to belly laugh because he knows he's doing something he shouldn't.

"Who do you think this one is going to look like?" Tate asks, handing Garon a piece of banana and then setting his son on his own two feet.

"I think he's going to look like me," Ellie says, accepting the big piece of mango her father offers her.

"I think he's going to look like a baby," Heidi puts in. She shakes her head when Tate offers her a piece of banana. "Pineapple please, Daddy." Ah, a girl after my own heart.

Tate and I start to laugh.

"Yes, you're probably right. He will look like a *baby*. But we're more wondering *who* he will resemble more once he loses his baby look. You guys used to look like babies, but now you look like kids. Will he look more like Mommy or Daddy?" Tate says, making room for Heidi on the blanket next to him.

Ellie comes over and squeezes in next to me. Her hand rests on my belly. "How much longer, Mummy?"

"About eight weeks," I say.

"And then we'll have another baby brother?"

I nod. "Yep, and then we'll have two boys and two girls."

Tate grins at me before he takes a bite of pineapple.

I pick up my own wedge and take a nibble.

Thank God this kiddo tolerates pineapple; I hadn't been able to stomach the fruit when I'd been pregnant with Garon. Pretty much since the moment of conception, even a glimpse or mere thought of my favorite fruit had made me taste bile.

"Two boys and two girls, just like we'd planned," my dashing husband says.

"You *planned* us?" Heidi asks innocently.

"We certainly did." Tate chuckles. "From the moment I saw your mommy, I knew I wanted to have babies with her. And I knew they'd be the most beautiful babies in the whole wide world. So I figured, why not make a bunch of them? We thought about two, but when we saw how gorgeous you two angels are, we figured we pretty much *had* to keep making more beautiful babies."

Both Heidi and Ellie giggle next to us while Garon drops his piece of banana in the sand and then stands there staring at it, contemplating if he should pick it up and continue eating, grab a new piece from the container or start crying.

"Will you keep having more beautiful babies after this baby is born?" Ellie asks, her sweet little hand rubbing gentle circles around the top of my belly.

Tate's eye catches mine. The man would have a whole soccer team of children if I'd let him.

"Ahhh," I sigh. "I think once this little guy is here, our family will be complete. Don't you think?"

"I love babies," Heidi says, digging her pink-painted toes into the warm sand and then wriggling them until they pop free.

"Me too," I agree. "But I think four is enough."

"Four is just right," Tate says wistfully, scooting closer to me as he swings his arm out and gathers Garon against his chest.

Heidi leans across her father's lap and rests her hand on my stomach, Garon mimics his sister, and soon all three of my children are feeling their little brother kick and squirm inside me.

Tate's hand lands dead center between them all, and I let my hand fall on top of his.

Our fingers intertwine, and we look up into each other's eyes.

"Four is perfect." Tears sting the corners of my eyes as my mind drifts back to seven years ago and how much has changed.

How much more complete, full and incredible my life is now.

And it's all because of Tate.

"Our life is perfect," he says. Just then the little boy in my belly does a somersault, and all three children jump where they sit and begin laughing. Tate tackles Garon onto the blanket and starts blowing raspberries onto his belly and tickling him while the girls climb onto their father's back and the four of them all begin to wrestle.

Both my hands rest on the dancing infant inside me, and I let that defiant tear sprint down my cheek as I take in my beautiful family.

Healthy, happy and everything I've ever wanted. "Yes, little guy, four is perfect. Life is perfect."

Grab Gavin McAllister's story, Quick & Easy, Book 2 of The Quick Billionaires

Here —> books2read.com/QEasy-QBS

If you've enjoyed this book, please consider leaving a review. It really does make a difference.
Thank you again.
Xoxo
Whitley Cox

DON'T FORGET!!!

Be sure to subscribe to my newsletter here: http://eepurl.com/ckh5yT

You'll get access to bonus content, deals, upcoming sales, giveaways, excerpts and all the latest news about my upcoming releases. I also sometimes post photos of our family adventures kayaking and camping.

No spam though because that's not cool. And I certainly don't share your email address with anybody but my dog and he's too busy forming grudges against dogs he's never me to do anything with your email address.

Chapter 1

Wasn't it supposed to rain at a funeral?

It seemed every movie that had a funeral scene took place in the rain. All the guests wore black and clutched big black umbrellas while the rain masked the tears that slipped endlessly down their cheeks; the gray clouds in the sky mimicked the dark mood in everyone's hearts.

But it wasn't raining today. Not even a cloud in the damn sky. What the hell?

Heather Alvarez smoothed down the skirt of her charcoal gray lace dress (she just couldn't do black, even today) and stepped out of her Volkswagen Jetta. The warm April sun hit her cheeks at the same time a gust of wind ruffled the hair on the back of her neck.

She loved spring.

Her dad had loved spring, too.

"There you are," said her mother, Rosemary, coming out of their family's Puerto Rican restaurant, Hola, Amigos. "I was beginning to worry."

Heather offered her mother a small smile as she swung her purse over her shoulder. "Sorry, Mama. There was an emergency at work. You know how busy tax season can get." Heather bent down and planted a kiss on her mother's cheek before following her through the full parking lot to the front doors. "Have you needed my help? Or did Lena and Aunt Florence show up?"

Rosemary's hand fell to her daughter's back, bringing the scent of cumin and garlic and very subtle lavender. Her mother always smelled like cumin and garlic from the restaurant and lavender from her favorite shampoo.

She rubbed Heather's back affectionately, maternally. "We've had loads of help. Don't worry, sweetheart. Besides, you were here setting up all last night. What time did you finally get to bed?"

Heather dismissed the question with a shrug.

Rosemary let out a rattled sigh and glanced up at her daughter. Her pale blue eyes were glassy and her strong jaw tight. "This is what he wanted. He didn't want anybody crying over him. He wanted a party. So, we're going to give him a party."

Heather swallowed past the hard lump in her throat and looped her arm around her mother's slender shoulders, tugging her in tight. "I know, Mama. We're going to throw him the best celebration of life imaginable. Blow the roof off the place."

Rosemary chuckled and pulled open the door to the restaurant. Voices, loud and cheerful, greeted them. She met her daughter's eyes one more time before tossing on a giant smile. "Show time."

"Heather!" half a dozen or more people cheered as she stepped inside the bright and spacious restaurant. Tables had been pushed to the side and chairs lined up in rows. A podium stood front and center below the sign for half-price daiquiris on Mondays, and a small table with the picture of Eduardo Luis Gomez Alvarez sat next to it. Food, piled high, dressed the tables, while beer, local and imported, nestled tightly into ice buckets. Yes, her dad certainly knew how to throw a party, even in the afterlife.

Just like her mother was, Heather slowly made the rounds of all the guests, accepting condolences and sympathy, hugs and hand pats. Everyone had a story to tell about her father, all good, most funny. And Heather listened. She nodded. She cried. She laughed. By the time the minister announced the start of the sermon, Heather was exhausted, all cried out and ready to go home.

But she couldn't.

Her mother needed her. It was just the two of them now, and she needed to take care of her mom, be there for her. Hold her.

She took her seat in the front row, her mother on her left, her mother's best friend, Lena, on her right. Her mother's sister, Heather's Aunt Florence, sat on the other side of Rosemary, their hands clasped tight. Slowly, the noise in the restaurant subsided as people took their seats, the din of conversation and the scraping of chair legs on tile receding with the clearing of the minister's throat.

Heather spun around to take in all the people who had come to say "goodbye" to her father, to celebrate him and what he meant to the community. She absorbed their love, allowed it to bolster her own. Her father had meant everything to her, and in the blink of an eye—a heart attack at the dinner table when they were out for her birthday three weeks ago—he was gone.

It was a packed house. Standing room only and well over the legal limit of patrons for the restaurant. But they'd closed it for the day, put up signs and purchased special permits. If Eduardo Alvarez did anything, he did it aboveboard and he did it right. She was just about to turn back to the front when a big body sneaking in at the back caught her eye. The entire atmosphere in the restaurant shifted, and oxygen left Heather's lungs as she watched him slowly edge his way behind people, sticking to the shadows and the back of the room. He was tall. Perhaps taller than she remembered and bigger, too. His shoulders and chest were broader, and the way his dress pants hugged his thighs told her he still liked to work out and probably ride his mountain bike.

All the moisture left her mouth as she continued to follow him with her eyes. His head was down, and when he accidentally bumped someone, he was quick to apologize and move on. Eventually, he found a safe space next to the bar, quietly ordered a drink, then stood back, leaning the wide expanse of his back against a wooden column. He tipped his drink up, revealing a very expensive-looking watch at his wrist. His suit was tailored to perfection and high quality, too. Heather didn't know much about fashion or designers, but she knew that thing wasn't from JCPenney. His impossibly deep blue eyes closed, and his throat undulated on a swallow as he brought the belly-warming amber liquid into his mouth.

Heather swallowed, too. Fuck, he was still as drop-dead gorgeous as she remembered, as she dreamed. He still hadn't noticed her, so she took an extra moment to check him out. His swath of dark hair was shorter now, tamer, though it still had that unruly wave to it at the front. He never had been able to control the curl. But she'd loved it. Loved twirling her fingers around and around the silky soft strands as he laid his head in her lap and they watched movies. His gaze shifted, and suddenly his eyes lasered in on her.

A gasp escaped her before she could stop it, and immediately Heather spun back around in her seat. Her mother squeezed her hand, then patted the top with her other hand. "You okay, sweetheart?"

Heather swallowed again. "Yeah, Mama. I'm fine." Even though she was anything but. The back of her neck prickled and heated from his stare. She knew he was staring. Just knew it. His gaze had always been fierce. Had always stripped her bare and made her submit to his will.

I can't turn around. Willpower, girlie, willpower. Ah, fuck it.

She craned her neck around to catch another glimpse, and sure enough, he was zeroed in on her like a dog with a bone. The corner of his sexy mouth crooked up into a sad half-smile. His head shifted in an almost indiscernible nod.

The minister cleared his throat again, forcing Heather to spin back around. Her chest tightened and her gut knotted. The minister opened up his book and began. But Heather didn't hear a damn word. She was too focused on the voices in her head, on the memories that involved the impeccably dressed man at the back of the room. Gavin McAllister, the love of her life, and the boy who broke her heart.

Grab Gavin McAllister's story, Quick & Easy, Book 2 of The Quick Billionaires Here —> books2read.com/QEasy-QBS

Acknowledgments

THERE ARE SO MANY people to thank who help along the way. Publishing a book is definitely not a solo mission, that's for sure. First and foremost, my friend and editor Chris Kridler, you are a blessing, a gem and an all-around terrific person. Thank you for your honesty and hard work. You really helped me with this one, and your feedback was spot-on (as always).

Debbie McDuffie, Justine and Krista for your honest and helpful beta-reads. I love that I can hand you the rough, unedited stuff and you'll read it and give it to me straight. Thank you.

Megan and EmCat Designs for my new covers. You are fantastic, your covers are fantastic and I so appreciate you. Thank you.

Author Kathleen Lawless, for just being you and wonderful and always there for me.

Author Jeanne St. James, my alpha reader and sister from another mister, what would I do without you? Thank you!!

Whitley Cox's Fabulously Filthy Reviewers, you are all awesome and I feel so blessed to have found such wonderful fans.

The ladies and gent of Vancouver Island Romance Authors, your support and insight have been incredibly helpful, and I'm so honored to be a part of a group of such talented writers

Author Cora Seton, I love our walks, talks and heart-to-hearts, they mean so much to me.

Author Ember Leigh, my newest author bestie, I love our bitch fests—they keep me sane. You helped me SO much with this book, and I am so very grateful for that. Sometimes it just takes talking it through with someone to have the lightbulb come on. Thank you for helping me find the light switch.

My parents, in-laws, brother and sister-in-law, thank you for your unwavering support. The Small Human and the Tiny Human, you are the beats and beasts of my heart, the reason I breathe and the reason I drink. I love you both to infinity and beyond. And lastly, of course, the husband. You are my forever, my other half, the one who keeps me grounded and the only person I have honestly never grown sick of even when we did that six-month backpacking trip and spent every single day together. I never tired of you. Never needed a break. You are my person. I love you.

OTHER BOOKS BY WHITLEY COX

Love, Passion and Power: Part 1
The Dark and Damaged Hearts Series: Book 1
https://books2read.com/LPP1-DDH
Kendra and Justin

•

Love, Passion and Power: Part 2
The Dark and Damaged Hearts: Book 2
https://books2read.com/LPP2-DDH
Kendra and Justin

•

Sex, Heat and Hunger: Part 1
The Dark and Damaged Hearts Book 3
https://books2read.com/SHH1-DDH
Emma and James

•

Sex, Heat and Hunger: Part 2
The Dark and Damaged Hearts Book 4
https://books2read.com/SHH1-DDH
Emma and James

•

Hot & Filthy: The Honeymoon
The Dark and Damaged Hearts Book 4.5
https://books2read.com/HF-DDH
Emma and James

•

True, Deep and Forever: Part 1
The Dark and Damaged Hearts Book 5
https://books2read.com/TDF1-DDH
Amy and Garrett

•

True, Deep and Forever: Part 2
The Dark and Damaged Hearts Book 6
https://books2read.com/TDF2-DDH
Amy and Garrett

·

Hard, Fast and Madly: Part 1
The Dark and Damaged Hearts Series Book 7
https://books2read.com/HFM1-DDH
Freya and Jacob

·

Hard, Fast and Madly: Part 2
The Dark and Damaged Hearts Series Book 8
https://books2read.com/HFM1-DDH
Freya and Jacob

·

Quick & Dirty
Book 1, A Quick Billionaires Novel
https://books2read.com/QDirty-QBS
Parker and Tate

·

Quick & Easy
Book 2, A Quick Billionaires Novella
https://books2read.com/QEasy-QBS
Heather and Gavin

·

Quick & Reckless
Book 3, A Quick Billionaires Novel
https://books2read.com/QReckless-QBS
Silver and Warren

·

Quick & Dangerous
Book 4, A Quick Billionaires Novel
https://books2read.com/QDangerous-QBS
Skyler and Roberto

·

Quick & Snowy
The Quick Billionaires, Book 5
https://books2read.com/QSnowy-QBS
Brier and Barnes

·

Doctor Smug
https://books2read.com/DoctorSmug
Daisy and Riley

·

Hot Dad
https://books2read.com/Hot-Dad
Harper and Sam

•

Snowed In & Set Up
https://books2read.com/SISU
Amber, Will, Juniper, Hunter, Rowen, Austin

•

Love to Hate You
https://books2read.com/Love2HateYou
Alex and Eli

•

Lust Abroad
https://books2read.com/Lust-Abroad
Piper and Derrick

•

Hired by the Single Dad
https://books2read.com/HBTSD-SDS
The Single Dads of Seattle, Book 1
Tori and Mark

•

Dancing with the Single Dad
https://books2read.com/DWTSD-SDS
The Single Dads of Seattle, Book 2
Violet and Adam

•

Saved by the Single Dad
https://books2read.com/SBTSD-SDS
The Single Dads of Seattle, Book 3
Paige and Mitch

•

Living with the Single Dad
https://books2read.com/LWTSD-SDS
The Single Dads of Seattle, Book 4
Isobel and Aaron

•

Christmas with the Single Dad
https://books2read.com/CWTSD-SDS
The Single Dads of Seattle, Book 5
Aurora and Zak

·

New Year's with the Single Dad
https://books2read.com/NYWTSD-SDS
The Single Dads of Seattle, Book 6
Zara and Emmett

·

Valentine's with the Single Dad
https://books2read.com/VWTSD-SDS
The Single Dads of Seattle, Book 7
Lowenna and Mason

·

Neighbors with the Single Dad
https://books2read.com/NWTSD-SDS
The Single Dads of Seattle, Book 8
Eva and Scott

·

Flirting with the Single Dad
https://books2read.com/FWTSD-SDS
The Single Dads of Seattle, Book 9
Tessa and Atlas

·

Falling for the Single Dad
https://books2read.com/FFTSD-SDS
The Single Dads of Seattle, Book 10
Liam and Richelle

·

Hot for Teacher
https://books2read.com/HFT-SMS
The Single Moms of Seattle, Book1
Celeste and Max

·

Hot for a Cop
https://books2read.com/HFAC-SMS
The Single Moms of Seattle, Book 2
Lauren and Isaac

·

Hot for the Handyman
https://books2read.com/HTHM-SMS
The Single Moms of Seattle, Book 3
Bianca and Jack

*

Mr. Gray Sweatpants
A Single Moms of Seattle spin-off book
https://books2read.com/MrGraySweatpants
Casey and Leo

*

Hard Hart
https://books2read.com/HH-HB
The Harty Boys, Book 1
Krista and Brock

*

Lost Hart
The Harty Boys, Book 2
https://books2read.com/LH-HB
Stacey and Chase

*

Torn Hart
The Harty Boys, Book 3
https://books2read.com/THART-HB
Lydia and Rex

*

Dark Hart
The Harty Boys, Book 4
https://books2read.com/DH-HB
Pasha and Heath

*

Full Hart
The Harty Boys, Book 5
https://books2read.com/FH-HB
A Harty Boys Family Christmas
Joy and Grant

*

Not Over You
A Young Sisters Novel
https://books2read.com/not-over-you
Rayma and Jordan

Snowed in with the Rancher
A Young Sisters Novel
https://books2read.com/snowed-in-rancher
Triss and Asher
March 4, 2023

•

Second Chance with the Rancher
A Young Sisters Novel
https://books2read.com/second-chance-rancher
Mieka and Nate
May 13, 2023

•

Done with You
A Young Sisters Novel
https://books2read.com/done-with-you
Oona and Aiden
October 13, 2023

•

Rock the Shores
A Cinnamon Bay Romance
https://books2read.com/Rocktheshores
Juliet and Evan

•

The Bastard Heir
Winter Harbor Heroes, Book 1
Co-written with Ember Leigh
https://books2read.com/the-bastard-heir
Harlow and Callum

•

The Asshole Heir
Winter Harbor Heroes, Book 2
Co-written with Ember Leigh
https://books2read.com/the-asshole-heir
Amaya and Carson

The Rebel Heir
Winter Harbor Heroes, Book 3
Co-written with Ember Leigh
https://books2read.com/the-rebel-heir
Lily and Colton
March 18, 2023

NATALIE SLOAN TITLES

Light the Fire
Revolution Inferno, Book 1
https://mybook.to/light-the-fire
Haina, Zane, Alaric and Jorik
•
Stoke the Flames
Revolution Inferno, Book 2
https://mybook.to/stoke-the-flames
Olia, Maxxon, Cypher and Alaric
•
Burn it Down
Revolution Inferno, Book 3
https://mybook.to/burn-it-down
Zosha, Knox, Shade and Tozer
June 3, 2023

About the Author

A Canadian West Coast baby born and raised, Whitley is married to her high school sweetheart, and together they have two beautiful daughters and a fluffy dog. She spends her days making food that gets thrown on the floor, vacuuming Cheerios out from under the couch and making sure that the dog food doesn't end up in the air conditioner. But when the kids are in school, and it's not quite wine o'clock, Whitley sits down, avoids the pile of laundry on the couch, and writes.

A lover of all things decadent; wine, cheese, chocolate and spicy erotic romance, Whitley brings the humorous side of sex, the ridiculous side of relationships and the suspense of everyday life into her stories. With single dads, firefighters, Navy SEALs, mommy wars, body issues, threesomes, bondage and role-playing, Whitley's books have all the funny and fabulously filthy words you could hope for.

Website: WhitleyCox.com
Email: readers4wcox@gmail.com
Twitter: @WhitleyCoxBooks
Instagram: @CoxWhitley
TikTok: @AuthorWhitleyCox
Facebook : https://www.facebook.com/CoxWhitley/
Blog: https://whitleycox.com/fabulously-filthy-blog-page/

Exclusive Facebook Reader Group:
https://www.facebook.com/groups/234716323653592/
Booksprout: https://booksprout.co/author/994/whitley-cox
Bookbub: https://www.bookbub.com/authors/whitley-cox
Goodreads:
https://www.goodreads.com/author/show/16344419.Whitley_Cox
Subscribe to my newsletter here:
http://eepurl.com/ckh5yT

Treat yourself to awesome orgasms!
This one only ships to the US.

https://tracysdog.com/?sca_ref=1355619.ybw0YXuvPL

Treat yourself to awesome orgasms! This one ships to Canada!

https://thornandfeather.ca/?ref=734ThbSs

39257561R00093